CJ WEBB

Green Eyes
& White Lies

When Love, Lust & Jealousy Collide

Special acknowledgements to my editor

Linda Olney Sikes

who's kind help and motivation, I am deeply grateful for.

In special memoriam to my friend
Tiffany S
You may be gone too soon, but your memory will
always be in my heart.

Love is Everything & Our Reason For Living

1

W hat the hell is *this* woman doing in here?" Brad Monroe's guttural hostility thundered from the end of the workshop. The sharp cold steel of his voice penetrated Jessica like a flock of daggers thrown straight to the heart. She froze, knees buckled, she hardly dared face the flashing light green eyes on the hunk of man rapidly approaching her. The flush of desperately needing to be thrown on the bed then manhandled till she couldn't walk, betrayed her. Was the overdue time clock on needing to give up on love and just get on and lose her virginity written all over her face? She hoped not - it was.

She stammered stupidly while investigating the nuances of her feet and fiddling with her long strawberry blonde plaits like a schoolgirl. "Oh, err, I was … l'm looking for my…" She couldn't find the words. She quickly realised this sudden masculine intrusion was the guy every girl in town had described as being an utter gorgeous God like creature that most likely never saw a pair of closed female legs in his life - a bit like a gynaecologist she mused. His tortuous mediterranean type good looks relinquished her to the back of the line of wanton females. Her eyes totally betrayed her - she was clearly not as impenetrable as she had thought - or hoped.

Mimicking a Sargent major surveying a pathetic failure in his squad, Brad strutted back and forth in front of her, fully aware of his hard muscular exterior and its effect on *all* women. Jessica squirmed as she continued to stare at the floor - he seemed surrounded by an intoxicating scent. She inhaled, clearly an expensive aftershave; a rich blend of Arabian musk with an undertone of Madagascan vanilla bean. As its lust filled infusion surrounded her, it fuelled fleeting pleasurable and whimsical carnal thoughts. Lucky he didn't *know* how suddenly wet for him she was - he did.

Brads' sarcasm ripped up then threw those enjoyable fantasies in the trash. He raised an eyebrow, the corners of his mouth flickering as though he were fighting not to smile. "Now let me guess, you came to see if your cute little car is ready?" Pointing a long tapered finger to the east side, he then hissed through gritted teeth. "The clue's in the sign that says *waiting room* - it's over there honey!" He flicked a tousle of raven hair away from his face, pivoted on one foot then strode away like an imperious arrogant king, immediately dismissing her very existence to text intensely on his mobile phone.

A mounting rage of humiliation crawled the length of her spine, but she couldn't help noting the well muscled curve of his butt cheeks as he left. She visualised his smooth skin, that perfect roman nose, and full lips, deliberately hostile, masculine, striking - she found herself imagining what he might like in the sack. Every girl would love to stare up into those amazing green eyes as he pushed himself hard inside them. Her mind was swimming with fantasies, him taking her virginity mercilessly, then crawling down her trembling nakedness, drinking her lust until she could take no more - oh yes! Suddenly breathless, she shook herself back to reality taking a cold shower in sensibility in a rather late and futile attempt to rekindle her disgust.

Jessicas' tempestuous spirit rose, if there was one religion she followed, it was to worship at the altar of 'take no shit from men' - not ever - even from someone as *intoxicating* and perfectly moulded as him - damn him. She shouted after him, but with not enough stamina so he could possibly hear. "Do the staff here really treat their customers so rudely?" Even though it was to the closed door she followed up, more to herself than anyone. "I'll make sure your boss hears about it you know!" A thousand insults pushed through her brain, but her tongue couldn't find the strength to voice them. It was too busy wrestling with her inner desire to lick him all over, tasting him till she heard him cry out in ecstasy. Goosebumps at the thought were immediately saturated by a wash of shame in the wake of wimping out so badly in front of the most shaggable bastard she'd ever seen - whoever he was.

Scott, a fit 20's something wiry mechanic hopped out of the nearby pit waving a large snap-on spanner at her. Dragging oily fingers across his face he grinned, unconcerned by the black sludge in his tangled hair. He spoke slow with deliberation, living up to his nick name *'pot head.'* "Yeah, you sure told him, *not*, but hey, the public ain't allowed in the workshop, glad, you mouthed off a bit to old green eyes though, even if he didn't hear ya - he'd fire us all in a second for that." He sidled up to her. "You're looking hot as ever."

He pulled her towards him, close, grabbed her hand pushing it gently between his legs. "See what you do to me?" Jessica closed her eyes for a second, if only that damned hard thing in her hand belonged to Brad Monroe. Scott, woke her from her fantasy. "Yeah, you really need some of that babe, a man can sniff it out, you're just oozing sexual need babe." She frowned, what exactly was he sniffing out? She pulled her hand away from his crutch, he pulled it back. "C'mon, you know you want it, besides, that film basic instinct is on with another 80's movie, something about eating and weight loss in nine and a half weeks, I think that's what it's called, supposed to be hot, at least it was in its day. Oldies are goodies - don't ya think?" Scott drooled over Jessicas' breasts, failing to disguise he was losing his eyes in the valley of the voluptuous.

Jessica pulled her hand from his hardened crutch again and cursed Scott through incredulous eyes; it was hard to believe how easily he forgave her constant honest rejections day after day - in fact almost every day for the last six months since he started working at City Motors. "Didn't you hear me when I said I didn't ever want to lay eyes on you again? And will you get it in your thick head, I'm not going to have sex with you, no matter how hard you are, or how hard you try. You just don't do it for me Scott Brennan - you're too damned young for a start, you're like a little boy." Her words showered him with a cascade of negative rain, deliberate in their cruelty. "I'm twenty five, with a baby smooth face, if that's a little boy to you, this ain't so little ay?"

He grabbed at his crotch. She threw her hands to her hips in mock defiance as Scott laughed at her expression of disgust, "yeah, yeah, you're like all the rest, a sugar daddy chaser. I saw you wetting your knickers over Brad, your pussy just throbbing for him, yeah you need it, I need it, just close your eyes and think of him, I don't mind." Jessica laughed at him moving away a little more, "you're *so* crude, honestly shut up now, I could have you for sexual assault. Anyway, I don't fancy him, he's too in love with himself." Scott didn't relent. "Yeah yeah, whatever you say babe, forget him, you'll be crying for the moon with the rest of the town. But when you realise just what *I* can do for you, you'll come running, besides, if you don't wanna lay eyes on my gorgeous smooth face again… then I gotta agree with Brad…what the hell are ya doing in here?"

He grinned winking cheekily, allowing his cow brown eyes to find their way back to wrap firmly around the fullness of her cleavage that had been perfectly arranged for male entrapment with an ever so subtle hint of nipple erection. Jessica opened her mouth to object, but Scott dived in feet first, "you know you want me, it's just a question of when, and I'll be waiting babe; god I love older women, you're so fucking sexy when you're angry, bet you fuck like a bronco." Jessica couldn't help but grin as she appraised Scott - giggling at his appearance; his usual surfer dude shaggy blonde hair was tousled and streaked with sump oil. His mechanics overalls were baggy like a clown.

She mused, she was now twenty eight, knocking thirty, Scott was from a well to do family, and not bad looking, should she stop looking for the perfect alpha male and settle for less? She laughed at him, "What're you going to the fancy dress party as? The organ grinders monkey?" She laughed at him, an exotic musical laugh inciting a further physical shiver of desire. Jessica couldn't help liking Scott, she saw him as a loveable brother, nowhere near man enough for her though; boyish features and weasel like frame just didn't do it for her and she hated the way he was always smoking weed with her brother, encouraging him to hang around with other 'stoners' or losers as she called them. Jessica sighed, she needed a *real* man, full of muscle and masculine sex appeal, someone she could love and respect. She sighed, men like that didn't exist for single women, they're either gay, happily married to a beauty pageant queen or complete bastards - she stifled a giggle, or all three.

A scream of laughter broke the loaded silence as her younger brother by three years, Kevin, emerged from a pit, blackened and oily from the four wheel drive he was servicing. She squealed in amusement, "Oh no, the return of the zombies!" Kevin walked stilted towards her, arms outstretched mimicking the undead, she jumped back in horror, he always took a joke too far. Kevin dropped the act in a make believe huff, "oh that's nice, well fuck you then, even my own sister won't give me a hug." Kevin turned to Scott, "you're right man, she *is* a sugar daddy chaser."

Kevin turned to Jessica, winking at Scott, "this is a man's world and no place for little prick teasers on heels like *you*." Jessica was in no mood for misplaced if not overly harsh patronising gender shit from her brother. "Well you can keep your mans' world' just sort my bloody car out before I shove one of my overtly feminine heels where the macho sun don't shine." The boys shrieked out a united high pitched, "oooh." She ignored them. "Don't take the piss, mums…my, Datsun keeps cutting out, it was so embarrassing this morning, cut out right at an intersection. It's a miracle I wasn't in an accident, and don't be so damned sexist you stupid arsehole."

She attempted to belt Kevin but he deftly dodged her hand. Kevin loved winding her up she was such an easy target. "That's no way to ask for a favour now sis is it? Anyway, you've got the money to buy a new one, better still, leasing is a better option - buying one is so, I dunno, old fart, yesterday. Anyway, why waste time on that heap of shit?" Jessica's eyes pooled grey instantly. "You know why and don't call it that." Kevin was feeling full of bravado. "Oh let me guess, you're keeping it because it was mums?" Jessica pulled out her plaits and tossed her blonde waist length fine hair over bare shoulders with an indignant air - it created static and rose like medusa. "I know you think I'm stupid, but mum loved that car, it was her *only* little bit of freedom to get away from dad - it meant the world to her and I feel close to her, when I…" She faltered as her baby blues welled momentarily. "You know how I feel, I just have to look after it!" Kevin fidgeted from foot to foot with male indifference, "She really doesn't need it where she is, unless she's making her debut return to earth in the walking dead." He started walking towards her like a zombie again. "Don't be so flaming cruel …"

Kevin' was about to retort but his face dropped as though he'd suffered a sudden stroke. He elbowed Jessica in the ribs and hissed out the side of his mouth, "you shouldn't be here." With a desperately sharp whisper he added, "pretend you're a customer." She was about to ask why, when she clocked the good looking bastard again. Brad stood like a carved statue, the wet mother of all sexual gods, but surrounded by an ominous black cloud of arrogance. He was silently eyeing the trio with holier than thou contempt - god only knows how long he'd been watching them.

Jessica decided not to allow him to intimidate her this time, after all, he wasn't *her* boss. As he approached, she tried to appeal to his manly instincts by gazing up at him with wide eyed innocence, which wasn't hard to do as she was five foot two and he was at least six foot. She puffed out her well endowed silicones at the same time; which usually engaged and controlled predictable males. Her feminine wiles bounced from a patriarchal bastard like force field as unemotional empty shark like eyes bored into her. She tried fluttering long lash extensions in another weapon from her female arsenal - it fell like bird shit on a parade.

Without uttering one word he successfully deflated her ego with his raised eyebrows and deadpan expression of disapproval. "Still here?" His eyes savagely undressed her as he appraised her from head to toe adding, in a slightly softer voice, "is there a problem?" He added with a flicker of amusement, which sent shockwaves through her system, "other than your hair of course." She quickly tried to dampen down her statically charged hair but before she could think of a suitably witty response, Brad switched his attention to Kevin and Scott. Jessica couldn't help grinning as she witnessed the bravado drain from *their* ghost like faces standing so pathetically in front of such an iconic god like man; they were both shivering like wimps - no hard ons anywhere to be seen - except her own.

She tried to stifle a giggle but laughed out loud; she always laughed at inappropriate moments, been like it since a child. Brad spun around like a headmaster to a naughty pupil, his glare anchoring her down like a pinned butterfly in a rich mans collection - she let out a girlish gasp of sexual excitement which seemed to somehow appease the Titan in front of her. The boys silence angered Brad, he turned his attention back to them and drilled, "I said, is there a problem?" He pointed at Jessica, "this girl to do with *you?*" He eyeballed Scott accusingly who was shaking his head in instant disloyal denial - he would have led her to any firing squad at that moment, and she felt the same way about him.

Jessica drew in a courageous breath then held out her hand to shake it. She smiled as sweetly as she could "Hi, I think you misunderstood my intentions back there, I'm Jessica Shackley, Kevin's older sister, just need my car looking at, damn thing keeps on cutting out." Kevin drew in a large disappointed breath, "for fuck sake" he whispered to Scott. Brad ignored her outstretched hand, eyeing her as though she was something smelly he'd just stepped in. She pulled her hand back, the flaming scarlet of his rude rejection sending her cheeks a humiliating crimson. Brad snarled, "I see, then continue your little family chats at home on your own time this is a restricted area for health and safety!" He pivoted on one foot and stalked back to the reception area, leaving Jessica choking on her own unexpressed anger.

"What the fuck? Who is this guy?" She gasped. "He behaves like Lord of the bloody manor. He's obviously the hot guy at the garage that the girls were talking about on facebook, but omg, what a rude arse hole, strutting about like a pompous twat that thinks he owns the fucking place!" Kevin was pacing up and down in a stress. "That's because he does!" He hissed, his annoyance at her behaviour was tinted with amusement, he always enjoyed his sisters rage even better with uncharacteristic accompanying bad language, for some reason the word, fuck, sounded so funny out of *her* mouth.

Jessica spluttered with fury. "Well, I don't care who the fuck he is or how much fucking money he has or how good looking he thinks he is, or how absolutely *amazingly* hot is body is, or how much I would like to…." She stopped short and tempered her voice noticing the boys expressions. "He just doesn't need to speak down to me like, like I'm his bloody bitch." The boys knew she had Brad fever. "Wow, you got it bad girl, me thinks love is in the air!" Kevin teased, ducking away from a predictable slap in the face. He laughed, "you're only angry cos you'd like to be *his* bitch and he ain't falling for none of those fluttering blue eyed silicone enhanced moves." He began twerking and shaking his chest. Jessica kicked out at him, he swerved, grinning, "gotta be faster than that blondie! So let me break it down for you. So, the most desirable bachelor in town don't fancy ya, so what? It ain't the end of the world, and you got Scottie here who's clearly knocking one out over you every night, so okay he's a fellow grease monkey, a few years younger and way less muscles, but hey, he's in your class, so stop behaving like you are some sort of celebrity or lady muck, you ain't, and you never will be."

He took a peak at Jessicas' deflated expression, her eyes brimming with self pity, then added, "anyway, Brads' bark is way worse than his bite - and actually, I like him, a lot!" He ignored his sisters dangerous expression. "He's hard but fair, and he's giving me and Scottie a great opportunity to do our apprenticeship with papers, so don't start fucking this up for us. I told you to say you were a customer and you dropped me right in it, I'll have to apologise to him later. I'll look at the car but you gotta book it in like anyone else and please stay away from here."

Jessica drew herself up, fighting to restore her tattered pride. Almost lunging at them she shot at the boys with her verbal gun, loading words as bullets; a little too angry, a little too loud and with far too much venom. "Not in his class? Are you fucking crazy in the head? *He* should be so lucky! As if I'd see anything in an arrogant 'A' hole like him, he's not even my type, mister bloody perfect, he's almost certainly gay, did you see his fingers? He's got a better manicure than mine. Gay guys are always so immaculately turned out, not like you two shit heads. I reckon if anything, its you two who are his bitches around here!"

She stopped, breathless, a deep frown furrowing her flawless tanned complexion, her chest heaving as she fought to control her breathing; suddenly embarrassed at the tell tale passion of her verbal onslaught. Kevin and Scott exchanged knowing looks again, she hadn't just been touched with Brad fever she'd been tied down, hung, drawn and quartered with it, like every other girl that came anywhere near him. Jessica back tracked, in an attempt to cut into the sudden weighted silence. "Of course I won't mess it up for you, if it makes you feel better, I'll apologise when I see him next. I'm here cos its a car garage and my car is playing up. Surely you can look at the old girl quickly before I go?" Kevin sighed, women are so annoyingly stupid,

"That's the point sis." Kev whispered, "I can't! I'm not allowed to do family and friends favours, Brad would kill me, it's the new rules." Jessica sighed too, "but Jesse used to let you, he was so kind, he always told me family first." Kevin looked over his shoulder and around to ensure Brad wasn't there, he reminded her gently, "old Jesse's dead and gone sis. Brad is Jesse's only son,

Jesse told us how he's built the entire WA group up alongside his dad without ever needing his money - he's a brilliant businessman with great plans for the group to be Australia wide."

Jessica could feel a stomach churning hatred building within, she stomped her foot in childish anger, "I don't care about his stupid plans, I just want my car looking at!" Relenting a little, she sighed wistfully, "can you come to my place tonight then? Give it the once over with your expert eye and I'll cook up a nice roast dinner." Kevin puffed his cheeks in and out with increasing irritation - he loved a roast. "If I got caught I'd be fired! It's a new policy, no private work, not even for family, and now you've told him who you are and shown him your bloody car you're gonna have to book it in like anyone else, period, or he'll guess I'm doing it, nothing escapes him, now I gotta get back to work."

Brad Monroe paced hurriedly into the workshop again, his brow creased as hard eyes reflected his disgust at Jessica's persistent presence. Jessica knew she should hold her tongue, but her mood invaded her better judgement. "My brother may be unfortunate enough to have to be subservient to a miserable task master like you, but *I* don't have to put up with your shit!" Kevin cringed, he whispered to Scott, "unemployment line, here I come." The oxygen seemed to deplete as they all struggled to breathe through a starched and concentrated atmosphere. Jessica maintained her defensive stance, eyes flashing hands on hips staring Brad down. He remained silent for what seemed like an eternity before a slow condescending smirk slithered across his mouth. He stared at Jessica like an Eagle to a mouse, his broad shoulders dominating the natural light which was flooding in through a small window behind him clothing his outline with a larger than life ethereal presence.

"You're a Pommie aren't you?" His words cut her with knife like disdain. Of all the replies she expected to hear, that was the furthest thing from her mind. What the hell had her British heritage got to do with anything? Kevin groaned and stepped towards his sister, he had to bloody shut her up or his apprenticeship opportunity would fly out the window, if it hadn't already. Jessicas' sapphire eyes flashed furiously. She pushed Kevin away and spat at Brad, "oh my god! Words fucking escape me, you're an arrogant bastard with a superiority complex, no scratch that, a god complex, you're a tyrant slave driver *and* a racist!" Scott stifled a laugh and whispered at a mortified Kevin, "words not really escaping our Jessica eh?" Brad ignored her, swivelling to face a shivering and white faced Kevin. "Didn't have *you* pegged as a Pommie!" His eyebrows raised and knitted together accusingly. Jessicas' face replicated a thunderstorm, she opened her mouth but Kevin quickly retorted, eager to restore Brads faith in him. "No, no, I'm not a Pom, I'm Australian - I was born here, in Perth, Mount Lawley, raised North of the river." Kevin renounced his heritage without hesitation. He avoided Jessicas' disgusted eyes as he delivered the final Judas like betrayal. "Jessica was five when our family emigrated from England, she was born there, so yeah, *she's* a Pommie."

"Ah, good on ya mate" a warm glow lit Brads' face up as he smiled appreciatively, slapping Kevin on the back in a friendly gesture. He shot a dark glare at Jessica as he added. "There's the difference." His name was called by the receptionist at the front office - he stalked away shouting out instructions to Kevin as though Jessica wasn't present. "Just get her out of here, health and safety and all that, if she wants the car looking at, book her in, but we're full till next Thursday." Kevin let out a relieved breath. "No worries boss," came his '*happy to be his slave*' reply.

Jessica pounced on her brother. "How could you grovel to him like that?" She swallowed a large lump in her throat, "for once I wish Amber was here, she'd have fucking killed him and eaten him for breakfast on a skewer!" The notion of eating him for breakfast made her blush a little and feel a little twinge. Kevin stared absently at his feet, "Be careful what you wish for, anyway, I was born here sis, I *am* Australian, and I'm proud of it, plus I really *need* this job." He draped a protective arm around her. "You're too sensitive for your own good - bloody pommies." Jessica stamped her foot again. "That's not funny. I'm not sensitive, don't keep saying that, I don't like being called a pommie, it's nothing more than a racist tag! You know I cannot stand *any* form of racism."

Scott grabbed at her waist and pulled her close to him. "It's just loving banter, it's in the Aussie Dictionary, did you know that? Anyway, it's a pile of meaningless words - who gives a fuck? What say I take your mind off this shit and show you a meaningful fuck with some proper Irish Australian love tonight - I'll pick you up at seven." Jessica nodded angrily then attempted to wipe Scotts' black hand print from her breast displayed on her delicate white broderie anglaise cold shoulder top.

Throwing her tamed hair back over her shoulders she stomped back to her car. Aware of a male admiring audience watching her on the forecourt she fiddled with the keys praying it would start first time - it did. She wound the window down and shouted, "Just so you all know, I'm British and proud of it." She then shot up her middle finger at the group, of car buyers, including a smirking Brad Monroe.

2

J essica cocooned herself into the worn soft velvet of her grandmothers chaise as the old grandfather clock in the lounge bonged nine times. Unwinding after a busy day in her salon, she recapped; three full slimming wraps, four cryogenic oxygen facials and two derma planes. Closing her eyes she brushed out her plaits, her hair was wavy like corn and fanned out with static. With long glittering gel nails she flicked the golden silky fine strands behind her ears. She mulled over the days events, she'd never wanted yet disliked someone so instantly and intensely as Kevins' boss Brad Monroe, more like Bad Monroe she mused. She'd be certain to post some negative shit about him to squash the excited female grapevine comments on facebook about him; new hunk at the garage? More like a new pig at the stye, she thought!

She giggled as she recalled her uncharacteristic bad language and manners, to the point of abusing and flipping the bird to a group of innocent strangers - how childish of her. She could still see Brads' face, standing there with them, like a God amongst a throng of pathetic mortals. Oh yes, he was perfectly formed, but he knew it and used it and that made him ugly - she felt as though she hated him so much, but couldn't really help wanting him to want *her* - being instantly forgettable, hurts.

Drifting into an exhausted slumber she fell straight into Brad Monroe's arms, tracing a make believe tribal tattoo that adorned the curves of his biceps she felt curiously warm and safe. In a deft move he scooped her up and threw her onto the bed like a rag doll. She writhed in ecstasy as he pinned her down and ripped off her clothes with a hungry mouth before lowering his head to her naked body. His lips brushed her thighs as his strong hands found the source of throbbing wetness between her legs. Without waiting he pushed his fingers inside her while dragging them in and out, back and forward rubbing her mercilessly he took no prisoners. Then lifting his head to her heaving breasts, cupping them while lowering his mouth to her nipples that he knew were begging for his attention. His tongue caressed them in time with his fingers slipping in and out of her. She began to fumble with his jeans but somehow he had already become naked.

He uttered words of love and affection then threw her on all fours bearing down on her with alpha male power and urgency. Without virginal fear she threw her body around enticingly, encouraging him to go all the way, to show her body no mercy. He smiled and stopped momentarily then plunged inside her. She screamed in twisted pain mingled with orgasmic pleasure; he was so big, so hard, it rubbed against a spot that begged him to go slow, but he drove it in, deeper, harder and faster - it was what she'd been waiting for all this time - *a real man.*

She gyrated manipulating his weapon of mass eruption to rub against the throbbing and tingling that was building, she was almost there, an unmistakable throbbing pulsated and intensified as he flexed his body. He arched his back as she raked her finger nails into his flesh. He whispered but his voice became a united scream of ejaculatory pleasure which somehow mutated into a high pitched and annoyingly constant ringing. A shrill doorbell chime resonated around the room awakening her in a heated sweat, she was wet and panting. "I hate him so much" she whispered to herself with a wry smile.

Dragging her spent body to the door she peeped through the spy-hole, it was Kevin. He bounced in, his usual youthful way, "forgot my keys again," he peered intently at Jessica, she was visually flushed, "you coming down with something? You look all hot and bothered and almost clammy, you're breathing fast, you got palpitations?" Swallowing a smirk she casually replied, "yeah I feel a bit heady, maybe coming down with something." "She had already succumbed to an extra strong contagion; Brad fever.

"You shouldn't have come to the garage sis," he started, unsure of the best words to use. "Yeah well Jesse used to like me there," she was vacant, still coming to terms with her sexually charged dream. "Jesse was *then* and Brad is *now,* you'll just have to accept it." She drew herself back into the realms of hating Monroe, it was easier. "You never mentioned I couldn't go there. How was I to know? Anyway, thanks for the support - not! You're a right pussy hole in front of that guy." Kevin smiled inside, yeah, she had been touched by Brad fever. "He's my boss, I ain't supporting *you* then losing *my* job, sorry, not sorry. Brad is an okay guy, you just have to get to know him!"

She smiled to herself visualising his toned naked body bearing down on her, "Yeah, get to know him, right, yeah, I really must do that sometime!" Kevin stared at her curiously. "You sure you're feeling alright? You look weird." He grinned looking furtively around the room for a half naked male, "are you sure I didn't interrupt something sis?" Jessica shook herself - busted. "Don't be stupid, I fell asleep, you woke me up, had a hard day yesterday. I'm fine, and for your information, I've got no wish to see that pig again let alone get to know him."

Kevin smirked knowingly, enjoying her embarrassment, "wow getting overly hot under the collar again, I thought you were Amber for a minute." Talking about their wayward sister was her achilles heel. "Don't bring her into it!" she growled. "I don't like the way he spoke down to me, that's all." Her face clouded to an indignant grey. "Anyway, I hate injustice especially racism - there's only one race, the human race." Kevin laughed at his sister always on some cause for humanity to love each other and world peace - whatever. "Blah blah blah, get off your sensitivity soap box, pommie is a term of endearment, nothing racist about it. I know you don't like me saying it, but you really gotta stop being so fucking touchy especially as we live in Australia for god sake - anyway, I guess he's got his reasons."

Jessica just wished she wasn't still single. "I don't give a flying fuck what his reasons are." Kevin raised a knowing eyebrow as she tossed her hair indignantly - the way she always did when she couldn't get what she wanted and she clearly wanted Brad Monroe. Kevin rarely had disagreements with Jessica, he fought tooth and nail with his other sister Amber, but never the quiet, peacemaking Jessica. Her aggressive behaviour punctuated by bad language was uncharacteristic - she's got it bad.

He mused for a second, was she really suffering a case of Brad fever? Or was he as bad as she made out? He shook off the notion and sniffed, "Oh yeah, I've got a message for you." She softened, squeezing his hand tenderly, "yeah, who from?" He grinned cheekily, "you sure have the power of the pussy over Scott, he says he'll look at your car Saturday! But I'm telling you now, if he gets caught, Brad will fire him for sure. I warned him, but he says you're worth it, the crazy loved up fuck." Jessica sighed, power of the pussy over Brad would be more like it, she wondered how incredible a woman would have to be to win over such a perfect male specimen.

"Who would fire anyone for helping a friend in his own time? Fire him? Over my dead body!" She cursed, her hormones still infuriated by her humiliating defeat. "I ought to march into that shitty little garage and sort Brad out once and for all." A vivid picture of her sorting him out over his office desk made her heart thump like crazed bongos. Kevin raised his eyebrows, "Oh please, gimme a ringside seat for *that* one." He chuckled, to her annoyance. "He's a powerful man in Perth! And that shitty little garage is the largest and most successful dealership in Western Australia! Anyway, I love that fucking job."

His soft kind eyes were pleading silently, in a way she could never resist. "Okay, take a chill pill Bill, tell Scott I'll ring him Saturday morning and I appreciate it loads, *and*, if he does a good enough job, I might actually go to the movies with him." Kevin grinned, "geez, you're such a prick tease. You're not really going to let him do it for you are ya? The car that is!" Kevin screwed up his face with mild smirking disapproval. "Of course I am, at least Scott cares about me." She felt herself begin to blush. He almost snarled back. "Then leave me out of any shit fall, cos trust me, you're helping a love sick guy lose his job, but as ever, you know best sis. Anyway, I gotta split, meeting dudes at the beach, surfs up - gotta grab my board." In a whirlwind he'd left Jessica to revisit her dream - Brad Monroe was absolutely perfect when it came to one thing - dream sex.

3

J essica fiddled with her hair anxiously awaiting Scotts arrival. Her mind focused on Brad for a few moments, she wished she could stop thinking about that almost ebony cropped hair, broad muscular chest, sculpted high cheekbones and such exotically Arabic light green eyes - she sighed - shame he was hateful inside cos outside he was *amazing*. She wished with all her heart that a man like *that* could take her into his arms and make her feel like a woman with his incredible body, she needed to lose her virginity, but Kevin was right, she was crying for the moon, when perhaps, if she gave Scott a chance, those stars were within her reach.

Pounding sexual urges dominated her thoughts as the biological clock marked her increasing need to become a woman, preferably in a whirlwind of clothes ripping passion - but with Scott? She needed to savour sex like the movies, she yearned to fall into the arms of a handsome hunk, a hero, who would do everything right, be blessed with plenty where it counts, to fill her up with his love, and know exactly how to make her scream with pleasure.

She visualised Brads body as he walked toward her in that garage, her subconscious mind recalled every tiny bit of detail. A gym body, rippling abs and a butt like steel what more could a girl want? She imagined him showing up when she wasn't expecting it just to tear her clothes off. Whispering chants of love and passion he would bear down on her mercilessly making her beg for more until she screamed and throbbed with the final ecstatic release. She smiled, he would then likely fly into the air back to Gotham City which is the only place men like that actually came from - comic books, dreams and City Motors!

Despite her crazy sexual fantasies, she needed to find a mutual emotional love, a husband, a life long partner - she described it to friends as *'me and you against the world'*. A close relationship was imperative to her which was why she had refused so many men along the way. She sighed, her sexual fantasies were just for the movies, handsome heroes like that weren't emotionally soft, they just played the field for what they could take, looking in the mirror more than *she* did. Life just wasn't like the movies, perhaps she should bite the bullet and be grateful for what she had. Perhaps Scott wasn't such a bad deal after all, and it was time to open the gate to her secret garden - wasn't it?

When the doorbell rang she was ready, sporting tight denims and a loose fitting and flimsy primrose yellow tee shirt. Scott gushed with youthful enthusiasm, "wow, you look lovelier than I could have hoped for, small yet perfectly formed." He clasped his hands around her waist, and kissed her fondly on the lips, before she tore away from him as a little vomit found its way to her mouth. "If you get caught fixing my car Kevin says you'll get the sack! I don't want you to lose your job." She bit her lip anxiously, why couldn't she even fake it with him? She knew she must try harder, but her fantasy man and rampant dreams felt more real and worthy than *he* did. Perhaps she should go to that Ann Summers shop and buy their top of the range electronic rabbit and a pot of KY after all.

He arranged her flowing hair, draping it lovingly across her shoulders. "You're so beautiful Jessica, it turns me on when you let your hair down, let it down with me now babe." He murmured, "I'll buy you a new car if you want, you know I got money my family trust. I'd do anything, pay anything, just to be with you." His breathing was rapid and intense, his pupils had widened, his retinas dominated by a wave of dark chocolate. He pulled her tight to him, his hot breath burning her cheek. "I want you Jessica Shackley, and I know you want me too, you just keep fighting the inevitable!"

She pulled away again, he was only a few years younger but to lead him on would be cruel. He came from a well known rich family, yet he was kind, gentle and patient. He was slim and hardly had the muscular physique she admired, but his pretty boy surfer looks made him one of the most popular young guys in town, or was it his money? His Meta facebook account had more than 1500 friends - mostly hopeful girls, yet despite everything, when *he* touched her, even if he uttered all the sweet nothings she so wanted to hear from someone else, an intangible lack of chemistry sent her red hot passion hungry fiery loins back to the ice age.

Scott searched her eyes for something, anything! "I want you so bad Jessica, don't keep me hanging' like this, it hurts." He swallowed hard, searching his limited vocabulary for the correct words. He pushed her hand onto his crotch, his breathing more urgent, "see? You do *this* to me every time I see you." She squeezed him, rock hard, throbbing and jerking about, she wanted *it*, deep inside her, making her scream, rubbing her ache, but she didn't want *him* at the end of *it* - that rabbit model was calling her name! She pulled her hand away, kissing him tenderly on the cheek, "I'm sorry Scottie, I can't, don't make me explain. I love you, you know that, but it's like a different sort of love, like I love Kev - touching you *that* way, it feels wrong."

The heavy silence of bitter rejection made her swallow hard with guilt. She tried to dig herself out of the hole, "If you still want to go to the drive-in tonight, I'll go - as a friend, but with no benefits, unless you see my company, popcorn and a hotdog with mustard as a benefit?" She squeezed his hand and smiled. Scotts starry eyes filmed over as his upbeat features dropped visibly to a snatch of anger, he looked at the floor momentarily then sparked back to life. "You *will* grow to love me Jessica Shackley, one day, I got time, the benefit of being young, anyway, anything worth having is worth waiting for."

True to her inappropriateness she stifled a giggle diverting her misplaced humour by raking her nails softly across his stubble free baby face. He resembled the iconic Leonardo DiCaprio in Titanic, so very good looking in a boyish way, his expression couldn't mask the knowledge of his fate - the doomed voyage aboard the sinking ship. "I'm gonna hurt you if you think I'll ever feel the same way about you," she warned softly. He pulled a face. "I'm a big boy babe." He shivered and grinned. "And you've felt the proof. C'mon, let me at that old car of yours, I'll have it purring in no time - yeah and maybe your pussy will purr for me."

Urgh, did he just say that? She felt sick. Desperately sad earthy eyes had now reduced to unemotional slits beckoning her to follow as he marched towards her bright orange Datsun. He shoved his head under the hood shouting out incoherent instructions to turn the engine on or off. Within twenty minutes it sparked into life. "If it stops again don't come to the garage just text me, sometimes these intermittent faults are hard to diagnose, and …"

His colour dissolved to a deathly grey. A bulging vein throbbed visibly down the length of his forehead as he stared over Jessicas' shoulder. She followed Scotts' line of sight, giggling. "Wow, you look like you've seen a gho…?" She clocked Brad Monroe as he pulled up right behind them in a 2023 model Nissan Patrol Ti-L - so much for saving the planet with that gas guzzler she thought. Her pulse began to race wildly, what the hell was *he* doing here? She stood, arms folded defensively, as an electric window wound down slowly. He didn't cast as much as a cursory glance at Jessica which dismissed her entire existence. Nodding seriously to Scott he rasped. "Disappointed in you bud, my office, 8am, Monday morning." Turning his attention to Jessica he appraised her momentarily; his wild, exotically light eyes undressed her, threw her down and penetrated her till she screamed. He cocked an amused eyebrow at her tell tale flushed expression. His voice uncharacteristically softer than ever drew her further in, "well Miss Shackley, seems we meet *again.*"

A herd of revealing goosebumps formed a stampede across her bare shoulders as her cheeks reflected the crimson sunset of wanton thoughts laid bare. He deliberately held his eyes somehow stripping her again of her clothes. His lips parted slightly, and he wetted them slowly and seductively - he knew *exactly* what women wanted - the bastard. He had her, transfixed, his puppet, to do whatever he wanted with, that is, *if* he wanted. Throwing his head back he scorned her weakness with a sexy but cruel smirk; he thought she was going to be a challenge - women were so boringly predictable. Without another word he accelerated into the distance.

Jessica was unaware that she'd held her breath, until she let out a huge sigh watching his patrol fading into the distance. "I really *hate* that man," she whispered half to Scott and half to herself. Scott grabbed her and shook her back to life, "Hate him? Are you kidding me? Your whole fucking world stopped when you laid eyes on him!" Jessica threw her arms around Scotts neck, "don't say that, it's *you* I like, don't you know that? Okay so I play hard to get, but that's because I want *you* to work for it, can't you see?"

Scott grinned and kissed her, "yeah?" Women, so deliciously complicated, maybe he was gonna get a root after all, "awesome." She immediately regretted leading him on when she felt his rock hard crotch digging into her leg. "You're so sexy, come on, let me make love to you on the beach tonight; promise I'll be gentle, you know you need it, it's time you gave it up to *me* babe, no more games."

He rubbed himself up and down against her as though the feeling of his erect penis would somehow conjure up the genie of desire, it served only to conjure up bile in the back of her throat. He whispered seductively,"the sounds of the ocean and making love to you, oh baby, it'll be magic." It would certainly need a magician to make her want *him*. Clearing the bile from her throat she squeezed his hand thinking quickly, "sounds wonderful, I want to *so* bad, but, I can't - damned monthlies."
Un-original, but always effective in an emergency - straight out of the 'girls handbook on how to deal with men 101.' His face dropped again, she could feel the heat of her cheeks revealing her lies, why was her bloody face so transparent? Attempting to make it better but actually re digging the hole she was already in, she added, "but we can go for a walk for awhile - Hilarys Marina? I love it there, there's a full moon tonight, it'll be *so* romantic." He tried not to let her see his disappointment, sex was on his mind. "I want you so bad baby, but nah, I'll give it a miss, I'm not into blood sports." He murmured, pushing her hand to feel the proof between his legs again, her expression revealed the answer to that one. "There's other ways a girl can please her guy you know," he winked licking his lips slowly.

She automatically recoiled, then pushed him out of her car with a playful smile, "go away, you sex maniac." He laughed tinged with a frustrated edge as he jumped into his jeep, "you know it babe, I'm hard as fuck and it's *all* yours." She tried not to show her repulsion at the thought. "I can't wait" she whispered, somewhat sarcastically, but swept up in his own virility he didn't notice. "I gotta pick up some smoke first, text me when you're there." He made a heart shape with his hands and sped off into the night; Coldplay blaring from his stereo. Jessica waved, wanting to return his un-heart felt gesture with her middle finger.

She was wondering how she was going to put him off without breaking his heart; she spat out the puke in her mouth shuddering at the notion of having any sort of sex with him, or even walking on a moonlit beach with a young idiot male who reminded her of her brother, but if it kept *him* happy, it's the least she could do for the repercussions he may face for fixing *her* car!

The car burst into life first time, with her foot hard down on the gas, she travelled down the West Coast Highway, her favourite scenic road. The moon threw silver streaks across the flat blackness of the dark mysterious Indian Ocean. Arriving at Hillarys Marina she got a text from Scott who'd had second thoughts about wasting time on romantic walks, especially as he'd just picked up a hot girl hitchhiker with a top rack needing more than a lift. "Babe, somethings come up, gonna be awhile, take a rain check on that walk yeah?"

If she'd cared about him she'd have been furious however she sighed with relief, laughing about what could have possibly 'come up', as long as it wasn't up her, she was cool. She grinned with satisfaction she'd at least got her car fixed. She turned the old key in the ignition but it just clicked - dead. She picked up her phone to call Scott back, the phone was dead too. "Beam me up Scottie." Locking the car she was thankful for the full moon that cast adequate if not eerie light across the otherwise unlit and deserted roads. She walked towards the nearest bus stop, all she could hear was the click clack of her heels on the road.
A large vehicle skidded around the corner skimming past her so close she had to run to the centre of the road - the car rudely sounded a two toned horn at her. She spun around to mouth obscenities to the driver and for a few stolen moments she reached into unforgettable eyes. Stuck in the middle of the road on an island, she watched the Patrol disappear around the corner. A familiar excitement mingled with the hatred of rejection overwhelmed her. "I don't fucking believe it, he might own the garage but he's taking his role far too seriously," she cursed - wishing it was *him* she was supposed to be meeting.

She crossed the second road, and waited patiently at the bus stop with no idea if there was a bus due; the two toned horn sounded out again. Her eyes searched and sighted the Patrol, parked in a lay-by further up the road - she wondered if he was playing some kind of sick and twisted game with her. She noticed a hand, beckoning her over - of their own volition her legs took her to him- trying not to run. "Get in," he rasped whilst staring at the road ahead. She wanted to say "stalking me yeah? Well jog on

buster." But, subserviently she obeyed, a shivering wash of
nervous excitement causing her heart to beat faster.
Climbing up awkwardly, her short skirt rose further up her legs
than she'd wished, Brads sharp eyes opened wider as he glimpsed
her perfectly rounded tanned thighs. His eyes twinkled for a
moment, and then returned to his mask of unemotional coldness.
She wanted to ask him a million and one questions, but her voice
was strangled by his superior presence - she made light
conversation. "Aren't these big gas guzzlers gonna be heavily
taxed? You know, climate change and all that?" She thought it was
a perfectly contemporary subject and one of intelligence. His
response was curt, "the Tesla is on order." She planted her face
against the window staring out of it, feeling like a prized lemon.

     Sensing she was feeling awkward, he couldn't resist
winding her up a little more, "wow, Scottie was right, you really
did need a ride didn't you?" He grinned to himself as her silence
said it all. As they headed up the freeway towards her home,
feeling irritated by his supreme arrogance, she tutted and added,
" so, how did you know I was gonna be there?" He smirked in a
jumped up know all way. "There's not much I don't know hon, and
I happen to be on my way home, this is my route; but I'm sure you
know that right?" She took a deep breath in order to argue. "Well
if you think I was hanging about in a bus stop in the hope of
glimpsing the almighty you, you can let me out of this vehicle right
now!"

     He laughed but didn't bother to answer; he knew she
wanted to be near him - they all did. Jessica peered out of the
window - neon lights and flashing colours whizzed by but she
found herself, stealing glimpses of the cruelly handsome driver -
there clearly wasn't a god, because men like this were only created
to punish women. She noticed his muscles were fighting against
the confines of his tight Hot Tuna tee shirt. Wearing only a pair of
beige canvas shorts, his legs were visible. A fine fluff of dark hair
ran softly from his ankle to his thigh. She tried to dispel her
growing excitement and wandering mind, wondering where that
fluff of hair went to. The increasing biological need to be with a
man influencing her intense eroticism.

     He put the air con on, her nipples stiffened suddenly
causing her to let out a slight sexually excited gasp, she hoped that

Brad hadn't noticed - he had. He put the digital audio radio on, and selected the smooth music channel, Barry White crooned, 'you're the first, the last, my everything.' The sense that the words had been written solely to embarrass her caused her to change channel. He frowned, but with a glint of enjoyment. An oldie screamed out the lyrics "the more I see you, the more I want you…".
She wanted to switch it off but pretended not to hear the words, which were totally written to explain her situation and clearly humiliate her in his presence. As he stared ahead she had a chance to once again appraise his face, this time closer. Such a perfectly symmetrical bone structure framing unforgettable eyes she openly pondered how he received the tiny scar above his right eyebrow.

He turned to her suddenly, catching her inquisitive stare. His face creased into tiny lines as his eyes smiled with a kindness that took her breath for a moment. She sensed a deepness - a raw honesty and vulnerability - she shivered weakly lost in her thoughts until his sarcasm crashed into them. "So why were you hanging about in a bus stop when there are clearly no busses? Argument with a boyfriend? She answered casually, her heart feeling lifted that he seemed to care. "I went to the pictures with Scott, but he tried it on, so I walked out on him!" It seemed a reasonable explanation, she wanted to send him a message that would make him respect her, like, she's not an easy lay - but it fell like a cow pat on a wedding cake.

Jessica watched with horror as his expression visibly recoiled, a new found darkness took possession within his eyes. He repeated her words in staccato, "You walked out on him?" His disapproval was obvious. She was confused by this man, she knew that it was not like her to keep silent, or to tolerate rudeness. She battled with the overwhelming urge to interrogate him and discover the secret behind those magical eyes. Her thoughts began to beg him to take her crudely to his bed or the back seat of his car in a lay by would do.

He drove right through those thoughts. "And you think to walk out on a man good enough to risk his job to repair your car, then take you to the movies, when you've led him on… is okay? Yeah?" She had to argue this one out. "Led him on? But how…" She didn't get a chance to fully explain, with sudden break force the patrol lurched to a halt. She was transfixed for a moment, stunned, they were outside her house; silently he waited for her to leave.

She turned to him in a futile attempt to regain her dignity. "But, I *didn't* lead him on." He just tutted, apparently irritated by her continued presence. She wished she had longer to explain, as she needed to reclaim his respect. She turned to offer thanks, only to notice he was absently admiring a passing lycra clad brunette girl on a push bike.

She struggled to get out in a dignified manor as her heels got caught in a gap in the step plate, she cringed and hoped he hadn't noticed her nervous awkwardness. Her fear was unfounded as he was busy texting; probably another woman. He turned to her before pulling away, his words destroyed any hope of developing a friendship or any further relations as he questioned the validity of her very existence, "I'm not surprised he tried it on with you. If you dress like *that* when you go out, you're gonna find yourself in trouble with *any* man." Standing on the sidewalk the patrol began to pull away - leaving her confused. She called after him, "dress like what ?" From the distance, shouting out of his car window, he shattered her world with two words, "A whore."

4

Jessicas mother used to dig the garden and spend time weeding or planting new flowers after a particularly bad argument with her father; she called it her earthly peace therapy. Jessica, in need of some earthly peace therapy after Brad destroyed her world, decided to plant out some Gerberas, her mothers favourite. But Brads' humiliating words haunted her, ripping away any hard earned self esteem in an instant; she wondered what he would think if he knew that this 'whore', was at 28 years old actually still a virgin.

She revisited her clothing, had she dressed like a whore? A really cruel judgement from a bitter and twisted bastard. She had to get it out of her head before he and his hurtful mouth destroyed her completely. That comment brought back a host of bad memories caused by her sister who was more deserving of the words - the effect on her psyche was devastating; Brad couldn't have said anything worse. She wanted to march into his garage and tell him how wrong he was, but common sense prevailed over such a pitiful and futile act. At least he hadn't fired Scott for helping her, seems he did have a semblance of decency.

A dark shadow loomed over the brightly coloured Gerberas' she had just planted, startled, she squinted up at Kevin's toothy grin. He rubbed 30+ sun cream on her arms, "It may be the start of spring but it's crazy weather, climate change and all that shit. It's hot today, c'mon, slip slap slop, you're turning into a lobster. Anyway why the fuck are you gardening of all things? You fucking hate gardening!" She wished that Kevin would go back to his own place instead of living at hers and visiting his! All he did was criticise her life, and although she adored his company, sometimes she wanted to be alone and miserable. She dragged herself up then sniffed the air, "you stink of ganja, will you please stop letting Scott encourage you to smoke with those pothead friends of yours?" He grinned and retorted, "in a word, no - you're only here once."

He pulled her into the kitchen. "Spill the beans, I know you fancy him, is it love or what? Are ya making babies yet?"

Kevin moonwalked elegantly across the terracotta tiles munching on a freshly stolen donut. "If you must know I find him arrogant and repulsive!" Jessicas' eyes flashed angrily in a way that amused Kevin profoundly. "Didn't you make out at the movies then? Wassup, he got a lil weaner? I know he's a dick…but nah, he ain't arrogant." He giggled at Jessicas' chameleon face as it turned several shades of purple. "He's hardly repulsive, I think he's perfect for ya, so he's a few years younger, nothing wrong with a toy boy n all that."

Jessicas face creased quizzically, "toy boy?" She let out a sigh, "Oh - you mean Scottie." Kevins eyebrows raised with interest, "so who did ya think I was chatting about?" Jessica snapped and turned her back on him so he couldn't see the heat invading her cheeks, "this subject bores me! I'll find myself a man, when, and *if,* I want one, or maybe even a girlfriend because women are clearly superior to men!" She threw a dirt smattered gardening glove at him, catching him square on the jaw.
Kevin couldn't resist pushing her, he loved to watch her get angry. "Oh my god, you thought I was talking about…" He ducked as she threw an orange at him. He chuckled with relish, "you really *do* have Brad fever." Before she could respond he grabbed his board, "surfs up, meeting Scottie, gotta split with a spliff!" He ran out the front door and down the drive to his car, shrieking with laughter while dodging the objects that Jessica was throwing at him. "And don't come back!" She yelled after him, attracting curious stares from passers-by.

Jessica tried to get back on track and focus on her business, she spent that night recreating her business social media pages, tweeting her new beauty premises. She set up a Meta Facebook and Instagram marketing campaign all from her Iphone. She ended up flicking through a host of childhood photos, the ones that she'd rather forget, but the ones that facebook insisted on reminding her were there. She drifted into a turbulent sleep - vivid, visual representations of the distant past flickered out of sequence in tangled black and white with bursts of colour. Her mother was always there, the trauma of such loss, caused her to protest out loud, her cries lost in the silence of darkness. Shadows of the past continued to invade her unconscious mind.

The corners of her mouth twitched into an involuntary smile, as she watched her brother celebrate his seventh birthday, Amber crying, why was she always crying? Dad always shouting at her. Kevins birthday party erupted across her dream, Amber ruined his birthday cake in a temper pushing her hands deep into its creamy depths. Involuntary tears tracked Jessicas' face ending in a pool of pain in her feather and down pillow. Her father was shouting at them all, while viciously hitting his mother, it was her fault for such bad kids, Amber, was *her* fault, his face blackened with disgust at his own daughter. Kevin and Amber were crying. "No!" She cried out. "Please don't hit my sister and my mummy." She sat up suddenly aware that she had once again been subjected to a recurring nightmare from the past; it usually haunted her when she was feeling emotionally low or extra tired. She tried so hard to put the anguish of her dysfunctional family behind her but it came to haunt her when she needed it least. She cursed the Meta Facebook photos and vowed to delete them, some memories need to stay forgotten.

The rest of the night consisted of wrestling with her quilt. Her father and mother dominated her thoughts. Drunken and enraged most nights, her father would torment and abuse his family. Yet she also remembered early years, Kevin was a baby, mummy and daddy spending days on the beach with them, laughing, splashing in the sea, daddy used to help Amber and her jump over the waves until mummy called them back because barbecue was ready. What happened to him that made him so horrible? And why did he pick on Amber quite so much as a kid? Her mother, gentle kind, once a strong intelligent woman quitting a successful medical career as a radiologist, became nothing more than a subservient slave to his every whim. She'd tried to heal him, to understand his anger and patiently tolerated it in the hope she could change him, but nothing she could do was ever good enough for him. When her body finally failed and her battle with cancer consumed her, it was only at her hospital bedside did he express his love and regret for his actions - when it was far too late.

Jessica wiped the tears that gushed and re-affirmed she'd never let a man hurt her the way her father destroyed her mother and broke up their family. After their mothers funeral, Amber lost the plot, seemingly unable to cope with the burden of loss, she fell down the slippery slope of drugs and alcohol too. Amber ran with a bad crowd she too was always angry, perhaps inherited more of her fathers genes. Jessica cried, when her mother died, she also lost a father and a sister, all she had was Kevin and a lot of historical emotional pain. Curled into a fetal position she drifted back off to sleep, determined to bury the destructive ghosts in her head.

Monday brought a new beginning, Jessicas' diary was deliberately empty. She'd taken her home beauty treatments to the next level and rented a professional room. With the social media in place, contracts signed, the day had come for her to pick up the keys. Full of excitement she called Kevin as she was driving to the real estate agents office in Wanneroo. She knew he'd be excited for her, as daft as he could be, he was her rock - her only family.

A bored female answered. "City Motors, Darlene speaking, how can I help you?" Jessica ensured she spoke in her most polite and friendly voice. "Hi, Darlene, it's Jessica… can I speak to Kevin please?" A short silence was followed by a nervous whisper. "I'm sorry Jessica, *he* wont allow the mechanics to get personal calls!" Jessica exploded, "Who is *he?*" The timid voice returned what she had feared. "Mr Monroe." Jessica's personal rage exploded. "I've had a belly full of that man, put me through to him now please." The telephonist was clearly afraid of him, "I'm sorry Jessica, he's out, business lunch I think, he's a high roller, not like Jesse, I'm just warning you, be careful, he'll cause Kevin grief!" Jessica fumed internally but changed her tone, "so what restaurants do high rollers go to these days?" She laughed matter of factly, hoping Darlene would be disarmed and spill the beans - it worked. "Oh he goes to loads, but I think Linda made a booking at the Fancy Affair for today, but don't quote me. I went there for my wedding anniversary, it's beautiful, absolutely awesome - they serve all that Masterchef type of food - very expensive of course, but if you are anything like me, you'll want a McDonalds on the way home."

Jessica exchanged some frivolous talk about weddings, then turned her car around to head for City Motors. She laughed to herself, while *he's* at the Fancy Affair he won't know if she visits Kevin - she'll pick up the keys later. Kevin was outside smoking as she pulled into the clients car park, from the deep frown plastered across his usually happy face, she guessed he was not aware that Brad was out to lunch - her turn to tease. "Pleased to see me Bro?" She mocked him cheekily, knowing he was definitely *not* pleased. "We could hear you coming a mile away, you've gotta fucking great hole in your exhaust!" He snarled. "What the fuck are you doing here? I hope it's to book the car in properly, or me and you'll have a problem!" Jessica was shocked, "wow, what a welcome, sorry, not sorry!"

She continued to tease him, enjoying getting her own back. Kevin turned a shade of purple his head jerking in every direction for fear of Brad catching him. "Jessica! C'mon, what the fuck are you doing here?" His exasperation amused her almost to the point of hysteria. She grinned, "I might be here to buy a new car, you said yourself I need one." He hissed at her, "you're not here to buy a car! You just won't be satisfied until I lose my job as well!" Jessica stopped in her tracks. "What do you mean *as well*?" Kevin lowered his eyes, shuffled his feet and gazed abstractly at a small bug that was nonchalantly crawling over his steel toe caps. His voice lowered to a hoarse whisper, "you don't know yet do you?" Jessica shrugged, "know what? Kevin?"

"Scott was fired this morning." He followed the bug on the ground with his boot for a while then squashed it, adding in a somewhat accusatory tone, "for doing private work to *your* car Saturday." He eyed his sister with hostility. She visibly stiffened, responding slowly and carefully, with staccato repetition. "He really fired Scott for fixing my car for all of five minutes?" She paused then looked at the time on her phone, "shit, look at the time, gotta go! Let's talk tonight Kev."

She looked up at him through eyes smothered by an obvious misty blanket of guilt. Kevin watched her leave through indifferent eyes, same old Jessica - unable to hide that she was up to something - but what now? Jessica ran toward the shelter of her car. Rusty and old as it was, it had proved it's worth over the years - today was no exception. Her eyes glazed, Scott had lost his job, and it was *her* fault! An acrimonious rage burned deep within her, as she drove to her date with the devil - she put the name of the destination into her Garmin sat nav and burned rubber as she screamed out of the carpark.

5

The Fancy Affair Restaurant a celebrity haunt, sat on the East of the City of Perth, situated in the heart of the Swan Valley. A rich contrast to the white hot sandy beaches of Perth, the undulating velvet green hills were dotted with sheep and cows and offered sweeping views of both rural and suburban areas. If Jessica hadn't been so angry she'd have stopped to admire the smatterings of bubbling brooks and magnificent snaking lakes offering a true rival to anything the English countryside could muster. Pulling into the gravel drive which curved elegantly around the Hotel and Restaurant, she suddenly felt a pang of embarrassment for her poverty, symbolised for all the world to see, by a back firing rusty and bright orange 1975 model Datsun.

As she parked next to a latest model Tesla, she made a conscious pledge to herself, to use her savings and get a new car. Stepping with awe into the lavish foyer her cheeks inflamed with scarlet shame, her loose purple cheesecloth shorts and cut off cotton surf shirt hardly conformed with the strict dress code. A short greasy haired Italian man, began to usher her out rudely, correctly guessing she was not intending to patronise his elite establishment - she looked worse than the hired help. Jessica hated to make a scene, and had already noticed several guests subjecting her to their stares of upper class disdain. She owed it to Scott to stand her ground and summoned every last fibre of courage to carry on. The Restaurant Manager approached her hurriedly trying to scoot her away as if she were a fly. "I'm here to see Brad Monroe, a guest dining here today."

At the mention of his name the overworked Manager scuttled off inside the restaurant, returning with a look of disgust on his shiny red face, "lo siento, perso, your name es señorita?" She "drew herself up pretending she was so upper class she did not need a designer outfit, "tell him it's Lady Jessica Shackley - it's important." Within minutes another waiter greeted her, "Mr Monroe is in the garden suite my lady, I will take you." He ushered her to a magnificent and grand room, with only a few empty tables lavishly set with the kind of silver even if you are not a thief, you want to steal.

Floor to ceiling windows sporting panoramic garden views acted as a backdrop. Jessica had rehearsed what she was going to say to him over and over again whilst in the car. And there he was, sitting alone, a strange look on his face, but sporting a glint of amusement in his eyes. The manager showed her to a different table on the opposite end of the room, and told her that Mr Monroe would call her, when he was ready to talk. In the meantime, she was to stay there, and have a drink with his compliments, the waiter arrived in seconds presenting her with a mai tai - seems he had already ordered it, whether she wanted it or not.

She sipped it, like a lady should, wondering what was going on, he wasn't on the phone, he was just sitting there, staring at her, for what seemed an age. Every second that went by felt disarming as she gazed at him, the him she wanted so bad. His face was serene, she wished he wasn't so handsome with a magnetism she couldn't explain, she had felt that as soon as she met him.

His eyes locked on her in a way that held her there, she was again a pinned beetle in a collection. She examined every nuance of his being, but there was something odd about his expression, it looked at times as though he was whispering to himself, gasping slightly, his face twisted, and he opened his mouth as though to gasp for more air. He ran his tongue around his lips, staring at her, then he closed his eyes as he threw his head back slightly. Jessica wanted to reach over to him, hold him, and kiss the lips that were now seemingly gasping and panting for breath - was he okay?

She was about to get up and check him out, when he opened his eyes and stared straight at her, breathing fast, panting in a somewhat strangulated way to compose himself in public - then with a final gasp, he visibly relaxed and gave her a drop dead smile. Still quite breathless, he called out to her, "nice threads , I like a, *lady*, who knows how to dress for an occasion!" He was definitely struggling to breathe properly - she felt pangs of guilt, perhaps he was asthmatic, it was common in Perth especially in Spring, so he was having an attack and that's why she needed to stay away from him for a moment - her heart wanted to hold him and love him. He *was* human after all, her heart went out to him.

Brad gestured for her to join him. Jessica downed her drink for Dutch courage almost forgetting why she was there or that she was crashing his privacy. Suddenly a beautiful young girl, likely younger than her, emerged from under the table - A willowy brunette full lips, big eyes, perfect skin and legs up to Jessicas boobs. The woman grinned and winked at Brad, "I found it!" She pushed a gold and diamond earring back into its sockets and sat opposite Brad who winked at her - she wasn't fooling anyone. He looked up at Jessica who then realised exactly what had just taken place - he wanted her to see him get blown, seriously? She could now add pervert to the growing list.

She felt a crimson rage flood into her cheeks. "Take a seat, Tanya was just going." He pulled out an ornately carved oak chair, with a red velvet padded cushion, and insisted she be seated, bowing in a mock servants fashion, "for you m'lady." Jessica continued to stand, angered by his patronisation, she spoke rigidly, her body language breathing fire. "I didn't come here to blow you, seems you got that one sorted already!" Turning to Tanya who was now clinging onto his arm in a sad display of ownership, he spoke gently and lovingly to her. "I'll call you later babe." Tanya took her cue to leave, kissing him tenderly on the lips. She swung her hips in an overstated and provocative walk to the door flicking long dark wavy locks over her shoulders. Before leaving she flashed Jessica a look, that would've killed a whole species. "What a bimbo," she muttered, wishing she had legs that went that far up! "She's not a bimbo, now will you sit?"

Jessica sighed, "and I'm *not* a whore." She spat it in retaliation. He ignored her and commanded, "sit", his voice impassive and cold. Relenting, she relaxed a little, secretly pleased that his intimidating model like girlfriend had now departed she had clearly performed her one and only use to him. She should've expected a man as wealthy and well renowned as him to have a woman hanging around every corner; but under the table in a posh restaurant? She sat, feeling a tinge of jealousy even if she did despise him. She turned to Brad, who was engaged in a conversation in Italian with an adoring waiter, "Another mai tai?" He asked abruptly. She responded in equal abrupt fashion. "Martini please."

He grinned, "Martini for m'lady, shaken but not stirred, of course." He winked at the waiter who grinned knowingly back he got a kick out of Brads kinky women. Suddenly conscious of the way she looked, she cringed realising she had no real right to just barge in on him - mouthing off about one of his staff. A surge of regret tingled through her too impulsive veins, but she was here now, she'd have to make the best of it. Perhaps if she were to impress him enough, she could charm him to give Scott his job back.

She looked him straight in the eyes - he was studying her face intently. She trembled as she spoke. "My brother told me you fired Scott!" She waited for a response, but he remained silent, which served to unnerve her further. "Well, if you fired him because he was fixing my car, it's, it's not fair - I made him do it and besides, it wasn't fixed anyway!" She stumbled awkwardly over her words, not able to articulate as perfectly as she was usually capable - it seemed more credible when she rehearsed her speech in the car. She went on, despite Brads continued silence. "Scott's a good mechanic, and…" She stopped short, noticing Brad rudely yawning. "Am I boring you?" He snapped back immediately, "as a matter of fact, yes!"

His words ignited a series of volcanoes within her head, dangerously loosening her tongue. "You conceited arrogant bastard! You don't care about anyone do you? Oh, except of course for total brainless bimbo's like that girl what's her face? Oh yeah blow job Tanya!" She took a deep breath, "you make me sick!" Her jealousy was obvious, she had it bad. Her face was ruddy with the heat of her outburst.

To her amazement he threw back his head and laughed, the kind of deep raucous belly laugh that one associates with a good but very inappropriate joke. The waiter busied himself pouring wine and invited Brad to test it. She inhaled his Portuguese Musk scent with those vanilla notes and appraised him - it was impossible not to admire his commercial gravitas; he was such an Alpha male, she thought. Sitting so close she wanted to run her fingers through his dark, short cropped hair, she adored the way it was perfectly shaved to the nape of the neck, he really looked like an Italian model - the front was slightly longer, but swept back off his face creating subtle height. His colouring was decidedly unusual, and quite striking, perfectly framing his face. It was his eyes that held the key to his innermost personality traits, she mused. They shone out like bright intelligent light green beacons, giving him the sexy Arabic Sheik look - dark hair and light green eyes, a perfect magnetic combination.

The waiter left - Brad grinned at her in open mouthed amusement, he seemed quite boyish for a moment, "you're a typical Pommie!" He said it in a tantalising friendly manner, but Jessica couldn't hear the humour she could only hear her own sensitive achilles heel stemming from childhood bullying. She saw it as targeted racism, his earlier comments sticking in her mind. Her face reflected her misplaced understanding. She stood up sharply bending down to his face, so that anyone who may be watching them would think she were about to plant a kiss on his cheek. "Go to hell you Aussie pervert," she hissed.

Tossing a defiant chin in the air she stepped away with dignity and poise. She felt great, finally in control telling him like it is. That was until she heard him laughing in the distance. She was filled with a renewed love, passion and hatred for the man who had hopelessly defeated her pitiful quest to save Scott, she wondered just how she was going to ever face Scott again. She was glad he came from a rich family but might have to give in to his sexual advances to dull her guilt. She kicked her car before getting in it, if it wasn't for that car, she wouldn't be forced into a romance with someone that she didn't love.

As she left the carpark she passed Brads gleaming two tone maroon and silver Patrol Ti-L, Scott had said was worth over $100,000. There it was sitting under a sign as arrogantly as its owner. "VIP valet parking." She cursed his wealth and status and cursed her own hot temper and poverty. How could she get him to re-hire Scott? She hated defeat but hated injustice more. She stopped her car and scrabbled in the glove box. That's it, she could slip a note under the windscreen wiper. A little desperate perhaps, but another shot at saving Scotts job was worth it.

She parked next to the four wheel drive, which seemed huge compared to her little Datsun. A man walked past as she jumped out he nodded as though she was one of the VIP club and so rich no need to even dress up - he patted her car walking around it grinning like a cheshire cat. "Wow, haven't seen one of these old girls since about 85." He looked at Jessica in admiration, "hubby collects?" She nodded in compliance and wished he would just fuck off. He patted the car again, "nope, they don't make em like they used to - good on him." He walked away whistling. Once he was safely out of sight she continued to ferret through her glovebox for a pen and paper. All she could find was one of her business flyers, reversing it, she wrote neatly on the back. She slipped the heart felt note under the Patrols windscreen wiper and left, believing that even the devil himself had to have a heart.

6

Kevin texted Jessica at 7pm that night. "Can't come over tonight - I gotta hotter than hot date." She knew he was probably with one of his many surfy crowd girls. She texted back, "who's it this time? Lemme guess, Shalana? Kylie? Caroline?" He responded instantly. "Nah, you don't know her - Tanya, a stunning model." Jessica froze instantly, remembering the holier than though look on the bitches' face as she emerged from under the table; surely it couldn't be the same girl, she was younger than her but around Kevins age she guessed. It must be a coincidence, there's got to be more than one Tanya in the world. "Call me now." Kevin obeyed. "Wassup?" Jessica was lost in thought and didn't speak. Kevin hissed impatiently, "you talking or chewing a brick?" She grinned at his verbal expressions, "yeah, yeah, I'm here."

She was praying the girl would be an aspiring model and an average decent type, working as a typist or something ordinary. She smiled to herself, she was being silly and over protective. "What's she like then this Tanya?" Kevin cooed with joy, only too happy to brag about his prowess. "Oh my god, she's amazing, I met her at the garage." Jessica froze as Kevin continued to gush. "One of Brads friends, he kinda left us together in reception and she …" He inhaled with excited breath, "well, she proper came on to me. I can't believe she's so into me." Jessica couldn't hide her disgust. "Neither can I." Jessicas' bile was rising. Kevin was too high to notice her sarcasm, "told you Brad was cool." Jessica spat at her mobile. "Oh he's cool alright, like a fucking iceberg."

She kept seeing the warning glare that said keep off he's mine on Tanya's' face. "Hey, what's the deal with this fucking hatred? I told you, he's a great boss, you need to get rid of that Pommie chip on ya shoulder. I told ya, he ain't racist, and thanks to him, I'm the luckiest guy in town." His chest puffed out with pride as he cooed. "I mean, every guy would want her." She couldn't resist the dig, "and they've probably already had her," she hissed back. "What the fuck? You don't even know her." Her anger was ignited all over again. "Yeah? Well I saw her today, emerge from under Brads dining table, clearly sucking the dude off in a posh restaurant, talk about gross, and you wanna kiss her after she's had her mouth around his…"

Kevin lost it. " I Dunno what's eating at ya lately but what the fuck were you doing at his restaurant? Do you *really* want me to lose my fucking job? My only opportunity to learn a trade and get qualified? You know how hard it is to get work in Perth." After a weighted silence, he added, "whadya want anyway?" His tone, impatient and clearly uninterested. "It doesn't matter, see you the weekend." He was angry at her. "Yeah, whatever." He clicked off, anxious to prepare for his very special date, he rubbed his hands with glee, she gives head in public places - awesome.

Performing several over arm swings, Jessica watched her precious Garfield collection hit the wall one by one. Various obscenities forming on her lips, but remaining unspoken. A light tap on the door, stayed her murderous thoughts of revenge. Shaking herself back to life she was surprised to find Scott on her doorstep gripping a large bunch of her favourite freesias. A wave of remorse at giving him any hope of a relationship with her, saw her drown in her own tears.

His ideas of a platonic relationship differed greatly to hers! She searched his eyes for forgiveness, before bursting into hot tears of guilt. Immediately wrapping his arms around her, he wiped them away with tender finger tips. They stood like lonely figures for some time, hugging each other silently. Neither one wishing to be the first to say what was on their mind. It was Scott that began, sensing Jessicas' recovery. "Monroe fired me," the gravity of the situation was punctuated by his unusual empty monotoned delivery. Jessica valiantly battled another surge of tears. Scotts' sensitivity kicked in; she was putting herself through hell over him - she *did* care.

"Don't worry babe," he whispered, stroking her hair. "I didn't wanna be a grease monkey anyway." He drew himself up releasing a confident smile and added, "my family has money. I was only working there to rebel against my father, there's some long running feud with the Monroe's you know how it is. Scottish versus Irish hot bloods, something like that - guess I was stupid even daring to work for him. My dad went nuts when I told him, even threatened my inheritance and trust fund. There's little work here and the apprenticeship was a good deal, but at least leaving will please the old man."

Jessica gazed up at him, "I went to that stupid place, The Fancy Affair. I tried to talk to him about what he'd done to you can you believe he had a girl sucking him off under the table in the restaurant?" Scott recoiled and re arranged a sudden huge bulge in his trousers just at the merest notion of such an experience. Jessica clocked it but chose to ignore it, hoping it would go away. "I tried to ask him to take you back on, but didn't get a chance," she hung her head, "I ended up telling him to go to hell instead - I'm so sorry Scottie."

Scott whistled between his teeth, "Fancy Affair reminds me of my family, full of upper class bull shit." He pulled Jessica towards him, "so you knew then?" She gulped, her guilt plastered across her face. "Kev, told me, and I …" He spared her pain, "good on ya for giving him hell, now forget the Monroe family of Scottish bastards, it truly is, just you and me against the world babe." She stifled the urge to gag or laugh hysterically, instead clinging to his warm comforting body, at least he didn't see her as a whore.

She felt his limited core muscles flex with pride, "you're everything to me, my beautiful princess." She knew Scott would turn to her affections for comfort, she was trapped, she daren't turn him away in his hour of need, especially as she was the cause of that need. She cursed the masculine gender, they were nothing but a source of misery in one way or another, her father had consistently proved that over the years. Scott traced his fingers from her brow to her lips, then cupping her heart shaped face gently lowered his lips to meet hers. Each second that he kissed her felt like an hour, but for the first time, she didn't move away, nor insult him with a slapped face.

She responded, dutifully, screaming repulsed tears of unhappiness, from somewhere deep inside her mind - now she knew how an escort would feel, as she transported her conscious being somewhere else and to someone else, so that she could return an almost heartfelt passion. Scotts' loving embrace was just the pressing of two lips to her, she felt a deep sense of nothingness. She would never love Scott, not in the way *he* wanted her - now, trapped by her own stupidity, she'd wait until things were better for him, then she'd let him down gently. "I love you so much babe," he crooned, occasionally plunging his tongue into the cavity of her ear as his hands felt the curve of her breast and squeezed. "I knew you'd be mine one day," he beamed, "and now you are! I thought losing my job made this a bad day, but gaining *you* - well Mr Brad Fucking Monroe, you've done me a favour, cos, it 's a very good day!"

Jessica groaned inwardly, rapidly questioning the validity of her romantic deceit. Hysteria grabbed her by the throat, "Scott, I…" He placed a hand across her mouth, exerting almost a little too much pressure as a surge of desire mingled with the fear and anger of the rejection he almost expected. "Please, shut up, don't say anything, don't ruin it, we'll just take one step at a time, okay?" Her eyes pooled with emotion as she fought for an excuse to leave his adoring gaze. "Freesias, need water," was all she could say as she wrenched herself from his grasp, to frantically search her kitchen cupboards for a vase.

Scott shook a silver mixer at her, he needed to get her to loosen up, she won't smoke so alcoholic loosening of the knicker elastic was the only option, and now fuelled by the picture of Brad being blown by some wanton woman under a table got him beyond desperate for it. "Pina Colada?" Grinning he poured a double shot of rum and threw the silver shaker in the air. "Perfect." Jessica giggled lightly, relieved that Scott had got off the subject of his undying love and devotion for her! "Hey, wouldn't you prefer a long slow screw against the wall?" I know I would, he thought to himself, re arranging himself again. He gazed at Jessica, she was deliberately showing off those large round breasts just wobbling out of his reach but on show enough to make him see and imagine what lay under that skimpy blouse. "You wish" she laughed. "Okay, we'll settle for sex on the beach then!"

He had to stop thinking about sex, she was driving him wild, any more and he would just take her. "So, how's work?" He chuckled to himself as he worked out his frustration by beating the cream - even the notion of beating and cream was turning him on. Jessica threw herself on the sofa. "Oh yeah, I've got news, the new rooms I rented at Wangara are ready, I move in tomorrow." Scott handed her a glass. "I think we should drink to you making shit loads of money then." They clinked glasses, and quietly sipped their Pina Coladas. "Mmm Scott, you really know how to make Pina Coladas," she murmured, appreciating the subtle taste of Pineapple and Coconut, mingled with white rum and cream. "I also know how to make love," he whispered sensuously, his snake like hand slithering up her thigh pulling gently at her panties. "Make love with me tonight princess."

She couldn't help herself, the word *princess* was so cheeseball, she couldn't control herself - nerves and her inappropriate laughing disease, caused her to laugh till she cried - shattering his heart and male pride. She hadn't noticed the purple twisted anger pulsating on his forehead or the fact he was gathering his things to walk out in a final statement of rejected fury. A heavy knock at the door made them both jump - she thanked her lucky stars for the intrusion, "I don't care if it's the devil himself, I'll kiss him!" she muttered under her breath. She pulled open the door still laughing inappropriately, stopping short as a waft of musk with a hint of vanilla invaded her senses.

Brad Monroe stood strong, his commanding countenance dominated the doorstep. Despite the hardness of his face and the way his chin jutted out arrogantly, his eyes told another story, twinkling enticingly. She stood catching flies with her open mouth in awe of him, she wanted to hate him so much, but her inner feminine self fell dead at his feet, like a beggar in unworthy idolisation. "Well isn't it customary to invite a visitor in or do Poms keep guests on the doorstep?" He flashed her a sudden bright beaming smile the type an orthodontist photographed as an 'after' picture for his marketing material she thought. With a smile like that, his handsome strong face could conquer an entire country - and he knew it. Her knees visibly weakened, guilty eyes betraying her. "Oh, I was just…" She hesitated, looking back at Scott wishing he'd be swallowed up by a big hole.

Scott approached still holding his cocktail glass sporting a pink umbrella. "Mr Monroe?" Brad raised a surprised eyebrow, his twinkling eyes replaced by accusatory lasers. He noted Jessica's teary mascara tracks - she'd been crying. "I'm sorry for intruding on you and your boyfriends' cocktail night." His engaging smile suddenly as cool as the crushed ice in her drink, his warm tone edged with frost. He paused, directing his attention to Scott and added, "yeah, the guys said you'd be here. The garage is too busy

to lose a good mechanic and yeah I guess, everyone deserves at
the very least …a second chance … maybe I was a bit harsh.”

He found apologies hard to verbalise. Jessica hissed under
her breath, “you can say that again.” Scott and Brad both frowned
at her. Brad ignored her and raised his eyes at Scott in male
agreement, “catch ya Monday morning bud, but if it happens
again…” Jessica couldn’t believe it. Scott jumped in. “Oh no, I
promise…” Despite his earlier comments about not wanting the
job, he bowed and scraped in front of him yet again like a grateful
slave to his master. Scott shook hands vigorously with Brad who
smiled momentarily and nodded at Jessica, amused by
her disgust at his grovelling employee. “I hope I haven't ruined
your evening of *fun*.” Scott jumped in again like the juvenile he
was, “of course not Mr Monroe, I was just leaving anyway. I
appreciate you coming all this way just to tell me. I know Jessica
came to see you to plead my case, and I’m sorry about that, it was
nothing to do with me. Women, always so emotional.”

He planted a wet soppy kiss on Jessicas’ irate and
humiliated face. If she’d had a gun she would have put him out of
his misery with one bullet. Brad replied staring straight into
Jessica's’ eyes, “oh I know how emotionally charged women are,
they’re *all* the same.” His tone was mocking and clearly directed
at her. But before Jessica could think of a suitable intelligent serve
back, he was striding to his car with Scott licking up to him like a
sucker fish - he was beyond pathetic.

As they left she noticed a large bunch of flowers thrust
deep into the thorny pink bougainvillea climbing up her veranda,
just to the right of her door. She fished them out and inhaled their
exquisite heady scent - blood red roses clearly very expensive
from the Subiaco Flower Shop. She stared into space and wrinkled
her brow in thought, why would Scott only give her the freesias
and ditch the much more beautiful roses at the door?

7

As Jessicas' head sunk into the soft comfort of her pillow, her thoughts transported her to the murky depths of an unforgiving nightmare. She thrashed and twisted fighting with her duvet as a watery despair drowned her unconscious mind in an invisible sea of emotional confusion. She awoke in an angry sweat - that utter bastard, he finally did the right thing for Scott, so he must have read her note, he could have at least acknowledged her efforts. She cursed her loose mouth, should she have thanked him? She decided, no, anyway the rude sod didn't even give her a chance. But did he really think she looked like a whore? That comment hurt, the pain that he thought so little of her, cut deeper than it should.

She sighed, he also had a problem with her because she was born in Britain. She hadn't ever come across hostility in Australia, she considered herself an Aussie. She remembered being five years old and starting school with Amber when they arrived from England - the other kids loved their funny accents. There was always friendly banter about pommies, but that's all it ever was - usually over cricket or rugby, stupid men. Never had she looked into someones eyes and found such bitterness and hateful resentment, it hurt.

As for Scott, sucking up to Brad like his little bitch, she felt nauseated, she needed to get him out of her life - she had nothing to feel guilty for now. Men were such selfish useless miserable articles - she didn't want one, not ever - so maybe she could lose her virginity without one - Ann Summers and the automatic pulsating rabbit was her only salvation - wasn't it?

The rest of her week was spent setting up her new beauty treatment rooms at Wangara, just a few miles away from her home at Edgewater. She had two rooms on the ground floor, bordered by flower beds outside to sustain plant life and a little colour. By Friday night, the sign writer had finished his handy work, it read 'JBS - Jessicas' Beauty Salon' The posters had been hung, covering the bare cream plaster. Telstra had installed new phones, and the all important fibre network for wifi. Finally, a new chapter of happiness could begin, if nothing else, financial freedom and a reason to think of anything other than Brad Monroe's physical male perfection.

Friday night was a miserable night, despite the elation at getting the salon together, she felt a cruel loneliness, a yearning to find a mate caused in most part by Brad Monroes physique and strength of character - she bet he was a real masterful lover. The nagging primal urge to fulfil her earthly desires of the flesh was dangerously escalating. She felt cursed, unlike her friends, she could not give in to her sexual desires easily. Despite the incessant throb of her growing womanhood, she didn't offer herself to just any man that asked, there were plenty on her case on Meta Facebook not to mention Instagram.

She only wanted to give her body to a man that she truly loved, the stereotypical hero you found in films. She was old fashioned in a modern world, she knew that, but she didn't care for selfies and naked pics that all her friends were eagerly sending to guys who asked. She wanted to save herself for someone special - but sometimes wondered if being pure, for love, was a stupid pointless exercise because in all probability, love at least like the movies, just didn't exist.

She considered Scott, a decent looking young guy albeit a bit wiry - physically and emotionally mature, but a weak 'yes' man to Monroe. He possessed the attributes of a future loving husband, rare these days, and he wasn't obsessed with social media - even rarer. Yet she knew she'd never love him, at least not in *that* way. She cast her mind to Brad, and rekindled her disgust. An alpha male, responsible for breaking many women's hearts, a complete arrogant playboy. She stood up to him, but secretly feared him, and in a twisted way, was hypnotised and drawn in like a moth to a flame by his *everything*. She could never commit to loving the decent husband type of man, because she found the strength and raw machismo in alpha males too attractive, but that's the type that would show no mercy - so she was doomed.

She was terrified of having her heart broken like her mothers. A large tear plopped into her drink, as her mothers grief stricken face manifested visually in her mind. No, she must throw herself into her work, she was best off without a man, she'd have to be celibate, was there something called a "Celibate Lesbians Club?" She would google it - if there wasn't one, she felt she should perhaps start one! Love always ended the same way, heartbreak; after all there wasn't a place called lovers leap for nothing. Perhaps she should become a lesbian, after all, her hormones told her she was anything but celibate, she imagined who she would turn gay for, even that turned her on.

Her phone sang out, playing a DJ Khalid number with Rhianna, yeah Rhianna was very sexy - she laughed, Kevin had obviously changed her ring tone from her usual movie score anthems. She pounced on it, pleased to hear from someone. It was Scott - he was surprisingly upbeat for a rejected man. She slumped with disappointment, didn't this prick ever give up? She hadn't expected to hear from him again, the night Brad came to her door, her laughter at a sensitive moment truly displayed her contempt for his love, and at that moment, he had chosen to realise it, in his own sweet way. She wished he would just hate her and do one. "Scott, hey thank you for the roses, why did ya ditch them?" She listened awaiting his own grovelingly puke ridden begging voice but he remained silent for a few seconds, then he coughed, "er yeah, just thought they were too much, glad you like em babe."

Okay, so he went over the top and bottled it, made sense, sort of, yet not so convincing considering their beauty and expense. "Jessica, I just wanted to tell you that despite you're obvious cruelty to me, I still love you, but only as a sister of course; I realise now, that you were right." Jessica gasped openly, words escaping her. "I met this beautiful girl, and man, she really digs me, the way I know you don't and like you say, never will, and if you ask me she's proper up for it, if you know what I mean." He took a deep and obviously excited breath, "you see, Tanya's a model…"

Jessica interrupted, "Are you fucking serious Scott? She was going out with Kevin. She's Monroes' plaything, she's the one I saw sucking his dick at the restaurant, what kind of disturbed shit is he playing at? You're probably nothing more than part of Monroes sick kind of game." Scott beamed, "wow, she did that? Even better, a woman who is in touch with her own sexuality and not afraid to use it, is a real turn on - but I didn't have you down for being *this* jealous. She already fessed up about Kevin, said they had some fun together, but it wasn't mutually exclusive and Brad's just a friend with benefits."

"I'm not jealous for fuck sake, I just don't wanna see you get hurt - that bastard has no friends, especially female ones."

Jessicas' warning cries were ignored, as Scott congratulated himself for attracting such a beautiful and sexually fulfilling young girl like Tanya. He was already booking the table where she could go down on *him*. As much as Jessica didn't love Scott, she couldn't hide her disappointment at losing him as a never ending admirer. The line went silent for a moment then Scott added, "look, it's over between us okay? You never wanted me anyway, you got what you wanted, so be happy." The line clicked off, he was gone.

Jessica stood for a few moments, shocked to the core, although glad to finally get Scotts affections off her back, she felt more lonely than ever. She'd got used to Scott being around for male support, but guessed Kevin hadn't rung her because he hated admitting defeat, especially as she'd warned him about Tanya.

Why was that bastard interfering in every sphere of her life? She couldn't work out why Brad Monroe was using his pathetic catwalk model type girlfriend to disrupt her brothers life and now Scotts. The more she thought about it, the more it seemed apparent he was deliberately antagonising her through any man in her life, did he hate her *that* much? Was he really *that* sick? She thought of his expression at the restaurant - while he was releasing himself into Tanya's perfect mouth - oh yes - he's *that* sick. She couldn't sit at home with her thoughts for company any longer, she would confront Mr Brad Monroe in person, at *his* home and make *him* explain exactly what he is up to.

8

A warm breeze of deliciously scented night air accompanied melodious crickets, all declaring their undying love under an ebony backdrop of a myriad sparkling jewel like stars. Frogs joined in the chorus offering varying funny croaks, they batted their calls to each other like natures tennis; it was a perfect spring night for romantics and lovers - Jessica hated it, it just reinforced her loneliness.

City Beach, approximately twenty minutes drive down the West Coast Highway from Edgewater was known as an exclusive area, five million dollars plus real estate there. The journey was a spectacularly scenic drive, along some of the best beaches in the world - usually Jessicas favourite drive, but tonight it was a dark and sad lonely hearts club journey. It was difficult to locate Brads' house in the dark, the street lights were few and far between, and the ones that were around seemed to leave slight patterns dancing abstractly around the globe shedding only a very dim glow.

Her portable sat nav had no signal so she had to dig out her old UBD Perth street map by torchlight, after doing no end of U-turns in tight cul-de-sacs, she finally found his house - set back down a sweeping gravel drive. She parked a little way down the street, not wishing to let him know of her arrival. Appraising his house from a safe distance, she sighed wistfully, a white rendered modern double storey and truly breathtaking mansion - it was a thing of beauty to behold. Designed in the latest Continental style and the height of modern fashion - it's cream rendered straight lines represented architectural perfection. Its splendour was surrounded by deep red Grevillea's and pretty pink tea trees with a stunning scented climbing jasmine that adorned its balconies.

She felt weak and insignificant all of a sudden, his house was as imposing as his personality. Perhaps she should just go home, to her small but homely Edgewater duplex; she felt so poor, a real loser. She turned the radio on low, a Radiohead song 'Creep', flooded her car with the exact lyrics that told her she was a weirdo and she didn't belong there! She forced herself to be brave and wiped away her tears of self pity that had formed. Refusing to allow the size of his house to intimidate her she drew in a deep breath to steady her nerves. She reminded herself, he was very clearly, deliberately and cruelly meddling in her personal life, and she had to stop him. She knew she should go home, she knew she was on a mission that was likely to hurt her even more.

As she exited her car she took a deep breath, despite everything, perhaps it was worth the humiliation, the utter emotional suicide, just to lay eyes on him again to inhale him. She almost tip toed up the street, breathing carefully and willing herself to harness her inner strength. Slipping through ornate gates that closed off the drive she followed a line of solar lights that lit as she approached. She could see a sparkling crystal chandelier and heard voices - her stomach dropped, she felt foolish what the fuck was she doing there? But her stubborn curiosity got the better of her - just who was he entertaining in his palace? Perhaps it was Tanya - she could finally get the proof to show Scott and Kevin that she was right about Brads' deliberate deceit.

She hitched up her skirt another notch to reveal a good amount of leg above the knee, and marched with renewed confidence past his triple garage to the double fronted hardwood door. A lions head brass knocker stared menacingly at her, she was sure it would bite. She shivered, but spent time admiring the lacquered double doors with spectacular inset glass cut stained glass. Questioning her sanity once more, she bottled it and turned to leave. A noise at the door, caused her to pivot around on one foot, she looked directly into a woman's' kindly face. "Oh, hello dear, what can I do for you?"

The lady smiled, bright white. " Oh, I was... er …" She stuttered like a stupid flustered juvenile. The woman smiled knowingly with surprising warmth. "It's Brad you want isn't it dear? We've been expecting you." Without waiting for an answer she called out. "Bradley darling, your girlfriend has arrived!" Jessicas' legs suffered instant paralysis along with her tongue, she wondered just what expression Brad would have when he set eyes on *her* - his girlfriend. The lady looked her up and down, appraising her thoughtfully. Brad arrived after a few minutes, wearing nothing but a white towel. The sharp eyed lady watched every muscle movement in Jessicas' face, as her eyes openly feasted on Brads' naked chest, and *oh my god,* what a knicker wetting chest. Her heart was rapidly beating out of control.

His mother broke the electrically charged but weighted silence. "Bradley, at last, you finally have an ordinary girlfriend!" Brad stared at them looking decidedly flushed like a naughty schoolboy. The lady looked from one to the other. "I know, I know dear," she laughed, "you two clearly want to be together, and what a lovely couple you make - I'll make myself scarce!" Her eyes twinkled with glee. "Well don't keep her on the doorstep Bradley, invite her in for god sake, you weren't born in a barn!"

Jessica gazed open mouthed at Brads' uncharacteristic friendliness as his mouth curved into a wide smile, displaying a disgustingly perfect row of unblemished teeth again. She wished her teeth were as straight and perfect - she made a mental note to go get them whitened and maybe a brace. Her eyes skidded around nervously as she awaited his angry marching orders. He was such a beautiful specimen of a man, and she couldn't help wondering if he had anything on under that towel - his nakedness almost stopped her breathing.

He didn't speak, still smiling, he beckoned her in with a rather aristocratic wave of his hand, intending she should follow him. But she wasn't sure what she should do and was left alone floundering for words in the entrance with the woman who had been curiously examining the dynamics of their interactions. Jessica wasn't sure that she liked being referred to as an 'ordinary' girlfriend, but she was sure that the comment was a compliment.

She had guessed the woman was his mother - she was very likeable. A petite 5 foot something, immaculately groomed in every aspect, she couldn't have been much over fifty, most definitely botoxed and perhaps had some fillers she mused; as she scanned the woman's face she made another mental note to top up her botox. "Oh dear, he's just so rude sometimes, I really don't think he realises we are not all his servants." His mother gushed, ushering Jessica inside, "Bradley is likely back in the spa dear, I will take you there."

Stepping into the marble tiled entrance, the wealth of her surroundings invoked an involuntary gasp. Abstract masterpieces dominated the gleaming white walls. Brads mother whom she later learned was called Julia, smiled knowingly at her. "First time here?" Jessica could only nod in agreement, Julia continued, "It's quite inspiring isn't it, Bradley decorated it for his wife himself, it's a little too sterile for my taste though, too much white, but I guess neutral is the style these days - I'm far too old school - give me leather, walnut, jarrah and lots of bookcases. But after Jesse died, I couldn't face rattling around the manor house on my own, so many memories, you know, so I'm here until he tires of me."

Jessica wanted to die, did she just say his *wife*? Julia took Jessicas' hand in hers and swept her through the maze of rooms, all equally as grand, until they reached an outdoor terrace. Mature cocos palms swayed romantically in the soft breeze and a breathtaking array of lush scented tropical shrubs and plants in pots surrounded a jacuzzi on a jarrah wooden plinth with steps up. "I guess his departure is his funny way of us getting to know each other, there's usually a method to his madness - I knew he'd be in there, waiting for you," she winked, "he's a dark horse, not always what you think - so sometimes, even if he doesn't deserve it, give him the benefit of the doubt, he's a good egg really, you just need to know how to crack him."

Mothers good advice she thought and oh how she would like to crack him - if only she really *was* his girlfriend. Brad was laying back, his strong heaving chest visible above the water line. His eyes were closed in quiet contemplation and relaxation. Jessica wished she could strip off, join him and kiss his Italian stallion hard body all over. Her mind began to float away with the imagination of him kissing her passionately back - she sighed. Julia broke the spell, "I forgot to ask your name Hon?" Julia drawled, in an articulate and well spoken voice trying to make small talk in the hope her son would stop being a complete ignorant arse and greet his guest.

Jessica whispered hoarsely, wishing the ground would swallow her up, it was definitely a *'beam me up Scottie '*kind of moment. I mean, what the hell was she actually doing there or going to say to a half naked Brad who was expecting the arrival of his girlfriend? Her voice cracked as she spoke, "Jessica, I'm Jessica Shackley."
"Why hasn't Bradley introduced me to you before? Oh, he's too secretive for his own good!" She threw Bradley a dark look which he ignored. Julia hugged her, "Well, welcome Miss Shackley, it's so nice to meet you at last. You're a little early though, we weren't expecting you for at least another hour, Brad said you're a croupier

at the new Casino in town - how exciting. I don't really gamble but hey ho!" She smiled at Jessica, "you certainly are *not* what I expected."

Brad ducked his head under the water then emerged, slowly, like Poseidon - all he needed was his trident and she sure would love to see that. Julia whispered, "the robes are in the closet over there dear, I'll leave you two to enjoy." Jessica couldn't deceive her any longer and with a sudden heated rush of honest emotion she blurted out. "Julia, I'm sorry for the confusion, but I won't be staying, I'm not Mr Monroes girlfriend, I'm just a - just a friend, I dropped in to thank him for helping another friend, but I'm intruding, he's obviously expecting someone special."

Julia was openly disappointed, "I should have known, you are *far* too grounded and decent to be *his* type." She shot a frown of disapproval at Brad who'd sat back in the spa eyes half closed, his expression a picture of male beauty and ignorance. Julias' face visibly dropped with disappointment, "you must come again dear, Bradley needs nice girl friends like you." Jessica wanted to cry, wishing with all her heart Brad would leap up and say yes, she's my girl. "Sure, definitely, I will," Jessica responded awkwardly. Brad suddenly called out, "it's okay, mother, I'll see my *friend* Jessica out." He shot Jessica a grin. Julia squeezed Jessicas' hand, "I'll see you again - soon I hope," she winked, and then with a swish of taffeta she was gone, deliberately leaving them together.

Jessica sucked her breath in as Brad once again emerged from the jacuzzi. Skin tight black speedos reminiscent of a seals skin clung to every muscular bulge and the most important one with no muscle. His body rippled confidently in the subdued lighting; yes, he was a god, in fact, now had become a literal wet dream. She tried to admire the huge potted tree fern that curled out majestically behind him, but her eyes of their own volition, led her attention back to the display of wanton knicker dropping masculinity that was forced upon her. He enjoyed the effect his nakedness was having on her, slowly and provocatively drying himself with a towel whilst his eyes remained locked upon Jessicas' face.

He was deliberately taking a mental note of her flushing scarlet embarrassment. She was openly spell bound by this display of male eroticism. He was aware of his physicality and its effect on women, he encapsulated alpha male magnetism and he was not afraid to use it like a weapon of mass orgasm which he used when it suited him, and now, seemed a good a time as any. As though pulling away from a bewitching spell, Jessica pulled her lustful thoughts back into order, and quipped sarcastically, "is that show supposed to be turning me on?" Never shifting his burning eyes away from hers, he murmured softly, "I don't know Jessica, you tell me - is it?" Her face flooded with hot embarrassment, he was staring her in the face, and taunting her with his raw sex appeal, how could any woman not be attracted to him, she thought.

She should have said, *'yes, now please just take me, any way you want.'* But she pulled back, regaining her strength, throwing her hands to her hips in defiance. "If you were the last man on earth, I'd become a lesbian," she rasped, "now, when you've finished playing games with me, could you see me to the door?" She was back in control. His eyes reflected no emotion, she couldn't see what effect her answer had upon him, he appeared as unruffled and calm as ever. It irritated her, because she wanted to get under his skin.

He grinned, unmoved, "So may I ask, why are you here, at my home, my dear lesbian friend?" At that moment Julia burst in, "Bradley, sorry to interrupt but Tanya is on the phone, she's very upset, she's been trying your mobile for the last hour but it's going to voicemail, why don't you ever charge the damned thing?" Without casting Jessica another glance, he clutched a towel and strode imperiously toward the study. Jessica stood awkwardly with Julia, "I'm sorry to have intruded, I'll see myself out."
Julia linked arms with Jessica, "are you sure dear?" Jessica nodded feeling even sadder and very foolish, she wanted to cry. "No, come on, I'll walk you to your car." Julia was eaten away with curiosity, she'd not yet fathomed this so called friendship with her son. She knew him only too well - he doesn't do female friends - only bed partners and it was clear, this innocent girl, had not been one, but she was sure of one thing, she wanted to be.

The gush of warm floral jasmine scented air embraced them as they walked arm in arm down the street. Jessica found her voice, "forgive me for saying, but you look way too young to be Brads mother." Jessica vocalised her thoughts finding strength in the anonymity of darkness. Julia squeezed her hand, "thank you dear, I'll be 60 soon and I so hate the idea of becoming a blue rinse queen, a good amount of Doctor Botox a bit of filler here and there." She laughed lightly then seized her opportunity. "So, what's the story with you and Bradley, no romance? Not your type?"

Jessica foolishly rebutted the notion a little too quick, for smart Julia, "Oh no, my brother works for him at the garage." Julia immediately quizzed, "which one?" Jessica had forgotten that Brad Monroe was a big shot with several garages to his credit. "City Motors" she replied. Julia stopped as they stood under a street light, she spoke with a sudden hushed voice staring intently at Jessicas' expression, "You're in love with him, aren't you?" Jessica gasped, a little too loudly, "gosh no! Just friends." Julia's interrogative stare was a replica of her sons. Her tone was distinctly disbelieving, "friends?"

It was time to fess up, she took a deep breath. "Actually, no, we're not friends. You're quite mistaken about my feelings for your son, it's quite the reverse actually. I hate to say this, but…" She took another deep breath and blurted it out with venom. "I can't stand him, he's an egotistical arrogant man, who treats people, especially women with little or no respect." Her outburst shocked Julia - Jessica drowned in the loaded silence for some minutes before Julia responded curtly. "I see!" Then she added, "It's simple then, you don't know you're in love with him, but give it time, you will." The voice of wisdom had spoken. They stood silently by the Datsun, Jessica unlocked it and got in, leaning out of the window, "I'm really sorry to say this, but all the time in the world won't change my mind about him" With a knowing smile, Julia waved her off, "okay dear, but one day, I know that you will tell me that I'm right - of that I'm quite sure."

Driving home, Jessicas' head turned upside down. She cursed Brad, it was apparent he held nothing but contempt for her, and she felt the same for him. So why would Julia Monroe say such a thing? Perhaps she was one of those women who just enjoyed drama, after all she was *his* mother plus lets face it when someone looks like a movie star, everyone swoons, how fickle and shallow humans really are. Why didn't women chase after a guy with a great personality? Julia was undoubtedly an astute woman, did she see something, a flicker, a spark, that she herself didn't see?

She remembered the way her breathing had quickened, and her pulse raced at the sight of his body. She then reminded herself that she should feel no shame regarding the needs of her own sexuality and it was that physical desire that Julia had almost certainly sensed, mistaking it for romantic aspirations.

Her feelings for Brad were nothing more than a primal sexual urge for a hot, well muscled, fit as fuck, near naked man. What woman wouldn't get the odd twinge? She sighed, as she thought about Scotts gentle and oh so loving embrace. He would have given her all she needed and some. No, Julia was wrong, she wasn't in love with Brad, because she hated him. Or did she hate him because she *was* in love with him?

9

Julia Monroe stretched, languidly tracing a french manicured finger against the raised velvet pattern of the maroon Jacquard chaise longue - she appraised Brad and his latest croupier girlfriend Danielle, another leggy stick insect with a stereotypical bland personality and overly sized breasts. She cursed Brad, she knew he was punishing himself, he couldn't let go of the hurt he'd suffered at the hands of his ex wife. As soon as Danielle made her exit to the bathroom, Julia launched her attack. "She's a coke sniffing mindless idiot, what's wrong with you Bradley? Why on earth do you keep subjecting yourself to these daft trophies, instead of finding a real woman?"

Brad was used to his mothers persecution of his love life. "My personal life is none of your business!" He snapped angrily - but the truth hurt. "Your happiness *is* my business! What about that girl? What's her name? Oh yes, Jessica, beautiful, big baby blue eyes, angelic little expression and a lovely curvy body, real, natural understated beauty with true blue Aussie grit, so tell me, what's wrong with *her*?" Brad leant over the bar and poured himself a neat whiskey, swallowing it in one gulp. His eyes narrowed, his expression, scornful. "True Aussie grit? That's a laugh, more like another deceitful pommie bitch." His words, razor edged, only his mother could dare to continue with the same line of questioning. "Oh don't be such a galah, calling her a pom, all my days. She likes you - a lot and she is definitely *not* a bitch."

He shot her a look that would turn a fluffy bunny to stone, she recoiled, "okay I'll butt out but…" She paused, "…she reminds me of the good that was once in Catherine and she is very similar in looks, does that bother you?" He shot her a look. "You haven't forgiven yourself, have you?" Her tone was softer. Brad drew himself up, "I forgot about that bitch three years ago, you would do well to do the same!" His mouth hardened until it was nothing more than a thin lipped grimace. "You're always trying to play the psychiatrist with me, reading into things that simply aren't there."

"She's in love with you Brad! It was written in her eyes. I told her, but she denies it. She doesn't realise it yet, and …" Brad stood up straight, fists clenched, "you told her she's in love with me?" His eyes flashed as his countenance became filled with a tormented strangulation of pain and rage. "You *told* her? Please, say you didn't do that, really? Just stay out of my personal life mother! I'm warning you!" Julia sighed deeply to see the pain laid bare in her sons eyes, but unperturbed she continued, "yes, yes, I've heard it all before, just listen to one bit of advice, Catherine was a one off, you can't tar everyone else who remotely reminds you of her with the same brush, open your eyes boy, look at what you're doing to yourself! Those meaningless girls like stick insects, they're gold diggers my boy. I'll not let you squander your fathers inheritance on bitches and coke so open your eyes and let your heart have another chance."

Brad wrapped a white towelling robe around his body, "why do you do this to me all the time?" He poured a whiskey and coke. "I work hard, I play hard - I'm not your little boy mum." Julia sat on the sofa, she held her soft hand against her head. "You're so much like your father!" Brad softened, "so you keep saying, but look, I make money, I know you disapprove of the girls I go with, but I'm a red blooded man, with Italian in me, and that's *your* fault. " He winked at her, disarming her with a smile, "if I need a woman, I take them, when I want them. They throw themselves at me, but don't worry, I have no intention of wasting dads money on any one of them. The trouble is, dad took the only decent woman on the planet, so I don't stand a chance!" He grinned, downed his drink and gave her a big hug sitting close to her.

"I miss him," Julia whispered, "I want you to know what real love feels like, like I had with your father, we were the toast of the town, everyone in Perth wanted to be like us, we had true love, so I know it *does* exist, you just have to open your heart to let it in or…"

Brad squeezed her hand, "I know you do, and I thought I had real love once, I *did* open my heart, I married her, but look what she did to it, she incinerated it. I lost my wife, my child and best friend all at the same time because of her betrayal, so yeah, my interest in women is for sexual gratification only, they have no other use to me now, and never will - period."

Julia sighed, "but that girl, Jessica, there's something about her." Brad shushed her with his finger tips to her lips, "she's frigid, so definitely *not* my type - now please stop the match making. I've enough women bothering me as it is." He swept his hair back and made a gesture from head to foot. "You can't look like *this* without having an entourage of bitches." He laughed at his mothers disapproving but amused expression. Julia muttered under her breath, "and here comes one of those bitches right now."

Danielle made her re-appearance, flicking her waist long hair extensions out of her face as she tottered towards them in overly high heels. Her oversized silicons were bulging like footballs begging to be kicked, a mini skirt revealed very long legs, her lips were so pumped with filler they would have made Mick Jagger jealous - she typified what young girls felt they needed to look like in order to attract males. When in fact they looked more like ridiculous cartoon versions of blow up dolls ready to indulge male fantasies. "Oh my gawd, you two are just such little old darlings." She whipped out her phone, "come on mom, selfie time," Julia visibly cringed, mouthing to Brad, the word, "American?" Julia reluctantly posed for a photo with Danielle, flashing a death ray stare to a grinning Brad standing in front of them.

Brad grabbed Danielle placing his hands around her bony waist, kissing her profoundly. "Is that the time? Wow, bedtime, already?" In a deliberate boyish display of rebellion - he winked at his mother with a wicked grin. Julia knew when it was time to retreat in defeat. "I'll see myself out, I'm going to Rosita's to stay tonight they're having a beetle drive card night! Goodnight Danielle, very nice to meet you." She scuttled out quickly before the lovely Danielle subjected her to any more selfies - she couldn't stand her high pitched nasal voice.

Brad closed and locked the door behind her, Danielle called him from the bedroom. As he walked in, she was already naked bending over the table preparing their love enhancement. She pulled out a bag and lined up four perfect lines of coke - sniffing two up in succession she laid on the bed. Brad inhaled his in seconds, and appraised her squirming naked for his attention, but he felt cruel, he knew he wasn't happy. "Not here, out on the terrace, I need a drink." She followed him like a trained dog to the balcony. "Got your toys?" Danielle smiled seductively, oh you're feeling kinky tonight. He hated that word, folding his arms he emphasised the word again, "I want the cuffs tonight" She could tell he was in a mood.

"Gotta robe? Ive got what you need in the car." He threw a silk dressing gown at her from the spa cupboard and walked with her to the car, "it's good to know you care" she purred - "I don't," was his reply but she didn't react to his cruelty. She pulled a bag from the car and opened it "will these do?" He looked inside to see a range of dildo's and handcuffs, "perfect, now call Tanya, lets make it a party." Danielle stared after him in dismay, she wanted his love, but was prepared to do anything to be in his life - she sighed, girl sex would require a few more lines.

When Tanya arrived she hugged Brad, she was so happy to hear from him. "So what're you thinking babe? Need some extras yeah? Lucky you got deep pockets." Danielle called out, "he's gonna lose control tonight Tanya, I've got his handcuffs." Brad pushed Tanya toward the spa gently, stripped off and stepped into the bubbling waters. With his manhood standing proud, he closed his eyes and let the women feast their eyes, causing both women to gasp as he stroked it gently. Opening his eyes slowly he half whispered, "what I want, is …" He stared into the garden over their heads allowing his imagination to transport him to another world where he would know exactly what he really wanted and where happiness could exist. He was sure he could hear Jessicas Datsun roaring down the west coast highway, the hole in the exhaust was easily heard for miles - it upset him for a moment.

The girls exchanged confused expressions, they'd never seen him quite so dreamy. It was Tanya who was on the clock, that piped up, "is this an all nighter cos if it is I gotta make a call." Brad came back from his dream and smiled at the two beautiful women as he rubbed his manhood back to life. He flexed his muscles in a hypnotic way, and held out his hands for the cuffs, "well what are you waiting for girls, come and get me."

As Julia drove to her friends, she thought about Brad, she knew her son better than he knew himself, she wondered if she'd pushed him too hard. Then she decided that she hadn't, it had been three years since Catherine left him, and for three years he'd thrown his seed around town as though his life depended on it. She knew he was doing lines of cocaine most nights, washing it down with whiskey. He was deeply unhappy, a lost and lonely soul with everything to live for, yet he was indulging in a slow heart broken and empty suicide. She was determined to do something about it - but what?

10

After only a month Jessicas' new beauty salon venture had paid off, she handled more work then ever, not having to waste time driving all over Perth. Her profit margin was high enough to cover overheads and still almost double her previous take home income. This was the time to purchase a new car! She chose a Nissan main dealership only two blocks away from her salon. Ambrose an eager to please young Italian his workmates nick named Casanova rushed over as soon as he saw her. His colleagues chuckled through the windows, this punter was absolutely perfect for Casanova. They laid bets as to whether he would be successful picking her up or not.

Jessica appraised him as he swaggered towards her, he didn't look like a typical car salesman. She figured he was from Italian or Greek stock, he carried himself with the pride of a Gladiator. He slicked back his raven black hair then flashed a bright 'come fuck me baby' smile. Jessica tried not to look into his eyes, he was an archetypal latin lover with seductive charisma hidden within dark cocoa eyes that carried a familiar twinkle - she had to admit, she felt something in his presence. He sported WA's typical work dress, smart beige canvas shorts with long socks but they didn't cover the ornate tattoo's which ran the length of his calf to his thigh - she tried not to admire his legs or his bulging biceps, she reminded herself he was likely around Kevin and Scotts age, and boys only a few years younger than here were so immature - and always only interested in sex.

She put on her professional expression. "How much will you give me part-ex for this Datsun?" Ambrose ignored her question, instead sizing her up from head to foot. "You a nurse mia bella?" He replied, his accent rather down and dirty Italian with a hint of completely spine tingling. He liked what he saw and made no attempts to hide it, pretty, with curves, "mama mia!" She looked down at herself and laughed, she was still wearing her white tunic. "Oh, no, I'm a beautician and masseuse, I own the salon on Prindiville Street." His expression changed into one of acute rapture at the thought of her hands rubbing oil all over his nether regions, "sorprendente!" She didn't know what he said but whatever it was, it sounded complimentary especially as he delivered it while smiling adoringly, "Oh, prego, you help er, il capo, boss - he has hurt spine. He is maestro d'amoure, er, uomo sexy." He grinned, "women love him - But I am better - maybe you give number, we, fai rumore, si?" He winked with a wicked smile then rushed back to the office. Jessica could feel her cheeks flush scarlett in another tell tale virginal flood of desperate for a sexy mans touch.

Jessica continued to look over a small Nissan leaf, the new electric model, good on fuel with self parking, DAB audio, a sensible option, reliable and economical, her mother would understand and approve. Perhaps if she were to offer the boss a free back massage he would give her a bit of discount - anything was worth a try. Ambrose rushed up behind her with his boss in tow - the both were enjoying the view that her lifting hemline gave them. They stood watching her bent over looking at the interior of the car. "Here she is, the masseuse." He winked at his boss, "la voglio." She wheeled around to stare into the haggard face of Brad Monroe. "You? This is *your* garage *as well?*" She gasped. "Yeah, one of many." He replied quietly, the usual energy and aggression was definitely lacking. He briefly addressed Ambrose, "I'll handle this one Ambrose." Ambrose couldn't help calling back to her, making a call me sign with his hands, "sei bella ragazza." Brad frowned at him and waved him away.

Jessica could see he was in intense pain. "What's wrong with your back?" She asked, pretending to care when what she really meant was, "serves you right you arrogant male whore!" His face twisted with pain every time he moved, "I think I twisted a ligament in my lower back," She threw sarcasm at him, "in bed with the new girlfriend?" She couldn't help herself, demonstrating that she *was* jealous that he hadn't gone for bed olympics gold with *her*.

"Actually, yeah, in bed." He smirked, sensing her mood. "I was alone at the time though, does that make it better?" His sensuous eyes drilled into hers - she instantly averted them. "I came here for a car not to see *you* !" But oh how her heart fluttered seeing him again. He ignored her, "My cousin says you're a masseuse, I was gonna call one but seeing as you're here, can you do anything to ease my pain?" For once he seemed genuine, his face creasing up intermittently as he moved. The thought of putting her hands on his body sent her hormones quivering.

"Cousin?" She nodded to herself, now the oozing sex appeal made total sense. He shook his head, they all loved young Ambrose but he would ensure Casanova went no where near this one ever again. Here was her opportunity to avenge herself , she threw her hands on her hips, "You want *me* a lowly Pom with a bad attitude, to give Mister high and mighty a massage, well that's a bit rich." She looked him up and down, as he quietly whispered, "yes please babe." He called her *babe!* Disarmed immediately she felt the increasing urge to throw herself at his feet and beg him to take her to his bed, but from the depths of her common sense she controlled it.

"Do you have a practice we could go to? I need you." The very words sent crescendos of latent desire screaming and kicking the length of her spine. Could his mother be right about her feelings for him? Surely not! Yet from somewhere deep in her unconscious mind, she knew - before she knew. Her professional ethos kicked in. "I'm at 125 Prindiville Drive, I'm free in about an hour as I need to look for…" He interjected with sudden masterful tones that send shockwaves straight to her knickers. "What's wrong with right now?" He cocked a quizzical eyebrow, his eyes raping Jessicas' soul and massaging every one of her erogenous zones. She responded gently, "I have to buy a car, remember?"

He smiled, "come with me," he hooked his arm around her waist and dragged her over to his Patrol. "Get in," he commanded. She cursed her weakness for obeying. "Where are we going?" She asked timidly. "To your salon of course," he replied softly, adding, "don't worry, I'll get you a car." He groaned as he hurled himself up into the seat, she wriggled with inappropriate desires, if not a slight urge to laugh. "You shouldn't be driving in your …" He placed his manicured finger against her lips - she inhaled a subtle waft of Portuguese musk and shut up. She felt turned on just watching him shift gear. He was the strong silent type, a man of few words. She trembled at the thought of laying his naked body on her table and rubbing him all over with her essence of ylang ylang and geranium. How would she feel? She began to tremble, terrified at the prospect, perhaps this had gone too far? Sex with him was a pure fantasy driven by hormones. She felt the panic rising as palpitations beat out her feelings from her chest; she needed to escape, but was trapped by an alpha male with a purpose. Was she a virgin because she was afraid of sex?

Once inside her salon, she relaxed, feeling more at home and more in charge. She sent him away to remove his clothes and get on the couch. She fought with her breathing as she approached him, only a fluffy white towel between her and his complete nakedness just like the night at his house. She applied an aromatic oil suitable for muscular relaxation and began to smother his entire back, pushing and gently prodding her fingers between his tightened muscles.

She noticed the tribal tattoo around his right bicep, her dream sex moment flooded her mind - how did she know he had a tattoo, like that, there? "Oh, you *do* have a tribal tattoo - how odd." He twisted himself to look up at, her raising an immaculate eyebrow, "and what is odd about it? Were tattoos on my body cause for some previous speculation?" She gently re-directed him to lay down flat again so he wouldn't detect her guilty secret with his eyes. She had a sense he could see everything she was thinking. "Of course not, I thought I saw some talk about you and a tribal tattoo somewhere in some random post. It was a throw away comment." He smiled to himself, she had been thinking about his body, of that, he was quite sure.

She focused again on stroking his back -her breathing was short and rapid and she found herself becoming extremely aroused by his presence, his occasional moans of appreciation, sending tidal waves of lust through her entirety. She had to keep it professional and forced her desperately wanton mind back to the job at hand. "I'm not a chiropractor, but from the general location of your pain, I'd say it's your SI joint. You need to ice it."

With an awkward jerk he sat up groaning slightly with the pain. He looked directly into her eyes, "sometimes, there's pleasure in pain - don't you think?" Jessica flushed scarlet, he continued. "You want me Jessica, don't you?" She recoiled and snapped. "Don't flatter yourself!" She was angered by his blatant display of conceit and even more angry with herself for making her sexual attraction so damned obvious - perhaps she really was a whore? He grabbed her, running his fingers along her arm, dragging them across her heaving breasts. "Well I want *you* so bad," he whispered, pulling her to his level.

"Kiss me Jessica, kiss my pain away." He moaned seductively. She was spellbound, anchored to the ground by her own desires that were mounting rapidly. He cupped her face with his hands, and pulled her lips to his, they met in a soft fluttering and trembling tentative embrace, that culminated into a deeper and more meaningful searching of one another's mouth. He lunged his tongue into her mouth and silently she rose to meet him with her own - and in that moment, the rest of the world stopped turning and disappeared. He threw away his towel, his male arousal there for all the world to see. She averted her eyes, but he made her look at him. "Don't be shy, I want to take your clothes off, I want to *see* you," he murmured.

She could neither agree nor decline, simply mesmerised by his eroticism. His hand reached out and slowly unzipped the front of her overall. She'd been holding her breath again and let out a sudden sigh as he deftly unclasped her brassiere, making her breasts tumble gratefully from their white lacy captor. Standing almost naked in front of him should have made her want to run, she should have shrunk fearfully away from his caress. Yet curiously she felt at ease, with the knowledge that it was time to lose herself, whether she loved this man or not was irrelevant, what she needed was his beautiful, hard, male body and she needed it now.

His fingers slowly and sensuously teased the curve of her breast until he found the hardened tip, stroking it firmly to full arousal. She threw her head back and arched her back as the thrill of his touch heightened the ache between her legs. "Touch me Jessica," he whispered, running his tongue along her neck and down between the valley of her breasts, and sucking with a sudden frenzy at her nipples. His hand guided hers until it met with a throbbing and twitching hardness; her finger nails raked against its shaft. This was *it*, this was going to be *her* moment, her virginity was about to become history.

She rubbed her hands up and down his length, driven on by the increasing volume of his cries. With a swift movement he ripped off her panties laying her down on the table. She closed her eyes as he stood over her, appraising her nakedness. She could feel his hot breath as he lowered his mouth to her skin. She writhed and moaned softly as his fingers discovered the wetness of her groin. Her aching was building into a crescendo as he pushed them further into her. Withdrawing suddenly he straddled his body on top of her, he grabbed at a pot of ylang ylang oil, and poured its contents over her breasts, and with both hands outstretched began an erotic deep massage, running his hands from her breasts down through her taut stomach, until he met the source of her lust.

As though an iceberg had suddenly submerged, a sudden fear and overwhelming wave of regret overwhelmed her. She struggled, sitting up pushing him away, "no, not yet, I can't, I'm, I'm so sorry." She grabbed at a towel rubbing the oil off her body humiliated at her nudity in front of him.

"Let yourself go woman, you know you want to." He was panting, lusting upon her nakedness. She grabbed at her clothes. "You don't understand, this was a mistake I, I don't sleep around - I'm not a whore." He withdrew in defeat, silently slipping his clothes on, wincing as he moved, the pain in his back unresolved - the air was stale with regret, "seemingly," he replied coolly. "Let's be honest here, you've made it exceptionally clear you want me, you may as well have advertised it on TV, you even travel to my home to throw yourself at me."

His voice was accusing, "so if you're *that* desperate to be with me, why are you such a prick teaser?" Jessica threw him off, struggling with her clothes, anxious to shield his eyes from her nudity. "You started it, anyway, maybe I wanted you to have a taste of what you'll never be good enough to have. I'm not like the rest." She snapped, deeply regretting her torrid passion of a few minutes ago. "I fixed your back as much as I can, now please just get out." He snarled "if you'd had any class you'd have been professional and continued to fix my back but no, you couldn't resist could you - says it all about you."

She walked away from his outstretched arms, away from the warmth of his body, away from the only person that made her heart beat out of control. She hardly dared look at him, she could feel his eyes, burning with rage and although silence would have been a better option she couldn't resist one last insult. "Just fuck off." His mouth curled into a snarl, "no worries honey." His words sent a thousand razors to her heart. Why did she say that? Why didn't she just go for it with the best catch in town? She hated her pathetic sense of morality, the need to be wooed, to be told how much in love her lover was with her. Love? It was an illusion she knew it, but it was an illusion she needed.

　　　She drew herself up. "We've seen each other naked, now, so let's call it quits, yeah?" Her eyes glistened with the humiliation she felt. "If you say so." He whispered, zipping up his trousers. Carrying his shirt, he looked back at her, "quits? Yeah?" He silently disappeared out of the door and out of her life.
She slammed it behind him, locking it with trembling hands, and then sunk to the floor sobbing like a baby.

　　　She'd allowed her heart to rule her head, she'd let a man touch her body in a way that would forever make her scream just thinking about it. She'd stripped in a second for him, was she really the whore he believed she was? Then she realised virgins can't be whores, but maybe she was a prick teaser, that was her problem. Should she have gone all the way? She didn't know, but what she did know is his mother was quite right - she was utterly in love with him, but now, she had lost the proverbial man of her dreams before she had even had him.

11

Kevin jumped onto Jessica's' bed holding a breakfast tray. "Here, scrambled eggs on toast - see I'm not always a shit." He dragged out the post. "Oh look, here's a letter for you. It's hand delivered, really posh envelope looks official." He stared at the writing screwing up his face in thought. "Wait a minute, it's Brads handwriting, yeah the address on the back is City Beach, that's where he lives." Jessica recoiled as though she had seen the devil himself, preferring to chase the egg around the toast - she couldn't let Kevin know the way she felt or that she had used his laptop to find out Brads address, and even worse, had been there!"Put it in the bin." He opened his eyes wide, "no way! Don't keep me in suspense, open it, but why the fuck would *he* be writing to *you* anyway? I hope you ain't been stirring more shit with him - have you?"

Jessica shook her head, avoiding his eyes, she knew he could read her like a book. But inside, her heart almost stopped, could he regret their interaction and was writing to declare his undying love? And how old school, to hand deliver a personally written letter - her heart was fluttering like a leaf in the wind, wondering which way the wind would blow. She mused for a moment, finding it hard to breath, as her mind relived the minutes when his hands caressed her, his tongue all over her body, his hard body writhing just desperate to be inside her. She shook herself back to the letter.

Kevin eyed her suspiciously. "Are you sure you haven't been causing more grief with my boss, you look mighty guilty?" Jessica snapped back, "don't be silly." Her stomach did somersaults, what would make the mighty Brad Monroe pen a handwritten letter and have it personally delivered from his home suburb. It must be important to him, an apology maybe? A love letter even? She couldn't dream any more, with baited breath she silently read it, each word sending her down with the Mary Rose.

Kevin was fidgeting on the spot, brimming with a childish curiosity, he snatched the letter. Jessica hissed at him, "don't bother reading it, it's not a letter - the absolute bastard - it's a bill!" She tried to hide her disappointment, he really was an class A bastard, why did she think for one second he'd have been sorry? "A bill?

what for?" As soon as he asked the question, he read out the answer, and shuddered to think what Jessica would do about it. He knew she was a spitfire when antagonised - often to her detriment, but this time, it could be to his! "We'll pay it between us don't fuck with him Jessica." If only he knew just how close she had got to fucking with him - it was almost laughable!

Jessicas' voice rose several octaves as she spoke. "It's the bill I requested him to send me, for Scotts repair work to the Datsun!" Kevins' face crinkled with disapproval, "when and why the fuck did you request a bill?" She felt stupid. "I put a note under his windscreen wiper, begging him to give me the bill and let Scott have his job back - guess it worked. I didn't think it'd be this much though - he's beyond taking the piss - it's not even properly fixed."

She broke off as her voice choked, her fluttering notions of the great man himself sending her a love letter dashed on the rocks, she was the fool on the hill - why was she so fucking stupid with men - lesbianism was beckoning. Kevin hugged her, "that was a great thing to do for Scott, but please keep the fuck away from him in future. He's a business man, that's how they operate, he's a playboy, and the most successful man in Perth, just like his father, all they care about sis is money. It ain't personal, we mean nothing to them - I'll pay half."

"Thanks for that, but he's got no heart - punishing the little people, what a great man - not. I hope he's really happy." She sobbed, her tears of disappointment overcoming her composure. She could see that by rejecting him, this was his retribution. Kevin wrapped his arms around her, "you think allot of him don't you?" She threw his arms off coldly, "why does everyone keep saying that? I hate him! I despise him! And whats' more, I'm going over there to tell him exactly what I think of him!" Kevin grabbed her, "hold on now, you can't lose it if you hate him the way you say you do, just ignore him." He stared at her ruddy complexion, she was flustered and mighty riled up. "I'll pay it all, I mean, how much is it?" He stared incredulously at the total for some time, adding up the lines again and again, "wow, five hundred bucks! He's charged weekend call out rates too. That's harsh man."

"Harsh, ya think? I'm telling you, he's a bastard of the number one order, and come hell or high water, I shall tell him tonight because we are *not* paying it!" Kevin shrieked, "don't, please, I mean it, he'll fire me like he did Scott, we don't have a rich family like Scottie. I actually *need* the job - *we* need each other, keep away from him, he's bad news for you." Jessica wrestled with her breathing for some moments as she digested Kevins pleas, then visibly calmed. "Okay, you're right, I can pay it, I'll be fine, I'll just pay it and forget he exists, don't stress."

Kevin hugged her, and relaxed, "you promise me? You'll stay away, no more bouncing back to argue with him? Are you sure you don't fancy him? All the girls at work talk about him all the fucking time, he uses women like they are sex toys, so don't get hooked on him, do you promise me?" She felt sick to her stomach, her younger brother seemed the more mature one right now. She hated lying to him, "I promise."

Hours later, Kevin was playing in the Metaverse with his friends, she seized the moment and slipped away - even her noisy exhaust got away with it - her escape was undetected. She trembled as she sat in her car, parked only a few cars away from Brads house. She'd watched Julia leave and was now fixated on his patrol dominating the drive. She wanted to go home and cry for being a no-hoper at love. She reminded herself of the cruelty of his bill and dredged up every ounce of strength; it was time to take back her pride and rid herself of his game of cat and mouse - she was gonna tell him to leave her the fuck alone.

She marched up the drive with renewed vigour, and raised her arm to bang on the door when it suddenly swung open. Brad was standing awkwardly, a tight smile matched his tight ripped dark blue denims and Versace shirt. He always managed to take her breath away, no matter how much she prepared for him, or how angry she was. He smiled as though greeting his best friend, "hey, you must of got my bill?" She nodded, unable to find any suitable sarcastic comments.

He sensed her distress and flashed a heart melting smile, eyes twinkling with amusement. "If I'd have sent you an invite, would you have come?" He raised a quizzical eyebrow. She spat with instant hostility. "No way," Unaware she was still the victim of his super intelligence. He grinned at her in an almost fatherly way, "but a bill and an unfairly harsh one, now that makes you angry doesn't it? You were so eaten away with hatred for me you just couldn't resist telling me to shove it up my rear in person, could you?" She remained quiet, still soaking in the knowledge that she had acted precisely the way he'd wanted, she groaned with embarrassment for her own gullibility - It wasn't a bill, it was more like a summons - how predictable she was, how in love with him she was - how fantastic *he* was. "Okay, so, you summonsed me, I'm here, so now what?"

"What do you want Jessica?" His voice reminded her of the hypnotic eyed snake in the Jungle Book - trust in me, just in me - coiling around her with a soothing voice whilst squeezing her to certain death. She stamped her foot with frustration to break the spell. "I came to ask you why you're trying to destroy me and my family?" He frowned for an instant, "what do you mean?" He seemed genuine. "You know full well what I mean! Why have you got your girlfriend Tanya to seduce my brother, and then dump him for Scott, after all they are hardly her type are they?" Her eyes flashed from baby blue to stormy grey. He stared deep into them and spoke softly, "what do you think the reason could be?"

His eyes betrayed his superiority with mild amusement. "Stop playing games with me, I don't like it. I'm going now, but I want to leave you with this - stay away from me, and my family, and leave Scott out of it, he doesn't deserve to be hurt, just because you seem hell bent on hurting *me*!" She wrenched herself away from the heady scent that surrounded him - from the urge to be held in his strong arms, to be kissed and loved. She began to walk away, away from the thorn in her side, away from the only man she has ever met that makes her feel this way.

"Jessica, wait.. " He stumbled and leant heavy against the wall, beads of sweat assembling on his brow as he wrestled with the pain. She ran to his side, his willing slave - immediately forgetting everything except to assist a person in pain, "can you make it somewhere to lay down?" He walked tentatively to the sofa. "I told you before I'm not a chiropractor, but try to lay on your front, I'll rub your back! Do you have any oils anywhere, any tea tree oil? An ice pack?" He groaned, "I've got some oils in the bathroom ensuite to the master bedroom. - ice pack in freezer, but don't bother with that for now." His voice strangled tight with spasms of pain that pulsed periodically through his twisted ligament every time he dared move a muscle.

She quickly found the oil she was looking for, and hurried down to her patient. She stripped him carefully of his jeans and shirt and laid a towel on him; her professional head on, she was worried, he needed a specialist, but she would do what she could for now. Luckily he was wearing a pair of Armani boxers, she wasn't sure she could handle any more nudity than that from him tonight. Her hands quickly found the knotted muscles, around his sacroiliac joint, she prodded her fingers into them ruthlessly, despite muffled cries of pain from Brad. She knew that he was in sheer agony and was impressed with his self control. After a rigorous fifteen minutes she had released the muscles somewhat, he appeared visibly relaxed. "Sit up *very* carefully, and tell me how you feel," she spoke softly.

Tentatively he turned over, she averted her eyes from his erection, which was quite normal for one of her male patients. They always got turned on by her healing hands, a perk of the job, she giggled to herself. He made no attempt to hide it, which was typical of one with such arrogance, she thought. He flashed her a sudden heart stopping smile, his whole countenance beamed with joy. "Oh my god, it feels wonderful, you're an angel." He jumped up, and touched his toes. "Wow, I never thought I'd be able to do that again." He laughed striding towards her. She backed away, sensing he would be trying to give her a reward also of the physical nature. "Okay, well nothing has changed. I've gotta go," She backed towards the front door as though trying not to aggravate a tiger suddenly escaped from the zoo.

She whispered, "you must relax more, your muscles are knotted with tension and stress, buy yourself a good aromatherapy bath oil, and soak in it and periodically have a regular massage; preferably with someone else. I've released some tightening of the muscles but it is far from fixed. It will almost certainly go again so see a professional chiropractor as soon as you can." She reached for the door, but he placed his hand across the handle. "Don't go yet, *please*, the night is young, after all, you haven't got what you really came for, have you?" His eyes glinted in the subdued light, and his chest seemed stronger and more masculine than ever.

She outwardly sighed at the thought of being taken to his bed - but it would be the wrong thing to do - wouldn't it? Her conscience argued with her hormones who believed it was time to give in now and just enjoy being his plaything - her overplayed sense of needing romantic love told her she must resist until the time felt right. He sensed her internal struggle and stroked her hair gently. "I owe you Jessica Shackley." She fought to control the throbbing urges within, and threw his hand off her shoulder, "no you don't," her tone was scathing. "I came here to tell you to stay out of my life. I've paid your bill by B'pay and as I said before - we're quits."

She pivoted on her heels without daring to look him in the eye. She held her head high and like the stubborn idiot she was she didn't stop, think, and listen to her heart. The pain of leaving his house and life struck her like a twisted rusty blade to her insides; tears falling with every step she took away from him. As she approached her car she began to breathe again, it was done - she had bravely purged Brad Monroe from her system, he was out of her life forever. She wished she wasn't so easily ignited. She wished she wasn't so pedantically moral. She wished she had the guts to turn around and admit - she was totally in love with him.

12

Julia Monroe buzzed happily around the office; her birthday celebrations was the latest hot topic in the society pages of the West Australian newspaper - Brad saw to that. This year he had planned something extra special for her 60th. She smiled down at Brad who was knee deep in paper work at his desk. "Darling you really are amazing - a private party and we have the whole of Rottnest to ourselves?" She grinned at her son, who wasn't listening. "It's a terrible crime that you're single - such a waste." He grunted in reply, nodding his head without listening, engrossed in paperwork. Julia waltzed around his office laughing, amusing the salesmen outside. "Rottnest Island, it's so romantic, the weather is lovely there this time of year, not too hot, don't you think? I've already made up the guest list plus one of course."

Her eyes gleamed with excitement - she frowned for a second, "you *are* going to make it this year aren't you? Because last year, I was so disappointed -you've gone to so much effort for this very special one, you *have* to be there - or else." Brad slammed his hands down on the desk, irritated by his mothers constant interruptions, "if you don't let me get this work done, no, I shan't be there!"

He added through gritted teeth, "why don't you ever talk to Linda? You know she is my rock! She has already said she'll send out the invitations, she's already arranged the guests air tickets from Jandakot airport - the private jet company has been informed and paid." Julia was used to his work place moodiness - just like his father. Ignoring him she continued to dance around him like a young girl. "I've always wanted to be part of a murder mystery event, and now I'm the star, and on Rottnest Island! I just can't wait till Saturday! It's such a shame I have to be 60 to do it!"

She jigged around the office, patting him on the head as she passed, "what shall I call it? Ten little Aussies? Oh I know murder at the Rottnest Lodge?" He slammed his papers down to make a point then rasped, placing his head on his outstretched arms. "What about the total and utter bloodied dismemberment of a mother on her birthday?" She laughed, nothing he could say could ruin her excitement. "You look tired dear, leave this place, come to Subiaco with me for lunch. If Linda is so great then get her to do that paperwork, isn't that what you pay her for?" He raised a disapproving eyebrow. She ignored it. "I'm meeting Davina and Georgie, you know how pleased they would be to see you."

He pulled a tired smile, and shoved his paperwork into his brief case. "You're right as always. I need a break, in fact, it's only a week until the party, I'm tempted to get away from the lot of it, and spend some time there this week - they got wifi so I can still work." He rubbed his index finger along his temple rubbing while in thought, "yes, damn it, can you finish the organisational details? Linda has other work to do as we have a lot of prepping for the new fleet contract. I've got the number of the Theatrical Company, and the caterers, here." He handed Julia a typewritten memo, with all the information she needed to complete her birthday bash.

Julia eyed Brad thoughtfully for a few minutes, then dismissed it, glancing at her watch. "I've got a lunch appointment to keep. Aren't you coming dear?" She pouted, already knowing the answer. "I'd love to honestly, but if I wanna take this break, then I *need* the rest of the day to organise work before I leave." He bent down and smacked a large kiss on each cheek. "Say hi to the girls, I'll see you on your birthday and I'll be bright eyed and bushy tailed as Dad used to say!" Julia shrieked with joy. "One thing before I go, the characters we have to act out, I'll ring you at The Lodge, and let you know who you are - I'll get your character outfit sent out to you." She giggled furiously, at his expression of disgust - dressing up was not his thing unless it involved hand cuffs, leather and beautiful women.

Brad strode out into the front reception area to wave his mother off. He was glad she was happy - when Jesse, his father died a few years ago, he didn't think she would ever recover. Their marriage was strong, they went everywhere together, still holding hands in public. How much he'd wanted to re-create that wonderful family environment by marrying the right girl. His brow creased into a deep frown, as he thought about Catherine, the British willowy blonde who sucked him in completely! He began to curse her under his breath.

A timid ginger, freckle faced temp interrupted his thoughts, "Mr Monroe, there's a call for you on line four." She was already terrified of him. "Who is it?" He hissed, a little too harshly, causing her to tremble more than ever. "I'm sorry, I didn't ask." She mumbled, almost at the point of crying. Sensing her terror he relented softening immediately, "okay darl, just put it through, but next time, announce the calls properly, okay?" She almost curtsied, "yes, sorry Mr Monroe."

Julia hurriedly arrived in Subiaco a favourite lunch time haunt, her friends were already there. "Sorry I'm late girls, he who thinks he must be obeyed held me up." She was out of breath and plonked herself down rather unceremoniously. Davina laughed a rather horsey laugh, she'd been brought up by a horse studding family on a large acreage in Yanchep north of Perth. Her dress was more conservative than Miss Marple. An ankle length red plaid skirt, which was probably the fashion in the 70's's, coupled with a nice frilly white blouse, that buttoned all the way to the chin. Her hair was pulled off her face in a severe bun, which gave her the look of a nun on holiday.

Georgie was a casual queen, always wore shorts and thongs with an incredibly expensive tee shirt, today was no exception. Julia however wore modern dresses and heels, always coiffured, botoxed and fragranced. She loved her oldest and dearest friends having spent her youth at Methodist Ladies College with them, it was always a trip down memory lane to be in their company.

After a great deal of hugging, cheek kissing, and food ordering, they settled down to their favourite subject, gossip. "Darlings, you just wouldn't believe what Father O'Leary has been getting up to!" Georgie began. Julia was fit to burst with her party information, and couldn't give a fig what Father O'Leary had been doing with his parishioners. "Never mind about him dear, you haven't forgotten about the party have you?" "Would you ever let us forget?" They chimed in unison. Georgie gushed with excitement. "So what's the theme, spill the goss? I didn't think Brad could improve on the Hot air balloon Party, I've never had so much fun, and it was hysterical to see Davina throw up over the side!" Davina let out a scream of laughter. "I'll never live that down, or should I say, keep it down. But last years Crocodile Cruise - he can't improve on that." Julia grinned triumphantly at the pair, "wanna bet? Brad has organised an amazing Murder Mystery Weekend at Rottnest and we're flying you all over. "

The girls whooped in unison again. "Observation City held those, I think they had to stop them, because they were too popular!" Davina giggled like a schoolgirl. "Georgie darling, please tell me how anything could be *too* popular?" Davina, winked at Julia who was enjoying the banter. "Darling, apparently the sleuths were having such a wonderful time hunting for the murderer, that hotel guests complained, drunken noisy players kept trying to arrest the guests." They all sipped their wine and mulled over the potential fun. "Well girls, I could do with your help, because Brad is going over there this week for a break. He's given me all the contacts if you would assist with the the last few bits. Seems wonder woman Linda Stevens is too busy." They raised eyebrows and winked. "So are you in?" She grinned at her best buddies eager faces. "Absolutely" they chorused in harmony.

Georgie whispered, "If you hadn't already agreed on the murder theme …." She looked over her shoulder as though about to impart a state secret. She then beckoned them to huddle together and whispered. "This is *so* new, I don't think it's even in Australia yet. Valinda my friend in London wrote to me a few weeks back, it seems as though all the rage in Europe is to hold a 'guess who your lover is' party."

Davina snorted out loud, sounding exactly like her horses. "Oh I don't think that would be at all appropriate for Julia, after all, she's no teenager." Davina was oblivious to the united frowns of disgust from both Julia and Georgie. Julia sipped on a fresh gin and tonic then added with intrigue. "What goes on at these parties?" Julia's mind was already whirring through many possibilities. She placed her drink down, and cradled her face on her hands, whilst Georgie recited the events. "The aim of the party, is for at least one couple to genuinely fall in love, apparently it works too! The company that organises it has a dating match computer, the kind of thing they use on all these dating websites. The players fill in online questionnaires about themselves and then the computer matches them. Next the computer takes each matched pair, and gives them an identity, usually well renowned lovers like for instance 'Samson and Delilah' or 'Romeo and Juliet' the list is endless."

She took a deep breath with excitement finishing her wine with one gulp. "Anyway those couples will be sent an invitation informing them they must at all costs dress as their character, and be unrecognisable as their real identity. All the make up is professionally done and outfits all supplied by the company. When all the guests have assembled they then have to find their counterpart, can you imagine all these crazy looking characters wandering around trying to locate their lost love? Actually Rottnest Island would be excellent, because you could have all the guests arrive, and head for strategic locations, so that their partners, whom they haven't met yet, are on the other side, you could use the whole island, you'd need a weekend for sure."

She quickly ordered another drink, "Anyway, once they have found their counterpart, they have to solve tasks together before heading back to a main gathering place, in your case it could be the lodge." Georgie gasped for breath, swigging desperately on her wine as soon as it was delivered. "Tell me more Georgie," Julia urged. Davina snorted again, "sounds like ridiculous tosh to me. I'd rather a wild western or something." Georgie flicked her with her fingers, "don't yout think about anything other than horses my dear?" Davina screwed up her face and downed her drink, immediately ordering another. "Err, no, I just find them far more reliable than men." She laughed. Georgie continued, "okay, when the lovers find their partner, they solve puzzles, like finding a lost trinket and guessing what significance it would have to them. I'm not sure about the finer details, but once they've done all that, then they have to identify each other, remember, up until now, neither of them must know who the other partner is in real life, they must speak with accents pertaining to their characters. I believe there's a prize for the person who cannot be identified by anyone, something good, like $5000, so it is in everyones interest to keep the charade going.

There is also a prize for the couple who correctly guesses the most peoples characters, I think they get a form to fill in or something. Then at the stroke of midnight, on the last day at the cupids ball, which could be Sunday, everyone is unmasked and by that time, many couples may have genuinely fallen in love. The matching software has a really strong track record of success?" Davina placated her, "maybe next year yeah?"

Julia clapped her hands with glee and danced on the spot. "I love it! I love it!" She sat down again out of breath and flushed with excitement. "Murder is *so* yesterday, so many of our friends are alone, divorced or single, this is amazing, I want everyone to fall in love - how can we make this happen this year?" Davina rolled her eyes and Georgie giggled.

Julia flopped her head in her hands with disappointment, "but we only have a week, it's *such* a shame, it will be impossible to organise it at such short notice - and Brad has already hired and paid for the murder mystery actors company." There was a pregnant silence then Georgie whispered again, "they're a slick organisation, you already have the island hotel booked and flights from Jandakot, so it's only a question of costumes and the finer details of the couples doing their questionnaire's online to match them, and then the tests they have to do."

Georgie screwed her face thinking of a solution. Julia was staring into the eyes of her lifetime friend with hope, Georgie always knew how to save the day. Georgie thumped the table and took on a positive grin. " That's it, throw enough money their way, I bet *they'll* make it happen. Have a think, but if you do want to do this, leave it to me. I'll ring you later on! Oh yes, one thing that you must be careful in doing, is making sure that *all* the guests are mildly compatible, you know, age, and that sort of thing and available! You don't want to start any affairs off, especially as your parties always make it to the press, so may need to add more singletons to the guest list if we can make this happen."

Julia grinned in a knowing way, "most of the guests are divorced or single anyway, I'll double check the list, but yes please, lets create our own love island - we have no time to lose." She clapped her hands to her face, "What about our married friends? There are quite a few couples on the list already." Georgie grinned. "They have their own place to assist the singletons along the way, it's so much fun and they are also secret characters, so no one, will be left out!"

Julias mind raced with ideas, her imagination bulging with potential scenarios, for what really would be the party of the century! Her mind temporarily turned to Brad, what would *he* think of the whole affair? She knew he would find it in *very* bad taste, but on *her* birthday he always made concessions. She smiled to herself all the way home - making out a new guest list would be a challenge but she was up for it.

By Wednesday of that week, everything had been fine tuned down to the last detail, and all the invitations were mailed by special delivery. Julia had joined Brad at Rottnest, and explained it all to him, in such a way, that he couldn't possibly let her down by not taking part. His vocals left no doubt as to his disdain, but after a heated discussion, he grudgingly conceded defeat, despite very strong reservations. Only the fact that he was in disguise made it seem worthwhile to him. He had already planned to slip off by himself, whoever the computer matched him with, he would avoid like the plague; he certainly wouldn't be falling in love with anyone anytime soon. Love was nothing more than a disease of the mind and he'd rather take poison than catch it.

13

Jessica signed for a crisp white parchment envelope amongst other letters which arrived at the salon. She stuffed them in her bag on her way home. Her mobile was vibrating in her bag as she unlocked the front door, she kicked it open rummaging through her bag. "Hello?" A familiar recorded voice played a message. "This is the West Australian State Correctional Centre…" She wanted to slam the phone down, but waited until the message ended and the female caller spoke. Jessica was silent, a familiar grating voice full of bad memories echoed down the line, "g'day sis, bet you're pleased to hear from me, seeing as absence makes the heart grow fonder and all that. "

Jessica stiffened, goosebumps consumed her. "Amber? Is that you?" She whispered, hoping she was terribly mistaken, perhaps this was a nightmare she was having in her sleep. "You got any other twin sisters doing time I don't know about?" Jessica's heart sank, "where are you?" She pulled up a chair, sinking down onto it. "So you didn't hear the recorded message for fuck sake? Where do ya think I am? Mars?" Jessica felt herself stiffen, typical Amber, hostility already. "Okay, I don't need an argument, let's cut the crap, what do you want?" Jessica was tired, all she wanted to do was have a quiet evening watching a little tv and maybe have a long hot soak in the bath. "Whoa, harsh words, and there goes my theory that *you're* the perfect little angel."

The voice inhaled smoke at the same time, occasionally blowing it, slowly and rhythmically. "Well, if you must know, I've some good news for you or maybe bad depending on your disposition - ya sitting down?" Jessica was not feeling tolerant. "Yes, get on with it, I'm in no mood for your mellow dramatics." She could hear the smoke being blown during a pause. "I'm getting out of this joint in a month, isn't that great?" A sticky silence ensued, as Jessica imagined just how great it would be. "I can see my news has you jumping for joy but that's not all, I decided after rotting in this dump for two years, it's time to focus on the family, so, to cut a long story short, I'm coming home sis, I'm coming back to Perth, so make my bed up, hope you ain't touched my clothes!"

The phone clicked several times as a recorded voice took over announcing the end of the allotted minutes, then nothing.

Jessica responded by bursting into tears, it had been five years since she'd laid eyes on her sister, the best five years of her life. The trouble that Amber Shackley had brought upon her shoulders had been tenfold. Now she'd started her own business, now that she had established a fine reputation, she was coming back! Her old memories began to haunt her, the taunts of 'slut,' and 'lowlife' that she would have to endure, for her sisters mistakes. She re-lived the visiting massage service that she had first started in Augusta, approximately 100 miles south of Perth. How she suffered when Amber posed as her, doing 'favours' of a sexual kind, bringing Jessica into disrepute and in front of a judge.

Kevin sauntered into the lounge wearing his precious 'Beats' headphones, the music so loud she could still hear it banging. As soon as he saw Jessica crying he ripped them off his head. "Hey, wassup?" He wrapped his arms around her. "Amber is being released - she's coming back to Perth." Jessica broke down, but Kevin seemed unconcerned. "It's okay, don't cry, she's probably reformed you know, these places rehabilitation the crime don't they? She went into some drug programme anyway, so stop ya worrying, she's gonna be a different person, I can feel it in my bones - well she can't be any worse anyway."

He winked with an innocent chuckle, his positive and cheery attitude made Jessica want to hug him more and never let him go in a childlike way. He'd inherited his mothers peace making attributes. She forced a smile and nodded, no point in distressing him too. "Hey, you haven't opened your mail or should I say bills?" He grabbed the pile of letters out of her bag and slung them across the table at her "hey, gimme that one," he grinned, "it looks cool."

He was referring to a thick crisp white parchment envelope, Jessica snatched it back. "I'll take that thank you very much," she said, cheering a little, "I was saving that one, it came by special delivery. I know you've always loved opening my mail haven't' you?" She grinned, waving the letter tantalisingly in front of him. "So what's it worth, if I let you open it?" Kevin always responded well to bets and bribes, "erm," he thought, scratching his long thatch of surfers hair profusely, "I know, I'll mow the lawn tomorrow." Jessica grinned waving the envelope under his nose, "Today, and once a week…for a month."

"Hold on sis, it's not worth *that* much," he protested. Jessica fanned it in front of his face, and he instantly changed his mind, his cat like curiosity enveloping his senses entirely. "Okay okay, you win… for a month!" He grabbed the envelope and gazed at it for some time, before slowly slitting it with a long sharp knife. "Get on with it you galah." Laughed Jessica, "it's not going to be *that* exciting, it's probably another invite for that Aesthetics Club they want me to join, so don't get your hopes up." He ran it under his nose like a cuban cigar. "Mmm, smells like money," he breathed, his dark eyes aglow with a fiery passion.

He pulled out the contents and surveyed them for awhile, his face lighting up with glee. "Come on, what is it?" Jessica snapped, her patience getting the best of her, "far fucking out!" Kevin started to read it out, "you have been cordially invited to Julia Monroes 60th birthday bash." Jessica smiled, but a jet of sadness ran through her veins. There was no way she would want to be with *her* jet set. "Oh, thats nice of her," she was somewhat surprised at Kevins excitement though. "Yeah but that's not all," he was gushing, falling over his words in his enthusiasm to tell her. "It's being held at the Rottnest Island, Lodge Hotel on Saturday!" Jessica wished with all her heart she could go, she really liked Julia. "This Saturday?" She quizzed, "I don't have anything to wear to a thing like that. I can't even afford to get there, no, it'll be way out of my league, all rich and powerful types. I def don't wanna go and your lord and master will probably be there." Kevin was watching her face intently, deep in thought.

"Anyway, remember when we got seasick on the ferry?" Her stomach was already feeling sea sick at the thought of seeing Brad being accosted by society girls dolled up and throwing themselves at him - she cursed herself, why didn't she just say yes to him, she will be a virgin forever. Kevin was dancing around the room, "No, no, look, here's the plane ticket, it says that you have to present this voucher to pick up your costume, the theme is a *lovers re- union*. Don't ask me what the fuck that means, but who fucking cares? Go find yourself a millionaire sis."

"Give me that, and don't swear so much." Jessica grabbed at the letter that came with the air ticket, her face beamed with pleasure as she read out bits of the instructions. "You'll be dressed up as a character, and will be professionally made up so that you are unrecognisable at all times, full details will be given at the costume shop where you must follow all instructions to the letter. A prize of $5000 is awarded to the character who cannot be truly identified by anyone, and a prize of $2500 to the person who can correctly guess the most true identities." She paused to take a huge intake of air, "however, in line with the theme, there will be a top prize of $100,000 dollars to the couple who legitimately fall in love, t's and c's apply. You will need to attend the full week-end, accommodation provided at The prestigious Rottnest Lodge!"

She was breathing hard with excitement, "Fucking hell - should I go?" It was tempting and despite the shock of Ambers return this was finally something good to be happy about. "Language sis - and of course you should go! You'd be mad not to! Look on the bright side, no-one will know who you are, so it doesn't matter if they're rich or famous, they'll all be acting out their characters. Besides, you could win five thousand bucks or what's that shit about falling in love and winning $100k? Now there's an incentive to get laid - wish it was me going!"

Kevin suddenly stopped still and stared directly into Ambers eyes, "how come Brads mother would even know you, let alone invite you to her birthday bash?" Jessica returned a non plussed shrug of her shoulders, "no clue." Kevin shrugged it off and they both danced around the house laughing.

All thoughts and fears of Ambers' return departed as the excitement of the society event of the year drew daily nearer. Only having a shit load of money could have made it possible to create an event with such extravagant prizes. Jessica took a deep breath, contemplating her poverty, then shook it off and assumed her naturally positive air - for once, she was gonna let her hair down and see how the other half lived. With a professional disguise she won't lay eyes on Brad and he won't lay eyes on her - perfect!

Friday night was a busy one for Jessica, she practically destroyed her bedroom throwing clothes around, debating what was good enough to take. Finally sorted with a bulging at the seams travel bag, she settled down to fill in her online compatibility questionnaire, she only had two hours before the deadline to submit. She grinned when she pressed send. Case packed, forms submitted - check - that's when she read, no personal clothes or toiletries, in fact they were not allowed to bring anything, but on the good side, everything was catered for!

She groaned when she looked at the state of her bedroom, but jumped into bed laughing, life was about to get exciting, and who knows, maybe the computer might actually find her a forever love! All her years in Perth, Jessica had only ever gone to Rottnest Island as a child and all she recalled was her father shouting at them and being sick on the ferry. It was too expensive to stay at the Hotel, and she didn't like the idea of camping. She decided to ring Julia to thank her for the invite, she knew that Brad would hate the idea he was far too bitter and twisted; but then again it was a special birthday for Julia, would he go? The only way to find out was to call and speak to him, her excuse could be that she needed Julias' number so it seemed a legitimate call.

She stared at her Iphone dialled the number then bottled out immediately; he might think she was chasing him, after all, she did keep turning up at his house uninvited then telling him to go to hell. Rottnest was big enough to avoid him even if he *did* show up - they'd be in disguise anyway, and she could thank Julia in person. She inhaled, full of excitement, it was time to live a little and in the spirit of adventure, the chance of winning $5000 or even $100,000, let Julia Monroes, game of love, begin.

14

J essica was clutching the invitation with white knuckles for fear of losing it. She headed across the road towards the costume shop located in a part of town that she loved, Subiaco. A quaint old bell - that deserved a place in any Dickens novel - rang mysteriously as she entered the curiosity shop. An old lady, with a positive twinkle, in her eye, immediately greeted her, putting her straight at ease. Another woman with a sour expression eyed her up and down suspiciously - Jessica didn't fit the mould at all. Jessicas' hands were shaking as she held out the invite, the miserable woman snatched it, "Name?" She was still shaking, "Jessica Shackley" she replied in a rather sheepish and unworthy cracked voice. The old woman spent what seemed an age to find her name on her list, at that point Jessica began backing away, step by step to the door. What on earth was she thinking trying to mingle with Perth's royalty as though she were one of them? And if Brad was there it would surely end in tears.

As she neared the door, the woman burst into fits of excitement and nudged the other, "she's *the one*." Jessica overheard and felt dizzy, "the one ?" A laughing stock was her first thought. Both ladies curtsied, "you are the Queen of the Nile, Cleopatra, and we are at your service." Jessica took the opportunity to quiz them, "so, who is my partner?" The women did tandem silent mimes of a zip across their mouths looking around them hurriedly as though they were secret service. Jessica immediately kicked herself for such common and shallow behaviour - but it was worth a try - she tried not to laugh hysterically and swallowed her mounting hysteria at their sudden serious pomp and ceremony.

A large set of plastic covered clothes were thrust into her arms. "Take these to Claras' Salon, it's two shops across the road where you'll be fitted." The women peered over their identical thin rimmed spectacles. The friendly one piped up in a hushed voice, "I hope you can sit still, your make-up will take awhile - good luck your majesty." Both woman curtsied, which Jessica thought was taking it all a bit far and struggled hard to keep the sarcastic laughter inside - the urge to laugh out loud was causing her to pull strange faces.

Glad to be leaving the women's' critical scrutiny, she staggered down the street, struggling to carry the weight. That's when the laughter came out, she laughed so hard she fell over, but quickly picked herself up, tears streaming down her face. She had a sudden urge to cry her eyes out, she often did that after a bout of hysterical laughter. She was grateful that Claras' Salon was only a short walk - she couldn't take the quizzical looks from members of the public wondering if someone had escaped the local psychiatric ward.

Standing outside the Salon, she took a deep breath, another old fashioned bell chimed her arrival as the heavy door opened and she fell inside the shop, clutching the weighty bagged up clothing. A young girl immediately ushered her into a special treatment room. "I don't think I'm supposed to be made up yet am I?" She watched two girls dressed in white, mix up a concoction of varying shades of bronze creams. "We have strict orders your majesty, you must be in full costume dress at all times - once you leave our salon, a waiting taxi will take you to Jandakot Airport, and you'll receive further instructions once on the plane."

Jessica gushed, "I feel like a spy or something," still in awe of the serious in depth organisation the event must have taken - the girls made no comment or conversation except for telling her off for fidgeting. It took two and a half hours to fit the clothes, be made up in the typical Egyptian style and finally be fitted with a fabulous black shiny wig. Looking in the mirror, she couldn't believe it was her own reflection. "Wow, one thing is for sure, no-one is going to recognise me!" She giggled, admiring her black outlined eyes, and pouting expressive red mouth. "I look like a bronzed Liz Taylor," she chuckled. "With respect your majesty," one of the make up girls tutted, "you look like *Queen Cleopatra, an Egyptian,* because that is who you are!"

"The taxi is here!" They began to usher her out of the shop. "I can't go out looking like this!" She exclaimed as they led her outside. Her cries fell on deaf ears. She stepped cautiously out of the salon, amidst a crowd of early morning Saturday shoppers; if she'd ever dreamt of being an actress in a blockbuster Hollywood production, her dream had come true. A crowd of onlookers held up mobiles and filmed, some took photos, teens sneered - but most gasped excitedly. Onlookers were impressed, thinking that they had perhaps glimpsed a famous actress at work. Feeling confident in her anonymity Jessica decided to play her part and held up her head regally gliding to the safety of her awaiting taxi - a white stretch limousine. She waved a slight movement of her hand, as one would expect from the Queen, and sat back appraising the crowds who had been mesmerised for a few fleeting moments - things like this just didn't happen in Perth at least, not to her!

Jessica had never been in a stretch limousine before - it showed. After playing with several buttons in the back, she realised that she could communicate with the driver via the phone, "excuse me," she spoke with polite caution, "am I allowed to talk to you?" At that moment, the glass window that separated them mechanically whirred its way down. "If it prease your majesty," he mocked in mild amusement. The driver was a rotund asian man, with a huge smile and merry eyes, which she could see glimpses of in the rear view mirror.

"Where are all the other guests?" she asked, hoping he might shed some light on the activities. "All been frown out - different times." He replied in his pigeon English. "When you get there, you go to room, where you stay until taken to starting prace." She gasped, " I've got to race?" Jessica took an intake of breath, surely she wouldn't be in a running race, she so hated running, anyway, it would be impossible in this get up. The driver chuckled, "my Englis, not so good, you go prace to start, not prace to run." He laughed at the notion of seeing the Queen of the Nile running anywhere in that gear.

Jessica seized her moment, "so anything you can tell me about it?" He shook a knowing finger at her, "they tell all when you on prane." She shivered. "When it's too late to back out - oh great." He grinned, "now now, my lovree Creopatra, no need nerve, it all be velly good." She smiled, "oh please, go on, tell me, there isn't any running or crazy physical stuff is there?" He just laughed, in a delightfully high tone, "I tell you what I know, but promise no back out, you make me trouble." She nodded vigorously, anything to glean a clue. "I promise," she grinned, flashing slightly uneven teeth at him. "You must find partner." It was worth a try, she pushed a little further. "Who is it?" She quizzed. "I not know your boy, all guests find partner hidden on island, you have map and clues - is all can say, and you velly beautiful."

He promptly closed the glass window, as they approached Jandakot." He winked at her in the rear view mirror as they pulled into the airports car park - she felt strangely serene as though she were fulfilling a weird pre-destined moment in time that would some how, some way, change her life forever.

15

Brad propped up the bar, thankful everyone around him was part of his mothers party wearing their ridiculous costumes - he never felt so stupid! Wearing a simple knee length toga made from unbleached muslin, he squirmed uncomfortably to fight the urge to scratch at his genitals - not a good look for a Roman General. He pulled at his mask like a schoolboy, Julia had made it quite clear he had to wear it at all times, making him unrecognisable, or he would ruin her special day, he even had to speak with an Italian accent, which luckily for him was easy as he was fluent thanks to his heritage on his mothers side!

He began to seriously question his loyalty to his mother, this party was not what he had in mind at all - his idea of murdering people was far more palatable than the daft notion of falling in love! Downing a large whisky and rye, and then another, he briefly glanced at his clue sheet, he had to find Queen Cleopatra - now there's a surprise - not. He couldn't imagine what the computer came up with from his entries on the online questionnaire, as annoying as the whole thing was, he had answered the questions honestly. Perhaps in the back of his head somewhere weighted down with an archaic and rusty anchor, the romantic in him hoped it would find him his Queen - for real. But his unconscious mind disagreed entirely - because it knew -before *he* knew -that he'd already found her.

He read his clue sheet: Thomas's boy lived where you might think, but Queen Cleopatra, is North in the sink! He wondered if he should bother to find her, after all, she had a similar clue sheet, she was bound to come looking for him, so he decided to stay put, and let his unrequited lover, find him - it was absolute fanciful bullshit anyway and even if she was a computer match, love was a disease he really had no desire to catch!

The flight to Rottnest Island was a bumpy twenty minutes in the air from mainland Perth, and the most spectacular coastline scenery Jessica had ever witnessed. She remembered going there once as a kid the cheap way - on the ferry. She giggled as she recalled how Kevin and Amber joined her hanging their heads over the side chucking up all the way. Her nerves were replaced by a longing to land on the magnificent Island, a popular holiday destination for Perth residents and overseas quokka hunting tourists. This weekend it was occupied solely by Julia Monroes' guests - that's what pots of filthy lucre can buy she mused, oh how the other half did live.

The pilot of the small six seater Cessna, filled her in on the history of the island, in a delightful broad welsh accent, "oh yes my lovely you're heading for my favourite little part of the world, other than Tonypandy of course - did you know the British Royal Mint is located in Llantrissant, just down the road!" He bellowed in loud sporadic guffaws, "oh but you are not interested in my beloved Wales, I know, so what about this then? Did ya know that the first Europeans recorded to have set foot on Rottnest Island were the crew of the Waeckende Boeij, it means The watching buoy."

She did this at school, time to score some Brownie points. "Wasn't it Willem De Vlamingh, who discovered it?" If she listened with her eyes closed, she believed she was listening to her beloved Sir Tom Jones. "Almost right, my lovely," He beamed, "but a common mistake, it was 38 years later that old Willem landed on Rottnest, he was the boyo who named it, thinking that the quokkas were giant rats, so he called it Rottenest, which literally translated means 'rats nest'. Of course the quokkas aren't even remotely related to rats, although I guess you could be forgiven for thinking so - personally I believe they are *Y Tylwyth Teg*, but maybe one day I'll tell you some Welsh Faerie tales." She was so excited, "I'd like that." She was too polite to ask what the hell *y Tylwyth Teg* are.

They sat in silence for a while as she stared out of the window, "how big is the Island?" She asked, staring down at the oceans vivid shades of blue to green - holding her stomach so as not to lose it's contents as they banked hard right. "It's about eleven kilometres long, and four and a half kilometres at its widest point, it's only a tiddler, that's what makes it such a magical place, the coastline which is surrounded by shallow reefs, alternates between rocky cliffs and sheltered sandy bays - not as good as Wales of course." He chuckled for a moment then continued, "I love Perth, but this place, with its five salt lakes, amazing weather, it's a unique place, so lovely and unspoilt!"

He closed his eyes for a few moments, lost in his own fantasies and memories, much to Jessicas' horror! He caught her expression and laughed heartily. "Don't worry yourself my lovely," he chimed, amused by the look of terror on her face in his mirror. "I could fly this thing all the way with my eyes shut, you're safe with me." She whispered to herself, "I'd rather you didn't." Moments later, she braced herself, for a bumpy landing, remembering all the light aircraft crashes that had recently been happening in Western Australia's outback. "I don't want to be a statistic," she cried as the landing gear began to judder. He must have had supersonic hearing for he answered her immediately. "There are plenty of shipwrecks around the Island, but I can assure you, you wont be visiting them without your scuba equipment, not on my watch anyway." He laughed aloud for some time at his own wit, before suddenly announcing that the Rottnest Island Aerodrome was five minutes away due north.

She planted her face against the window mesmerised by the sight of several shades of turquoise blue waters framing miles of white golden sandy beaches. She pulled it away quickly realising she had left a makeup mark on the window. No sooner had they landed, the pilot threw open the door, and they were greeted by a solemn looking man, dressed in a typical chauffeurs uniform, he spoke with a decidedly posh British accent. "Queen Cleopatra, I have instructions to take you to the lodge so you may acquaint yourself with your royal suite, after which you will be taken to your starting point." He handed her a clear view file containing a great deal of typewritten instructions and maps. She wrestled with rising hysteria, and stiffled many giggles, especially when the serious chauffeur tripped over a tool bag stubbing his toe and was literally hopping mad. He then completely lost his cool with a young aircraft mechanic, who was responsible for leaving it there. It was then that she noticed the chauffeur was wearing a toupee, which after his fall, was flapping in the breeze held on by one strand, quite precariously. She opened her mouth to tell him, when the young mechanic, flashed a wicked smile at her and winked. She agreed with him, and let the miserable driver carry on, not knowing just how funny he looked!

The Rottnest Lodge Resort, was a rambling rustic affair, comprising of a large and stately looking main red brick building, with beautiful majestic wide verandahs surrounded by individual log cabins adjoining fountains, trees and the Australian native bush at its best. Immediately ushered to her room upon arrival, Jessica almost passed out. Her room truly lived up to the title of a 'Royal suite', she was amazed by it's huge size and splendour.

A smart tap on the door and she was greeted by a young woman with the longest red hair she'd ever seen. When she saw Jessica she squealed with joy, "wow! You look *amazing*, I'm so glad you are traditionally Egyptian bronze rather than the white skinned version which is so unrealistic!" Jessica had forgotten that she looked like Cleopatra having become accustomed to the wig and heavy clothing.

"Thank you," she responded weakly, wondering just why the girl was hanging around outside her door. Guessing Jessicas' thoughts the young woman explained "I'm your guide, you're not allowed outside the room until it's time to be taken to your starting point, and then the game begins! It's so exciting." Jessica beamed. "I haven't been given a clue sheet yet, when will I get one?" The girl cocked her head to the side "How do you know about that?" Jessica recalled the drivers warning about his job, "oh just guessing there must be something like that, am I right then?" She convinced the girl that she hadn't been given any advance information and she continued.

"As soon as you're taken to the starting point you'll be given the clue sheet, did you know there's a prize of $5k, up for grabs and a crazy $100 k if you genuinely fall in love but there's obviously lots of conditions around that one, of course it's just pin money to most of you here." She hadn't noticed Jessica wince uncomfortably, feeling so poor again. The girl continued, "my advice, don't let anyone trick you into giving them any hints as to your real identity, but there are about four Jessicas on the list, and we haven't put surnames on, so it makes it even harder. If you want a chance to win the money make sure you disguise your voice also, mind you, I expect you're donating it to charity anyway - you guys are out of my league, I'm just a lowly bar girl."

"I bet I'm as rich as you are," Jessica grinned, glad that the girl didn't know her sad financial state of affairs, "but that's all I'm telling you," she giggled. Anyway, what's your name?" Harriet laughed, "Oh silly me I forgot to introduce myself with all this excitement, I'm Harriet, I usually work in the bar downstairs, but I've been loaned to Mrs Monroe for the event. I was going to be one of the dead bodies for the murder weekend but now I'm your personal guide and helper for a love fest!"

Jessica glanced at her watch, her stomach completed a few somersaults, "when do we start?" "At 1.30 pm, every guest will be led to their starting point, it's only an hour away, so I suggest you study the map you've been given for now, the sooner you locate your partner the better chance you will have." Jessica was feeling really nervous, "what do we do when we've found each other?" Harriet smiled, "you go to the designated area, you'll be shown before you leave, and when you've found your correct partner, you'll find a task sheet, and an identity sheet, you have to find a special object together, and perform certain tasks, when you've done those things, you bring them back to the same area, and you'll both be given a guest list, which will contain everyones real identity, all you have to do, is be the first person back to have correctly placed the identity of the character to the true identity in couples, so for example Bill and Ted characters, might be James and David in reality! We have men dressed as women and women as men, so it won't be easy."

"Oh my god, I don't think I'll ever manage it - my head's spinning." Jessica was feeling more terrified by the minute. "Of course you will," laughed Harriet, "but you must rest now, or you'll be too tired later!" Jessica perched on the edge of her huge oversized king bed and studied the tourist map of the Island. Her heavy heart wandered to thoughts of Brad, she wondered if he was taking part? Then decided he would never stoop to such revelry - he was far too miserable to have such fun, and even if he was there, he'd never recognise her in her outfit under her cement like make up. She wondered if he did join in, would she recognise him?

A tinge of sadness overtook her as she had a flash-back of her encounter in her salon, why did she stop him making love to her? She answered her own nagging question, because it *wasn't* love and it was the right thing to do. She *was* in love with him, but he was only in lust with her. She wondered just who would be matched with him, knowing it certainly couldn't be her, she had answered honestly, about her yearning for truth and true love; they were complete opposites on that score.

Her costume was beginning to annoy her, the wig and head dress was itching, but she'd been warned not to take them off until she was ready for bed. The heavy gold bangles that were forced up to her biceps were cutting deep into her flesh. She longed to wrench the whole outfit from her body, wipe off the bronzed face cement, throw away the heavy gold neck collar, and bathe in asses milk in the marble surrounded spa bath, that beckoned her. For what seemed like an age, a light tap on the door, made her jump, she looked at the clock inset into her bed - she wasn't allowed to bring her mobile or have a watch on, her stomach completed another more serious series of somersaults, it was time for the games to begin! Her heart insisted on strangling her confidence, would she see Brad? Her heart hoped, her body yearned, her mind disagreed.

16

Julia puffed out her chest with pride as she appraised Georgie's organisational skills which were so far working like clock work. She spotted a sad Roman General scratching at his shaggy wig, hunched over the bar and hurried towards him. "What on earth are you doing here Bradley? For goodness sake stop scratching your head." She whispered, not wishing to give anyone a clue as to his identity. "Damon should've taken you to your starting point! I knew Sheila shouldn't have hired him he seemed such a galah," she cursed a stream of Italian unrecognisable words under her breath - worried her plan would fail. "Don't blame Damon, Mother," he whispered back, "I told him I'd find it myself, after all, my starting point is only five minutes from here, what's the point of me sitting there like an idiot for an hour, while some sheila comes looking for me? And do I *have* to wear this ridiculous wig, it's killing me?"

"Bradley, you *have* to wear it, your hair is too recognisable, this longer tousled look will disguise you, but honestly you really haven't embraced the spirit of this event have you?" Her confident air diminished immediately into that of an unhappy widow, "the sheila as you so eloquently put it, will be waiting for her male counterpart to find *her*, so unless you go find her you'll never meet her." She sighed, "a very sophisticated computer has found a match for you darl, I don't know who it is, any more than you, so give it a chance son, and even if you are not interested in her, have some fun for god sake! You work hard, and it's time to play hard, the old fashioned way. You're not backing out and ruining my birthday fun are you? Your father would have loved this party, I miss him so much, words can't express the pain I feel." Her eyes pooled with genuine tears.

"I miss dad too, don't be upset, I'm here aren't I?" He tried to sound kind but the tone was cold and hard hearted. Guilt consumed him, feeling bad, he grinned at her, brandishing his sword, "alright, alright, I guess I better go find this dumb desperate for a man, Queen." Julia laughed, "good, find her, before I have you beheaded!" Brad swept a bow, "oh yeah, great costume, your majesty, Queen Victoria, never looked so hot." She beamed at him, "neither did Marc Antony! I must say the mask does well to disguise you. Remember, Italian accent you don't want her to guess who you are, you need to get to know her without the interference of pre conceived ideas of who you are in reality, so be anonymous and don't be afraid to be vulnerable and honest."

She could sense his irritation as he itched his crutch, "go on, try not to scratch your genitals dear, it's most unbecoming of a Roman General.Oh and just watch where you put that sword." She laughed for ages watching him stalk away non plussed. Brad was determined not to participate the way his mother wanted him to, but for now, he would comply with the full disguise, he didn't want people knowing who he was at all, especially dressed like a dick, so that was *some* comfort, and now, he focussed on how to find this stupid Queen!

He sat cross legged on the grass at his starting point, and studied the map he'd been given; although he knew every inch of the Island, he couldn't work out the clues without it. He repeated his clue over and over again in his head, until it clicked. "Thomas's boy, lives where you might think, but Queen Cleopatra is North in the sink, ok, let's see, Thomas's boy, that's Thomsons Bay and Cleopatra is North in the sink?" Following the line north from Thomsons Bay, it didn't take Brad long to discover the sink, was referring to The Basin, a sheltered snorkelling area, with the most unique view point on the Island. Brad laughed to himself as he paced quickly along the road, passing Charlie Chaplin, Ronald Reagan and Miss Marple, all of which looked totally lost.

The basin was only a ten minute walk from his starting point at Thomsons Bay, he was convinced that his mother was making it all far too easy, still, who was he to complain? After all, mother knows best. He bumped into a blonde bombshell, a knock out Marilyn Monroe lookalike, complete with incredibly full pouting red lips; he instantly wished he was *her* partner as his loins forgot about his itch and thought about another pastime, whoever she was.

"I think you're looking for me gorgeous?" He said, sweeping a bow, and not taking any care to disguise his accent or voice. The shrill voice returned with a breathy but delighted version of Marilyn, "we should definitely be together, especially as we share the same name; Brad Monroe, that's you isn't it?" She immediately scribbled down his name on her form. "How the hell can you tell with all this junk on?" He asked, annoyed with himself for not being more of a mystery. "Your voice is unmistakable silly, if you don't want anyone else to guess who you are, then put on an accent - surely *you* of all people would know what to do."

"Do I know you?" He cooed in his playboy voice, sidling up to her and stroking her soft tanned bare shoulder openly admiring her white swirling dress and heels. "Because, yeah, I reckon we should get together some time, maybe call me later hun - you know where I am right?" Before she could answer, her jealous partner ran over, "Marilyn? Lets go!" The two of them hurried off together. He watched them with disgust - he never chased women but she was something else. Brad shouted after the guy making off with his blonde bombshell."Who the hell are *you* supposed to be anyway?"A distant reply was immediately returned. "President Kennedy, of course." He murmured to himself "of course.

He hadn't realised just how serious the guests were taking the game, $5000 was a nice little prize for anyone to win and $100k was the ultimate demonstration of his mothers flamboyant generosity. He knew all of Julias' friends were rich enough anyway so it would almost certainly go to charity - well in most cases. He sighed, it was gonna be a long and painful weekend. Trudging in what felt like overly hot heat for Australian Springtime he approached the basin via the small sandy winding path that snaked around the dunes; he spotted his prey, she was sitting calmly and rather regally on a rock, gazing dreamily out to sea.

Jessica gazed at the tranquil waters that lapped gently and rhythmically against the shores edge forgetting and not caring why she was there, just spell bound by the rhythmic repetition of the tide against the rocks. "Cleopatra I presume!" Brad was now standing right behind her. She turned slowly still under the hypnotic spell of the breathtaking beauty of the Island. "Oh, yes, that's me." She whispered in a decidedly sexy rendition of an Egyptian lilt, as though afraid to disturb a nearby flock of scavenging sea gulls. Also remembering to disguise his voice, he spoke in a more convincing Italian accent. "I 'ave been looking for you, why are you not looking for me? Do you not want to win ze money?" Jessica raised an eyebrow as she clocked his strong muscular legs but turned away, unimpressed with the idea of abandoning her view from the rock.

"I just love this place, when I see something as breath taking as this, I can't bear to part company with it, for fear my eyes would become blind to anything that is less beautiful." Brad opened his eyes wider for a moment, and crinkled his brow, had he at last found a female to which money was not a consideration? Or was it that she was just so rich that more wealth was a bore? There was something else about her, he couldn't quite fathom; was she just acting out her regal status, or was she truly as imperial as she sounded and looked?

He stood quietly by her side for awhile, taking in the beauty of the seascape with her. He was struggling with his memory, to think of one of Julias' friends who would behave in such a manner, after all, they had all holidayed on Rottnest many times, most people in Perth had, so why was she behaving as though she had never beheld such a view before? She was indeed mysterious, and not at all what he had expected. He silently appraised her, enjoying the open wonder and awe that she displayed. He felt as though there was something familiar about those eyes, despite all the heavy black eyeliner, but he couldn't put his finger on it. He'd looked into many blue eyes in his life time, but he couldn't shake the feeling that those eyes meant something to him - but what?

He silently appraised her, running his eyes over her body. Petite with a delicious curviness so much more sexually enticing than his usual, as his mother puts it, 'stick insect' dates. Her legs, tanned and smooth jutted out from beneath her long white robe which had risen up enough to give him a generous view of her rounded supple thighs. She was intriguing, an enigma to him. Had he ever dated this woman? Surely not, but she felt *very* familiar, if he had he would never have let her go. As though destiny gave him an almighty shove, he suddenly felt an overwhelming determination to genuinely get to know her.

"Would my queen like to walk along the beach with her humble servant?" He asked softly, almost afraid of shattering their moment of shared silence. Jessica threw her legs over the side of the rock, allowing Brad to take her hand for support, as their skin touched he felt a shiver of excitement, unusual for him. "what about the competition?" She quizzed, looking at Marc Antony in

earnest for the first time since they'd met. "As they say in ancient
Roma non progredi est regredi," he laughed, then added,
"Cleopatra, we ave our love to keep us warm so we must go
forwards or we go backwards." She smiled broadly, he hadn't
noticed her slightly recently whitened but uneven teeth.

"I don't think that makes sense, are you really Italian?"
"No Senorita, are you really a beautiful woman wis a very odd
Egyptian accent?" "Si senor," She replied before breaking into
laughter so musical, so profound he felt the notes of her melody
burn the name Cleopatra into his soul. They walked idly, hand in
hand, bare foot, enjoying the sensation of sand between their toes,
leaving combined imprints on the sand. The tide at its most gentle,
allowed them the luxury of paddling without being blasted by huge
waves. The greedy flock of sea gulls followed above them
screeching for food. They ran laughing, avoiding a direct hit.

"The weather is so perfect today," Jessica murmured under
her breath, throwing her head back and gazing up at the china blue
sky. "Not a cloud in it today, I love Australia, the clarity of deep
indigo skies on a summers day, the breathtaking stars that gather to
pay homage to the black velvet of the night." Brad stopped dead,
swivelling her around to look at him. "Cara mia, sei reale? Or are
you ze Botticelli - carved to perfection but far from a cold sculpted
vision of beauty?" He stroked his finger across her face, and pulled
a face when he looked at his finger, it was thick with makeup. She
immediately flushed a deep scarlet that wasn't visible under the
pan stick foundation. "I'm sorry," she started, "it's not my idea of
fun wearing ridiculous make-up like this."

He smiled kindly, "I can tell you are even ze more bella
under zis," He whispered, wiping his finger unceremoniously on
his muslin skirt. "Oh you flatter me, my General, but you don't
know me at all, I'm not what I appear to be!" Her insecurity was
like a submarine resurfacing. "You mean you're not ze Queen
Cleopatra?" He laughed and almost completely dropped his accent.
"Guess what, I'm not really ze Marcus Antonius, but hey, can we
pretend a while? I'm kinda getting into this role play?" He winked
and shot her his most polished 'come on' smile that sent overtures
running through her mind.

"Let's go sit under ze shade of ze old date palm over zere,
its too 'ot wandering all over ze beach dressed like zis!"

Brad felt a heat alright, but not from the Spring sun, it was the inner heat that generates when a man is confronted by the unstoppable chemistry of being in the presence of a compatible woman. He hated computers but wanted to kiss the one that matched him with her, perhaps his mothers party wasn't so stupid after all.

"I feel as though I've found my little piece of heaven," she sighed, "what shall I call you?" He inhaled, puffing out his chest. "Call me Marc my Queen, and si, zis is a piece of de 'eaven. Do you mind cara mia, if I take zis face mask off? It's a burning my face off, but of course, you will zen know oo I am." Jessica laid down in the sand, a slight shade fell on her face from the palm. "Lets just get out of the sun, I don't think we should know each others true identities, yet, can we enjoy this role play for awhile?" She was secretly afraid if he revealed *his* true self she would be forced to reveal *her* true self and his interest in such an ordinary person such as her would be squashed and the game of love would be over too quick.

She already felt faint but would rather die in the Australian heat as a Queen, than endure the pain of a right royal rejection. "As your loyal servant and historic passionate lover, I'd fight to the death for your honour, as indeed I died for you, so let my entire face be turned to ash if your wish be my command." He squirmed and used a date palm leaf as a fan - clearly a hardened woman used to getting her own way - obviously a wealthy young lady.

Changing the subject he decided to see if he could catch her out with some well put questions - she intrigued him, completely. "C'mon zen my lady, give zis honourable Italian a clue, I know you work for ze lady Julia do you not?" She guessed he was trying to work out who she was. "What makes you say that?" She answered, forgetting to keep up the accent. "I'd have known if Julia had a friend wis a daughter like you, no, you must work for her. So give your humble General a clue, what department are you in?"

Jessica flustered a little, she didn't have a clue what Julia did, let alone what departments she had! She imitated his accent with a sarcastic air. "You seem to ave all ze answers, why don't you tell me what department I'm in." He laughed, a carefree laugh that made her want to laugh as well. " Ha! I guess zat you are not so ow you say, stupido, after all cara mia!" Jessica felt so at home with this guy, already, "now, zats the best thing you ave said all day," she giggled, continuing to mimic him. Trying to thicken her accent she asked, "So ow, do you know of ze great Julia? You work for her also, no?" He grimaced under his mask, "no!" His response was a little too emphatic, but she hadn't noticed. "Okay, zen let me ave a good look at your face, perhaps I can recognise you zat is if it 'as not cooked too much." She half heartedly grasped at his face mask, causing them both to fall back with laughter. The glimpse of his most perfectly angled jawline made her gasp - Brad? He couldn't be, could he? Her mind began working overtime.

Brads lips were now within an inch of hers, he wrestled with the overwhelming urge; to take her into his arms and kiss her passionately; was it the costume or was chemistry at work? This woman had an effect on him and he felt compelled to find out *why*. Sensing what was on his mind, Jessica struggled to her feet. "Come on Marcus Antonius, lets go and get our instructions, I feel ze need to win $5000, that's if you're Centurion enough for it."

They ran laughing still hand in hand, towards The Lodge, Jessica was feeling a strange warmth toward this man, his hand in hers felt right, like coming home. He was gentle, yet manly, his physique was as breathtaking as the Basin, but she didn't want him to know that in reality, she felt like Cinderella, unworthy of his princely love. She was afraid that if she were to unmask him, and he were to disrobe her, he would be terribly disappointed; after all, she was so different to the sensual Cleopatra, with striking bronzed skin and raven black hair. She wanted to stay in her role as Cleopatra forever, so that *he* would continue to be her lover. After all, the computer matched him to her, so Julia couldn't have had anything to do with it - so as much as she got a sense that the similarity in features were Brad like, he was softer and kinder, so she discarded the wild fantasy that it could be him.

She felt safe in the knowledge that here and now, there was another man in the world that she would *feel* something for. But could she dare let her barriers down and allow a romance to happen *here*, on the Island as Cleopatra? And could she dare allow him to know the real her without running away when the clock strikes 12pm? She was sure that if she did, she'd end up hurt; she

couldn't allow that to happen. A fleeting moment of ecstasy
wasn't worth an eternally broken heart - her fluttering fragile heart
turned to the thought of being with Brad once more, or was it?

17

As they approached the main square, Jessica wished she'd kept Marc back at the basin; she spotted a very curvy and physically perfect Marilyn Monroe, exchanging mutual admiring glances - she even performed a sensual wiggle and song, 'I wanna be loved by you…' just for his benefit. Daggers hurled involuntarily out of her own flashing beautiful eyes, her jealousy obvious to all around. She glanced at Marc Antony, who seemed to have eyes for every other woman around, except *her*. He slicked back his unkempt shaggy mane of raven hair with his hand catching her unmistakably green eyed jealousy - if only she knew how loud and desperately his heart already beat for her.

He murmured in her ear, dragging his parted lips across her cheek softly sending overtones of the promise of the ultimate sexual thrill. "Zey cannot 'old a candle to you my queen - wiz zem it is games, but wiz you it is …" His voice trailed to a sigh, with no disguise, "… something else, that I can't explain." Jessicas' heart stopped for a second, that voice - it meant something, she shook away the notion, allowing her heart to beat in time with her mystery partner. Neither of them knew why they felt such an instant bond, as though serendipity had worked its magic through the genius of modern technology; but their hearts knew, the truth before they did.

Carrying on the charade in the spirit of the game that brought them together they eventually found their way to the second post and the person giving out the next level instructions. Marc read them out loud still maintaining his Italian/Roman accent. "It says we ave to find ze jewel of ze Nile, situated in a cave off of ze Queens partners town?" They sat musing on what it meant, solving the geographic puzzle was imperative if they were going to be able to solve their couples task. "The Queens partners town? Well, the Queens partner is a King, surely?"
He grinned and touched her nose. "Right on Queenie, it's Kingstown - I know the cave, I used to play there all the time when I was…" His voice trailed to a whisper "… a boy!" He'd dropped the accent in his excitement, causing Jessica to look at him quizzically. He caught her brief stare - did she recognise his voice? She didn't appear to, she was busy scanning the map. He didn't

care anymore, he was finding happiness just being by the side of his beautiful mystery partner.

Grabbing two bikes, they fought for their breaths as they tried to cycle in bulky costumes, while screaming with laughter - having to stop periodically to rest for breath and to chug water from their bottles - although only 24 degree Celsius Spring sun, the heat was devastating in full dress. Jessica couldn't believe the fun she was having with Marc, he was everything she wanted in a man - the chemistry was clearly shared, in no time at all she wished with all her heart it wasn't just make believe.

The cave they were seeking was located at the base of a rugged group of cliffs, they had to negotiate a difficult path down to the beach below. Brad made the journey with ease, he'd climbed down to that particular cave many times in his life time, usually if he wanted to be alone. This was the first time he had shared its secrets with another, despite attempts from the many women in his life. Taking an unknown Queen Cleopatra to his special place felt strangely right. He hated to admit it, but the computer matching had worked - *she* felt right.

Jessica threw her arms around him as they stealthily made their way into the mouth of the cave, it's cold darkness and damp atmosphere, was a welcome reprise from the heat of the sun, but it sent shivers of fear up and down her spine, causing her to shudder violently. "You'll be alright," he comforted, "you're with me now, I won't let anything bad happen to you." He was so masterful, she shuddered again as her heart did somersaults. He squeezed her waist, then threw his arms around her, and in the dark pressed his lips to her mouth, which was already opened in eagerness, for the moment that seemed as though destiny had dictated would have to happen or the world might end.

He pulled away from her suddenly, painfully, and spoke with deep feeling. "Why do you feel so special to me? I know it sounds real stupid but I feel as though…" He paused to swallow. "…I've already met you in my dreams." He paused for a second, then whispered, "Am I crazy?" He ran his extended fingers across her chest-bone, stroking her flesh as though his life depended on the warmth of contact that he found there. Her chest heaved as her breath shortened with every stroke of his hand, "not crazy." She stumbled over the right words. "Somehow, it feels like you're my destiny."

"I'd like to be." He murmured, kissing her neck, his loins raging with desire. The fluttering of dark unseen wings diverted their attention momentarily. "You're not afraid of bats are you?" He asked, despite the darkness, she could tell he was smiling. "I can't say I've ever been near one before," she broke off, as a pair of wings brushed against her wig, a little too close for comfort - she squealed involuntarily. "Come on, we must go deeper." Brad clamped her hand in his, and pulled her firmly, until they were in the middle of the cave. The roof of the cave opened up, and a solid beam of light pierced the darkness like a shining star. Jessica stood in awe of the fabulous stalactites that hung precariously from the roof and gasped at the equally impressive stalagmites that looked as though they had forced their way up through the floor from the centre of the earth, creating a strange new world effect.

"This is incredible Marc," she gushed, throwing her accent away - he caught it and squinted at her in disbelief, that unmistakable twang - could it be? He threw the notion away - but his brain computed the facts in lightening speed until he knew it made absolute sense. The pillar of light that streamed in from above, cast an eerie shadow on the rock formations, surrounding them with a soft back light, just enough for them to see each other. "You are so beautiful, I wish they'd let us bring our phones, I'd like to capture this moment forever," he said softly.

Jessica blushed, and was grateful that the light flattered her features, she was quite sure that her makeup was a mess by now, and was not in a hurry for Mark to see her in the harsh light of day - she would definitely feel like Cinderella as the clock struck twelve and her face falls apart. Except she would be the one that turns into a pumpkin. Brad found his old table and chairs, a large flattened rock, coupled with three smaller equally flattened rocks. "Hey look, my old table and chairs." He led her by the hand and sat her down on the most comfortable stump and was about to show her the carvings he had made twenty five years ago when he realised that if he did she would see his initials BM, working out his name would be an easy calculation. He felt safe with his anonymity, and for now thought it better to continue on as Marc Antony, if she knew who he *really* was, perhaps she wouldn't truly accept him and would judge him by his well documented playboy reputation. He couldn't take the risk, in case he lost her before he'd won her.

Jessica smiled alluringly at the man she was beginning to idolise. He looked funny in his face mask, he reminded her of the scarlet pimpernel, a brave, dashing hero, his identity never to be revealed. His eyes were not easy to look into, for there were only narrow slits for him to look out of, Julia had thought of everything she marvelled. "You can take that mask off if you want," she remarked casually, as if she didn't care who he really was, but this time it was Brad that wanted to avoid the truth for fear of losing his Queen. "I think it has fused into my skin - anyway, it'll be more fun if we don't learn each others true identity until the dance tomorrow night. How romantic if at the stroke of midnight we're unmasked and we can truly adore each others vision."

He stood as close as he could to her side, "there is nothing I would like more than to see you completely unclothed, but for something so special there is a time and a place, let's enjoy each others soul today, and make a date for our bodies tomorrow." He sighed as the words tumbled out, he barely had time to think before he spoke, merely echoing the stirrings of his rusty heart. She crossed her legs, as her womanly aching accelerated with his every word. "Wow, that just took my breath away. Have you always been a sensitive and poetic speaker?" She could see him grin cheekily, "me? Poetic?" He threw his head back and laughed, a magical sensitive laugh, that made her tingle with latent desire and stirred up something else, a memory or was she imagining things that weren't there? But, wait a minute, it *had* to be him.

"I've never been accused of *that* before." He admitted solemnly. "Well, there's a first for everything my handsome Roman General." He pointed to a place in the corner of the cave, "look, a parcel." He weaved around the formations with ease, his familiarity with the cave a pleasure to behold. He waved a small white package at her, as he returned. "For my Queen." He bowed, and handed over his booty. She ripped open the small white box in excited anticipation, eager to behold the secrets of the 'Jewel of the Nile.' She took out a typewritten letter, and a small black velvet lined jewellers display box. Ignoring the letter she opened the box, her curiosity overwhelming her. She let out a huge gasp of admiration, as she gazed at its sparkling contents. Brad placed his arms around her waist, and kissed her ear, delicately nibbling on her tender lobes. He then took the ring from the box and slid it firmly onto her outstretched finger.

"The shining brilliance of this ring is but a faceless piece of glass in your presence, but I want you to keep this, and remember me *always*…and I'm *not* play acting." Jessica could feel hot tears of emotion trickle down her cheeks, no-one had ever said such moving words to her before, she struggled to gain her composure, but merely crumpled in front of him, sobbing with breathless embarrassment. He laid her head against his chest, and comforted her silently, allowing her the dignity of a shared silent moment. Once she had overcome her tears, she looked up into his face, his strong angled jaw jutted out proudly, and that classically roman nose, she wrinkled her china doll painted face for a moment in thought, was she so in love already with Brad that every man reminded her of him?

She spoke, slowly and deliberately, daringly abandoning her masking accent. "Have you ever been in love before?" Brad paused, and then took in a sharp breath before answering her question. "Yes and no, I thought I was in love." He whispered gently tracing her face with his manicured finger tips. She didn't question him further, aware that he would tell her about it, if he really wanted to. He returned the sentiment, "What about you? Ever been in love?" She immediately retorted "I've always avoided it, I've no inclinations to become embroiled in teenage fantasies of tall dark handsome lovers of the night."

He recoiled, "is that how you see romance?" His disappointment was clear. "Yes," she replied, immediately regretting it, for fear she was putting him off, she quickly added in a very soft and inviting voice, "well, that's how I *used* to see it." He was quick to jump on it, "and now, Queen Cleopatra, how do you see it *now*?" His breath burned, as his lips brushed fleetingly across her flickering eyelashes." Her heart was beating out of her chest again, only one man had ever made it do that before. "Now, I…" She stumbled awkwardly on her words, afraid of expressing her true feelings for fear of rejection, and terrified not to, for fear of losing him.

She wrenched herself away from the warmth and security of his arms, perhaps if she were away from his magnetism, she could answer him sensibly. Faint music floated in with fresh pockets of air wafting carelessly through the cave, "someones' having a good party," Jessica laughed lightly, anxious to avoid answering Brads probing questions. "Yeah, it's getting pretty late." He sighed, approaching the pillar of light now from the moon, to look at his watch he had sneaked in his pocket, and returned with a broad smile, "we've been in this cave for hours, guess what the time is?" She screwed up her face as she tried to think, "oh it must be about 7-30." She murmured, letting out a big breath, relieved for the temporary reprieve from his inquisitive stares. "Try 9-45, I guess we're not the first couple back."

He smirked, his mouth curling tantalisingly as his tongue wetted his lips. He lowered his mouth to her ear and whispered "I never want to go back." She shuddered, feeling apprehensive at the thought of the unmasking drawing nearer and nearer and so too, the rejection. "I think we'd better be getting back Marc, Julia will be worrying about us!" Brad noticed the typewritten letter that came with the ring, he immediately bent down to pick it up, his back clicking loudly. He moaned in pain, a deep forlorn moan, a very familiar moan. "Are you okay?" Jessica enquired, her brain working overtime. "Yeah, it's just an old war wound," he laughed, rubbing the base of his spine vigorously, "can you believe it, I play squash, jog, lift weights, eat a super healthy organic diet, and don't smoke, all in the name of good health and what happens? I turn over in bed and tear a ligament or something, I've been told by a reliable source that it's my sacroiliac - I guess I'll get over it."

His words and accent free voice went straight to her subconscious, as the pieces of the puzzle slotted together all at once marching the obvious evidence to her conscious mind. The hero standing in front of her, the sensitive creature that both spoke and moved with celestial poetic grace, was unmasked in her head. How stupid was she that she had not recognised him long ago, his true identity was now unmistakable.

18

Jessica watched Brad read the letter, and appraised him once more. This time with a more critical eye, even though the moonlight was dim in the cave, she could see him quite clearly. Strong broad shoulders, framing an athletic countenance, muscular legs covered with the same soft downy black hair that she had admired when he had given her a lift home in the Patrol She screwed up her eyes, trying to picture his hair, she giggled, he must be wearing a wig. That was the only thing that really threw her off.

Her heart beat louder than any tribal drum, as she fought back the tears of humiliation! She should have known him in an instant! Was he deliberately trying to deceive her? No, the sensitivity and openness he had displayed were not acted out for her benefit. Brad Monroe was not falling in love with *her*, the poor wretch Jessica Shackley, he was falling for Cleopatra, the black haired sensuous image a beautiful powerful Queen, that she was portraying so well, but simply didn't exist - except in history and like Cleopatra, she knew she would die for him.

Brad interrupted her thoughts as he strode over to her he was laughing lightly, "Hey read this my Queen, it says once we discover the Jewel of the Nile, I must slip it on your finger, and kiss you for at least a count of twenty!" Who the hell wrote all this shit anyway?" He took on a sudden serious air, and pulled her with all his masculine strength to the close proximity of his body "Let's try that kiss shall we?" Without waiting for her to either agree or disagree, he pushed his open mouth towards hers, this time teasing her lips with his tongue. "I want you." As he moaned, she felt a pang of anger, the same words said in the same soft moaning hypnotic way, he didn't want *her,* he simply wanted dress up sex with Cleopatra, after all, he didn't even know who she was, and there he was, spinning a line like any polished actor - prick.

She pulled away, angry that once again she'd allowed this man to penetrate her armour. She wanted to scream, but he pulled her with unbridled passion towards his mouth, at which point she allowed herself to enjoy the hot lusciousness of his tongue, searching her mouth greedily - why couldn't she resist this incredible male chauvinist? She knew why. She abandoned all resistance, responding with a hungriness for him that made them both groan with throbbing desires. In the darkness of the cave she was safe, as long as Brad was unaware of her true identity she would remain his, but she knew, he must never know the truth, she was hurtling toward heartbreak city which was only hours away!

It was Jessica that eventually forced herself away from the safety and warmth of his body. She shivered, as the coolness of the night air enveloped her. Brad wrapped his arms around her, their mingled body heat creating a dangerously hot fire within her. "I think we'd better get back Br…" she stopped short, checking herself, "Marc" she added weakly, hoping he hadn't detected her mistake. He clung to her in a way that was boyish and needy, yet at the same time possessed a heady masculine rawness. "Yeah," he sighed, like a true romantic. Was she wrong? Could this *really* be Brad the bastard bad boy?

He gushed with breathy words. "It's time to share the velvet blackness of the eternal skies, and marvel at the wonder of a thousand flickering heavenly bodies, but I can only appreciate it, if I'm with you." His words could melt the Ice Age, along with her heart - if only they were really for *her*. She was battling a bloody war in her head, imagining all the scenarios, if Brad were to discover that she was none other than Kevins' sister, whom he had taken an instant pleasure in disliking! She couldn't believe the other side to his personality. Her mind fluttered back to the sculptured objects of beauty that he surrounded himself with at home, she'd thought then that such creations could only be appreciated and admired by one who possessed the same intuitive sensitivity as the sculptor who created them. As Julia had once said, Brad was indeed, a dark horse.

Brad led her away from the dimly lit cavern, and they cautiously stepped through the dark towards the mouth of the cave. The sun had already set, and the sky was dark, the moon hid behind a cloud, making their task harder, with no outer light to guide them. Brad called out instructions periodically, so she could avoid holes in the floor, that she had easily seen before. With a sudden lurch, she lost her footing, and plunged to the caves hard rocky floor heavily. She hit her head against a stalagmite jutting out, and a blackness engulfed her, rising up like the sea to drown her in an unconscious slumber - just like sleeping beauty.

Brad came to her rescue as best he could, but the blanket of darkness made seeing her impossible. He called her name several times, feeling the floor, but the stagnant silence and fluttering of bats were his only reply. His blood ran cold at the prospect of losing the one girl he needed all his life to find. Groping carefully in the dark his hands suddenly felt the cloth of her robe, she was lifeless. He held her close to him, as he wrestled with his thoughts. He found her mouth and kissed her hoping it would somehow bring her back to life, but once he realised that had failed, he lifted her up, ignoring the burning pain crucifying his back and gingerly making his way out.

The moon had thrown away the clouds and shed enough light for him to see her face clearly - he almost dropped her. "Jessica, I knew it, I knew it." He laid her down in the sand, and felt her pulse. He sighed a huge sigh of relief to find one - at least she was alive! He felt her arms and legs to determine if she had broken anything but no bones were out of place. He pulled out what seemed an endless stream of clips that held her wig in place, and carefully removed it, her own flaxen hair tumbled out gratefully. He remained still for a moment, as he drunk in the truth of her identity. Then he examined her head, and found a nasty bump, he guessed she was suffering concussion, and the best thing he could do, was to bring her round, and get her to the Islands Medical Centre.

He carefully placed the wig back on, cupping her head delicately, not wishing to wake her just yet. Once it was in place, he admired her natural beauty, despite the tracks of mascara that had migrated down her cheeks. He knew that somewhere deep inside him, he had guessed her identity from the get go, the false accent that she let slip every now and again, gave him clues, but it was the way she moved and the honest down to earth unpretentious way she spoke, that truly gave her away. She would need more than a wig, and heavy make-up to disguise such a fabulous character. He'd been in love with her from the very first moment he laid eyes on her, yet, all he could do was to reward her with a constant stream of criticism and hostility, because he was afraid of the power she would have over his very damaged heart.

He cursed himself, as he strode quickly down the path toward the Lodge, cradling Jessica gently in his arms. He knew she'd be furious if she found out that it was *him* that had been kissing her in the cave. After all he had said and done, and the callous treatment she had received from him, she was hardly going to believe that he really did love her with a passion! In his unguarded moments of truth he felt as though he could have told her anything! He couldn't bear the thought of her directing anger toward him, he *needed* her love. She had single handedly resurrected feelings in him, that he'd resisted for so long. For now, he would keep his knowledge of her identity a secret, and make sure that she wouldn't recognise *him*, until he could work out a way of convincing her that he wasn't the playboy bastard that he'd been, because for her, he would move mountains and in that moment, he knew she was, his person.

19

Tipsy revellers wolf whistled and clapped at the sight of a Roman General breathlessly carrying his Queen into their midst. "Wow, he's loved her to death! Hey, I think you've conquered that one Marc!" A drunken Dr Spock chuckled, who'd already seen them together on the beach that very afternoon. Brad ignored them, beads of sweat across his brow betrayed his intense pain. "Where's Doctor Hartman?" The crowd immediately parted, and a tall man with an equally long beard dressed as Merlin pushed forwards, "take her to the lodge, I'll be with you in a minute."

Jessica had come around enough to be aware she was being carried, she relaxed into the strength of the arms that held her in their grasp so tightly. The pounding yet rhythmic beating of his heart mingled with her hazy thoughts, as she allowed herself to drift in and out of a painful throbbing sleep. A sudden disruption to her new found peace forced an excruciating light into her heavy eyelids as muffled voices discussed her health. She caught a glimpse of a strange man above her, "Merlin?" But before she recalled any dialogue, sleep enveloped her again.

She awoke hours later in a sudden sweat, a cold flannel was pressed against her brow. "Where am I? Is Merlin here?" A sudden surge of vomit pulsed into her mouth, she hung her head over the side of the bed launching her stomach contents into a bucket already waiting for the inevitable. She raised her hand to her head wincing as she found the source of the dull throb. A feminine voice seemed to echo from afar. "You were out cold, we're arranging your transport to the Royal Perth Hospital for observation, the doc says you're concussed with a slight contusion, should be nothing to worry about."

Her eyes flickered unresponsively for a few moments, as she tried to deal with the bright burning light that seemed hell bent on blinding her. With a final effort she opened her eyes, squinting at first, then becoming accustomed. She looked into the wide eyes of her personal helper Harriet."Gotta get Julia and the doc, won't be a minute." As she turned to leave, Jessica grabbed her arm with a vice like grip. "No don't! Stay, tell me, what happened?"

She creased her head in her efforts to remember, but fell back breathlessly against the pillow. "I can't remember a thing she cried, "I feel as though there is something important I should know, and I can't remember, you have to help me." Harriet smiled as she appraised her, she was a refreshing change from the pompous rich people she often had to endure at the bar downstairs. "I'll help you if I can, what do you want to know?" Jessica, struggled to talk, "who brought me here?"

"Mark Antony carried you all the way from Kingstown, he's a strong man, apparently he overcame a great deal of pain to bring you here." She sighed dreamily, oh yes, my Roman warrior, "Marc Antony?" She rubbed her head and closed her eyes as she half smiled to herself. "You know who he is don't you?" whispered Harriet. "You mustn't let anyone know that I know, it's very important, do you understand?" Harriet grinned and squeezed her hand, "no worries, safe with me girlfriend." Jessica was still worried, "there's one more thing - was my wig in tact? He can't know who *I* am." Harriet could see Jessicas breathing was too fast, "yeah it was fastened tight, you're unrecognisable, and your make up is like waterproof cement - I could do with a foundation like that. I wanna get the doc for you though."

Jessica was visibly relieved, "thank God." She heaved with immense satisfaction, as the memories of her night of romance flooded back. "I'm getting the doc now." Harriet grinned, the large gap in her front teeth, giving her an air of mortal friendliness. Jessica almost had a panic attack at the prospect of leaving the island and her Centurion, she needed his arms, his lips, his love, just one more time. "Please cancel the airlift to the Hospital, I don't wanna go, tell him, go, now!"

Julia sat by Brads' bed, her brow creased with the increased strain of worry for her son. "You must see a specialist, I'll have one flown out tomorrow morning, it's ridiculous to ignore such a thing! You of all people know how important it is not to aggravate the situation, although I have to admit, I admire you for bringing your partner back the way you did." Brad flexed, "my partner?" His eyes misted briefly, "my partner is *Jessica,* you know full well it is! You organised this whole charade with your incessant meddling! I warned you not to interfere with my love life, but you ignored me, you deliberately threw us together - didn't you?"

His accusing eyes narrowed, his face appeared grey and dull, but Julia remained steadfast hiding the pangs of regret and guilt she felt for meddling incessantly. "So what if I *did*? But I'll have you know, in *this* instance, it was the computerised matching system that did it, I simply invited her and then got you two to submit your answers. I thought, if you really were a match, it would put you together, and it did! Are you really *that* angry with me or are you finally going to admit your feelings for once in your life?"

"There's only one thing I have to say to you mother," he threatened, pointing his finger in her face. His voice wavered to a mere strained whisper before adding "thank you - I love you mum." Julia shrieked with joy, "I knew it, I knew it, you're in love with her aren't you?" He smiled, "Don't push it, mother." He warned, hating hearing her shout out his most private thoughts. "Just tell me Bradley, have you told her how you feel yet?"

"No! And as painful as it is for me to say that you were right once again, please for god sake, now leave the rest to me, no more divine Monroe intervention! I mean it! Please, okay? Say it!" Her joy was evident, "okay." She beamed, her eyes simply glowing. "This is the best birthday ever." That statement made him happy, to see *her* happy for the first time in a long time. "Can you do me another favour?" He whispered. "Well that depends on what you want." She grinned cheekily, squeezing his hand, desperately wishing Jesse was here to see his son.

"This is important, you have to just let her think that I don't know who she is, and under no circumstances let her know who I am, because at the moment she doesn't know." Julias' face dropped, resulting in her mouth opening in a blank look of amazement. "Are you saying that you spent *all* that time together, and you didn't let her know who you really are?" Here it comes he thought. "I have my reasons." He snarled, a little nastier than he had meant. Julia relented, she had given Bradley the opportunity of a lifetime to make it with Jessica, she had to back off, and leave the rest to him! "Well if you want to blow it, I guess it's your prerogative. Don't forget to take your Naprosyn tablet." Brad raised his eyes to the ceiling in a display of boyish rebellious disgust watching thoughtfully as Julia slipped out of the room.

Julia quizzed the Doctor as she saw him leaving Jessicas' room, "is she alright Ted?" Still dressed as Merlin he looked funny. "She was lucky, she sustained quite a contusion, she'll have a serious headache for awhile, and may suffer some confusion, but I'm satisfied with her recovery. She has concussion and I'd have sent her to hospital but apparently she's insisting on staying, so I'd like to keep her here for observation for at least the next 24 hours." Julia grinned to herself as she watched Ted make his way towards Brads suite, perhaps Brad would listen to *him* about his tablets, she mused.

Jessica was sitting up in bed looking quite bright by the time Julia entered. Her hair was hanging around her shoulders in a tangled and stringy mess. Julia held her hand and looked deep into her baby blue eyes. "Are you feeling better dear?" she asked softly. "Yes, thank you, I feel much better, the doctor said I need some rest, and by tomorrow I should be right as rain. I desperately want to go to the Sunday night ball, it's your birthday tomorrow - I wouldn't miss it for the world." Full of curiosity she couldn't resist asking, "What happened in that cave? I've heard of love struck but you've taken it to the next level!"

They both laughed. "Other than a bump on the head, did you get on with your mystery partner?" Jessica looked her straight in the eye, "I think my contusion is proof enough to say I've fallen head over heels for him." Julia was bursting to say I told you so, but had to contain her opinions, for Brads sake. She added casually. "Oh I'm glad about that dear, who is the lucky guy?" Julia thought she detected a flicker of a frown for a second, then Jessica answered, "That's the thing you see, I don't know who he is, that's why I want to go to the ball, then we can really get to know each other." Julia was still convinced they were meant to be together. "Only on the stroke of midnight," Julia reminded her with a cheeky grin, thinking she would give a million dollars to witness Jessicas' face, when she finds out her lover is none other than her son!

"It's almost midnight now, past an old duck like me's bed time, she yawned, "I'll visit you tomorrow." "One more thing Julia," she called weakly, "How is Marc Antony? I heard he was in pain from carrying me." She flashed Jessica a beaming smile. "He's fine, he pulled a muscle that's all, you'll see him at the ball, I promise!" She promptly left, turning off the light, allowing Jessica to dream of Brads arms, his kiss, his body, his everything - if only Prince Charming was real but on the stroke of midnight tomorrow in true fairy tale style, her fantasy would come to an end - the Queens true identity would be revealed, and her heart shattered into plain old pieces.

20

The next day Jessica languished naked in bed, thankful the doctor agreed, it would be "more relaxing" to scrape the thick foundation off her face and relax there. Harriet guarded her from any inquisitive guests - the whispers about the witnessed beach love tryst, not to mention Marc Antony carrying his unconscious Queen back to base, was the topic on everyones lips - surely it must have been staged? But who were these actors? Or are they real?

The excitement was turned up a notch by whispers it could be Brad Monroe, his name sake Marilyn couldn't keep her mouth shut. Literally imprisoned in the royal suite, Harriet and Jessica played every card game imaginable while Jessica eyed the clock desperately willing it to hurry up - she needed to be held again, to feel his heart beating, to feel the passion of his lips smash against her own - to become Marc Antonys Queen, if only for a night.

Finally, the day had passed to night, Harriet had left Jessica to soak in a solid marble steam bath, Jessica poured more of the exquisitely sweat pea scented bath creme from her guest toiletries pack - they'd thought of everything she mused. The aroma was heady and she laid back dreaming of the night ahead until her new make up artist arrived, and then the pushing, pulling and statue like behaviour began in earnest, she would really be a Queen for her King if only for one last night.

Despite efforts to be brave even Marc Antony cried out in pain as Julias' latest expenditure - a top Chiropractor, pushed, squeezed and pulled every living fibre in his body - he mercilessly manipulated his lower back until he was closer to crying than he'd ever been before. The results were outstanding though, as with a final twist and crack that would make most grown men beg for mercy, the searing pain that weakened his otherwise iron man strength disappeared completely; it was a trapped nerve around his sacroiliac and was now released.

He couldn't wait to usher the man out who insisted on giving him more drugs and a serious warning about what *not* to do when he got back to Perth. Finally alone with his thoughts, he sank gratefully into his hot bubbling jacuzzi bath. His mind fluttered back to Catherine - the beautiful British seductress and love of his life, or so he had *once* thought. He grimaced as memories of how she delivered the ultimate betrayal sent a jagged anger juxtaposed with strangled and excruciating emotional pain. He had sworn whilst rising from the catastrophic heartbreak that lay bleeding in the aftermath of her betrayal - he would *never* love again.

A sudden overwhelming anxiety of a new disloyal relationship enveloped him. What was he thinking? He swore to the memory of his father he would never let a woman destroy him so totally as Catherine had, yet here he was racing headlong into danger, again and with another English blonde woman? Was he really *that* stupid? Perhaps he should go with his first instincts when he saw her in his garage, and insist she leave, get out of his life, for fear of what powers she would hold over him. But how could someone so innocent, so petite and lovely, be dangerous?

He shivered with anticipation - he couldn't help it, she was his heroin like drug, her tender kiss, her feminine curves, the musical naivety of her laugh, sent weakening signals to his knees. He shook himself back to life in an attempt to mentally prepare his emotions but his imagination wandered, he could feel her warmth and oh so gentle touch. He inhaled as though her florally scented skin was next to his. He felt empty if she wasn't in the grasp of his arms. How could he bear to lose her now?

As the bubbles surrounded him he rehearsed phrases that he would say, poignant words to impress her, making sure that she would be so deeply in love with him, that when she discovered the cold light of truth about his identity, he wouldn't have to endure the pain of her bitter rejection. This feeling was alien to him, he never allowed women to invade his heart, preferring to run around with promiscuous empty socialites or stunning high class hookers. He thought about all the women he had dated since his marriage to Catherine was dissolved; not one of them had meant anything other than a sexual conquest and many he paid handsomely for their company during outrageous partying and sexploit's - gaining him a playboy reputation. They always feasted on his body, performing his every whim and all of them so eager to please him - he knew they were secretly harbouring the hope that he would pick them to be his new wife.

He was quite a catch around town; 'The rich successful physically perfect playboy' was the headline in a National magazine. Two years ago he was reputed to be Western Australias' most desirable and eligible bachelor, according to the polls! He grimaced as he remembered all the empty marriage proposals that flooded in after the article revealed the extent of his own personal wealth! Only Jessica was pure enough in heart to tell him and his money to go to hell. He laughed to himself at her spunk, why had he been so cruel? He knew why. Despite his external cruelty, inside he yearned for her, in every possible way. That's why he had to expel her from his life; the overwhelming chemistry, so magnetic, he was sure it would destroy him if he dared surrender to it - but now, like a moth to a flame, he was drawn, captured, he *had* to win her over.

Drying himself he remembered Jessicas' face when he taunted her about being born in Britain; he cursed his impulsive behaviour, punishing her because of his venomous British wife Catherine. He intended to lay his heart bare in a bid to rectify his mistakes, if only she would give him the chance and he only had one chance - tonight.

A rather serious assistant called out solemnly ringing the bell - it was time to be fitted into his new regalia - fit for a ball. Tonight he would be transformed into a dashing Roman General fit for his Queen. His outfit comprised of a plain chiton-tunic, with a fancy engraved metal breastplate then a large adorned belt bearing pictures of roman emperors rested at the waist along with his scabbard and sword.

His arm tattoo completely hidden by a type of armour like sleeving. The metal skirt was heavy but just long enough to hide his signature strong muscular thighs. His shaggy mane like wig was first clipped into place and then a helmet instead of a mask, was pushed over his head, a shining compact version of the typically Roman helmet adorned with a bright red plume - the mask had been doctored to add more facial disguise - leaving only slits to look out of - I'm gonna be the fucking man in the iron mask he cursed, imagining how hot it was going to be, lucky there was a lot of air conditioning in the ballroom. For a cape he wore a simple square of red cashmere wool matching his helmets plume, attached at the shoulder with a monogrammed brooch. He looked in the mirror admiring his new look, rather dashing, not a dry crotch in the house when the girls see this he mused. Best of all, no one would recognise him, his mother had certainly pulled strings to attain such fine costumes.

He took one last long deep breath then strode confidently down to the dance hall to find his Queen. He was a Roman General and leader of men in every sense of the word and he would go into battle with any enemy to win Cleopatras heart - he didn't know how he was going to reveal his identity to Jessica without infuriating her. He feared that rather than seeing it as part of the game, she would at first see it as yet another deception. But he was going to do everything in his power to let her see, the man who carried her back from that cave, the man whom she openly admitted she was hypnotically attracted to, was the *real* Brad Monroe.

Jessica twitched nervously as she tried to sit still for the make-up girl, who was trying desperately to smear a large amount of thick bronzed foundation across her flawless tanned skin, making her skin so much darker and exotic looking. Once her black eyeliner and deep magenta lipstick had been applied, she was ready for the placement of her ceremonial head-dress, she had a choice of two, one being a white plume which rose from a gold band, and the other a vulture head-dress, in gold and white feathers, she chose the stunning vulture one, which was matched with a larger neck collar than the one she had worn yesterday, this one was encrusted with a fabulous array of precious stones.

She stood in front of her full length mirror, and gasped at the majesty of her own reflection. There was no doubt in her mind, tonight, she *was* Cleopatra, and she was determined to enjoy her last evening as Marc Antonys' lover, before she was banished forever, to the reality of her Cinderella life. There'd be no glass slippers for her, but at least she got to go to the ball. Cautiously she peered out of the room, it was clear - she practiced walking carefully with her head held just so, completely upright, so that her head-dress wouldn't tumble to the floor. Her long white flowing tunic was secured high up under her breast, with a thin embroidered belt, it emphasised her small waist, and pushed out her chest provocatively, she had never felt more sexy.

If only this wasn't all make believe - she sighed, she knew when they were unmasked at midnight she would see his disappointment, if not rage, at his new love being the lowly Jessica Shackley, not a high flying executive or well heeled tycoon. She tried to forget her true status as she stepped with grace and elegance towards the hall but with every step she felt her heart sink.

The hall was teaming with colourful characters through the ages, Jessica spotted Julia immediately, dressed as Queen Victoria. She didn't seem to have a male counterpart, but was quite content laughing and talking with Miss Marple and her partner Poirot, and an incredibly good looking Scarlett O'hara matched with Rhett Butler! Jessica felt a pang of sudden awkwardness and panic - what the hell was she doing there? She felt ridiculous, she didn't know anyone in the room other than Julia, and hated the idea of crossing the dance floor in full view of everyone for fear of ridicule. She felt as though somehow her innermost thoughts and insecurities were displayed on her back. What if she tripped on the long toga?

What a fool she would look falling over in front of everyone as they laughed and laughed and made a mockery of such a pathetic fool. Her heart began pumping out of time, she was having panic driven palpitations, her head began to throb, what should she do? She noticed a bar on the south side, and made a beeline for it, hoping she wouldn't need any money to grab a drink, or three! She was immediately accosted by characters eager to question her, and guess her identity. She was vague with them, as she didn't want anyone to know who she was for fear they would tell Brad too soon.

She was horrified when she was handed a form to fill in, which identified the real identities of every guest but not their character, her first name was printed clearly on it with her last initial and she noticed other Jessicas and even another Jessica S. She could only pray that Brad would not have noticed, he hadn't seemed interested in the game anyway. She felt someone blow into her ear, and wheeled around expecting to see yet another inquisitive and annoying character. She was greeted by the heart melting sight of a wonderful, tall, dark and breathtakingly handsome General of the Roman army.

21

A group of musicians burst into a slow smoochy love song, high lighted by a soulful saxophonist. Brad took his cue, diplomatically escorting Jessica to the dance floor. He wanted to hold her, tight, close, never let her leave his arms again. He could feel her hand tremble as he held it gently, upright - she was swooning beneath the makeup, wrestling the urge to laugh hysterically at the ridiculousness of the pomp and ceremony again, but as soon as Brads hand clutched hers, a disarming tidal wave of desire drenched her amusement - this was no laughing matter. She grasped his hand, elegantly moving her body to his lead; both careful not to allow their bodies to connect, for fear they could not guarantee what would follow next and in public.

The magnetic force between them was obvious causing multiple gasps as guests admired the splendour of this mysterious and magnetically hypnotic, couple. Poirot leaned and whispered to Miss Marple, "I told you my dear, zey are not actors, non, you cannot, make such ze pretence of ze obvious, zey are, ow you say, absolumont in ze amour." Marilyn Monroe cursed President Kennedy, compared to Brad Monroe he was a typical politician all wind and no sails.

The guests were all wearing incredible disguises, their excitement exhilarating - as they threw themselves into their final acts of deceit and investigation for their form before the ultimate event, the unmasking. Suddenly the band launched into, dance like an Egyptian - all eyes fell on Brad and Jessica - they *had* to dance to please their audience. They laughed so much as they performed for the crowd together, unashamedly, abandoning any fear of reprisal, both feeling protected by their anonymity.

As the music merged into an another upbeat song, a Samba, Brad kissed her hand bowing low - he tried to conceal the fact he was panting, the wig and the helmet even in air conditioning were uncomfortable to say the least. He led her to a corner table in the hope of evading multiple sets of eyes that were firmly rooted on the couple. Jessica looked him up and down, silently rewarding him with a dazzling smile. "You should bump your head more often," he smiled admiringly. His hushed voice sent tingles the length of her spine causing her to shiver.

"My Queen, you look even more amazing than you did yesterday and are by far the most beautiful woman here - and anywhere." He stroked her shoulder lovingly with his finger tips and whispered "you're my dream girl." Jessicas' eyes stung, but she managed to control the pooling sadness, if only this was real but there, he had said it, it's just a *dream*, and she's his dream girl - nothing more - the whole thing staged for a rich lady's birthday.

She managed a regally courteous smile, she wanted to blurt out her undying love, and beg for a thousand pardons at her ridiculous farsical behaviour in the restaurant and at his house, she even wanted to offer to go down on him in every restaurant in Australia if that's what he wanted, but all she could do was whisper. "Thank you for saving me Marc." Her eyes searched for any nuance or twitch of recognition, hoping he may have known her true identity all along, yet still love her despite her bird flipping inappropriate bad behaviour. But even though she had dropped her disguised accent on occasions there was not *one* flicker of recognition from him, he was completely ignorant of her true identity. A negative wave of hostility washed over her - she was clearly so forgettable she had never meant anything to him or he *would* have recognised her.

Brad wanted to fill in the blanks as he felt her yearning to ask him who he was. He summoned up all his courage, he couldn't bear the charade any longer. He wanted to scoop her up in his arms and tell her how he felt, how his heart had stopped the very first time he had seen her at his garage. He wanted to explain why he had to tell her to get out that day, for fear he would lose his heart and head that very second and fall to her feet - his heart captured.

"There's something I need to tell you," he whispered, caressing her hand, "it's about us." Jessica felt her knees go weak, her pulse beginning to race wildly - her breathing became erratic with fear and anticipation. She took his hand in hers and squeezed it hard. She wanted to scream out how much she loved him, she wanted to tell him to take her to his bed and be the first man to take her virginity and complete her. She wanted to beg him to never leave her side again. But from the depths of her own heart, she knew the reality was that he could never be hers. She was not part of his top tier group, she was a mere mortal and it was time to tell him.

She whispered, "if only this dream was real," more to herself than him, but he heard it. He opened his mouth to tell her who he was and how he feels, when a large lady with bulging breasts dressed in a convincing costume of Marie Antoinette grabbed hold of Brads' arm and hauled him away, shouting her apologies as she left. Brad frustrated and bemused, kept looking over his shoulder at Jessica; pulling faces of helplessness as the lady pulled him to a group of Julias' friends - he was instantly surrounded by a group of coiffured female socialites who *all* wanted his attention. *He* was clearly the belle of this ball. He called out to her, "wait there." Jessica looked at the clock only 15 minutes to midnight - the unmasking.

She took a deep intake of breath. Brad was covered with hot looking women, but then she saw Marilyn Monroe dancing close to him, her lips pouting, she was slithering all over him and he didn't look too bothered by it. Jessica seized her opportunity to chicken out of telling him who she was, to escape the ball before Brad learnt the damning and embarrassing truth. He clearly didn't read the guest list as her name was there, albeit with a few other Jessicas so perhaps he really hadn't noticed. She reminded herself that he was an arrogant playboy, so likely only indulged the party for his mothers sake.

But, how could he be so intimate and real? Perhaps because he thought he'd found someone else real, that was as well connected as he. She justified her actions with every step out of that place; she'd rather die than see the disappointment in his eyes, she had no intentions of turning into a pumpkin - she imagined their gasps of shock and disgust in a public unmasking of the glamorous Queen, who was nothing more than a disappointingly average girl working as a beautician and masseuse in her one man band business.

Acting swiftly and precisely she scouted the room; Julia was sipping a drink with Romeo and Juliet in the far corner but as the band played they left her alone to dance! She hurriedly made her way over to her - she pulled off the ring that Brad gave her. "Darling there you are, where's Bradley, isn't he with you?" Julia clamped her hand across her own mouth looking over her shoulder frantically in case anyone else heard her faux pas - she was clearly flushed with guilt. Jessica smiled kindly she guessed that Julia had hoped they would get together. She flung her arms around her and kissed her, whispering in her ear. "Thank you for everything Julia, I can't ever repay you for allowing me to be part of this amazing experience." She fought with her emotions as she could feel her voice crack and waver to little more than a rasp.

"I'm feeling overly tired, probably the concussion taking its toll as my head is hurting more than it should, I should have listened to the Doctor and gone to hospital. I'm going to retire to my room now to lie down, it's really been a wonderful party, I'm not going to last until the unmasking, I'm sorry. Oh of course, I forgot to say Happy Birthday your majesty!" She kissed her politely on both sides of her cheeks and then curtsied.

Julia was an astute woman, she could see that behind the smiling eyes, and carefree chatter, Jessica was hurting like hell and it was more than her concussion. "What's wrong Jessica?" She asked, in a hushed motherly voice. Jessica looked at the floor momentarily, taking in a huge intake of breath before handing Julia the ring from her finger. "Here, you must have this back, I can't take it - I don't deserve it. l'm so sorry, I have to go now, I shall be leaving first thing in the morning."

Without daring to look into Julias' piercing eyes again, she uttered a final tear choked whisper, "I want you to know that you *were* right - Goodbye Julia." She swiftly left, holding her head up in a dignified manner, praying that Julia would have the good sense to let her go without an inquisition. Julia stood looking at the ring in shock, she called after her, puzzled, "Right? About what?" But Queen Cleopatra had left the ball. Jessica heard Julia call out, but kept walking, she knew she would work it out soon enough. As soon as Jessica was out of the claustrophobic atmosphere of the ballroom, she picked up her long flowing gown and ran, sobbing.

It had only been fifteen minutes but it felt like hours as Brad tried to wrench himself away from the loud and enthusiastic group, of women clamouring to be his next girlfriend - they bored him, all of them, useless socialites, even Marilyn Monroes efforts fell short. Striding ceremoniously through the hall, Brad searched for his Queen. There were heads everywhere it was very difficult to see in the subdued lighting. He felt a wave of panic go over his head, as he feared she'd uncovered his real identity and fled. He sighed with abated annoyance as intermittently girls would make a bee line for him, throwing themselves at him in a ploy to take his eye. He only had eyes for Jessica, he wanted her, and he couldn't find her - where the hell was she?

He could feel his heart thumping out of control as he crashed into people becoming ruder in his attempt to thrust his way through the crowds, ignoring people who greeted him. He *had* to find her! Meanwhile Julia who was desperately searching for Brad, spotted him. "Bradley there you are, wait, I have to speak to you." Brad ignored her, calling out, "can't stop, I've gotta find her." Julia ran towards him and grabbed his arm with a vice like grip. "What did you say to Jessica? Why has she left?" Brad stopped in his tracks, beads of perspiration shone on his forehead, he panted, "she's left? Why? Where is she?"

"She left a few moments ago Bradley, she was clearly upset, what have you done to her?" His shoulders slumped with disappointment, "she said she was tired and her head hurt, so she is going to lie down but, her eyes, I fear, they told a very different story." The band stopped and the compare began a countdown - the unmasking. Julia and Brad stepped outside, "she gave me this." Julia handed him the ring. Brad caressed it, recalling the love they had shared in the cave, the sense of timelessness and how right it felt when he had slipped it on her finger.

His brow creased into tiny lines, his eyes losing their intense sparkle. "She's left because she's found out who I am, and she hates me." He ripped off his helmet and wig. "Damn this irritating fucking thing," he snarled bitterly. "I should have told her who I was straight away, perhaps then …" His voice strangled to a whisper, as he controlled himself in public. "Oh my darling Bradley, I should have told you …" He snapped to attention and saluted at a passer by, "told me what mother?" He bellowed, quite uncharacteristically, causing a few heads to turn.

"I think she knew who you were, I don't know exactly when she found out, but when I spoke to her just now, I asked her where's Bradley, and she didn't bat an eyelid as though it was no surprise." Brad was furious, "of course she didn't mother, she's too polite, but that's why she's left, you just had to open your trap and let it out - I needed to tell her *my* way and now you've stampeded all over my love life, *again*. I should never have agreed to this ridiculous charade!" Julias' face dropped, "oh Bradley, I'm, so, sorry - but if she really loved you - she wouldn't do that would she? Run out on you?"

He softened and hugged her, "It's not your fault," he sighed, "it's my fault, I was the one who behaved so badly before, I did, unspeakable things, and behaved like a damned porn star, no wonder she ran out on me." Julia smiled, "you must go to her," she said, in a sudden wave of new enthusiasm. Brad exhaled with emotional exhaustion. "She doesn't want me mother, she doesn't love me, she's left me, remember?"

Julia clapped her hands on her face excitedly, "but she *does* love you, I didn't know what she meant at the time, I called out but she didn't answer, my brain just couldn't make the connection quick enough." Brad let out an exasperated breath. "What on earth are you talking about now?" Brad snapped, his tolerance for her misplaced good intentions all but depleted. Julia was grinning from ear to ear, "She said something that didn't make sense at the time, she said she wanted me to know that I *was* right! Now it makes sense, oh my god, she was referring to the time I told her when she first came to the house, I could see that she loved you and she told me she didn't and I said I was sure one day she would tell me I was right. Tonight she told me, I was right! Don't you see? Go to her, find her. Do it now, she knows exactly who you are, you galah, and from her own lips, she told me I was right, she does love you."

Brad wanted to tell her off for interfering with his life, but compliantly he kissed his mother on the cheek, before saluting proudly - then he was gone. Praying the alcohol hadn't induced his mothers memory of Jessicas parting words he couldn't wait for the lift to take him to Jessicas' floor, so he ran, taking five flights of stairs in his metal regalia, even a fit man like him arriving breathless. He composed himself, and re-arranged his hair, before knocking gently on her door. No answer, he knocked louder. Still no answer. He backed up then kicked the door in - the room was empty, she was gone. He saw her things, all packed up, great, it meant she was still somewhere on the island. He sank to the floor and cradled his head in his hands in despair. But did he have the right to look for her? After all, if she knew who he was, and that made her leave…

His brain worked overtime throwing around possibilities. If she had told his mother that she loved him then why the hell did she run out on him? He controlled his thoughts and focussed on where she may have gone in her moment of despair. He climbed upon her bed and sat quietly gazing up at the stunning pictures of Rottnest Island hanging proudly on the wall. Then inspiration hit him, he knew exactly where his Queen was, and he was going to find her, capture her heart and make her his forever, or he may as well die by his own sword!

22

Jessica walked with deliberation, barefoot in the sand, eyes stinging with unbridled shame. Failing at love seemed to be a recurring trope she was destined to suffer. She inhaled the aromas of the Island; frangipani infused with the natural scents from the ocean. She stopped, eyes closed letting her lungs fill with the heady fragrance. She replayed her fathers cruelty to her mother, his drunken slurs and unfounded accusations. As a little girl she was witness to the way he systematically slashed her mothers self confidence beyond repair. Her mother was an optimist and proud, she remained externally strong and seemingly unaffected, but her coping mechanism was internalising the pain of his repetitious hate speech. Jessica was sure those drunken words and his cruelty caused the cancer that eventually killed her.

Jessica let the tears flow, she needed to indulge in a pity party. She relived her moments of joy with Brad, recalling the sensory ecstasy of his touch - how she longed to let herself go and submit to the raw primal desire of his body - what better specimen of a man could she choose to finally make her a real woman. She shivered at the thought, but his so call love for her had been an act, cruelly staged for others pleasure - the elite. She was nothing more than a pathetic pawn, an actress dressed up like a xmas turkey and pushed onto the dinner table for the rich guests of Perth to feast upon. She punished herself again and again by reminding herself that her story was like her mothers, doomed from the start - she was defined by her genetics - a failure at love. All she had left was a glimpse of what a perfect love story felt like.

The tears came thick and fast as she recalled the moment, somewhere in time, when her heart was revived by the one man that would also stop it. A zillion tiny stars flickered in the velvet black skies of Western Australia. The memory of walking barefoot through the sand, laughing talking, and falling deeply in love with Brad the day before, faded before her eyes. Her love life was beyond tragic - she blamed herself - she was unloveable. Salty tears plopping out of her eyes were blinding her until she had to stop walking. She threw herself onto the sand, convulsing with sobs releasing her pain in a miserable abandonment of pained constraint.

Vivid images of her mothers sorrow, flashed before her, wickedly twisting the knife - it was clear - she was destined to be alone. She'd broken her own rule, she'd fallen in love with the one man that could never return it - she simply wasn't good enough. She wanted to return to the party, dance with Brad, let him kiss her so tenderly, make plans with him, love him, but she knew she couldn't face the inevitable coldness that he would subject her to. She'd rather remember him for the warmth and masculine strength he possessed, coupled with a sensitivity that only a god could have. She'd cling to the memory of the way he was with her, loving and attentive. She couldn't begin to imagine the pain she would endure if she were to witness his face drop, and his eyes narrow with hostility, as his once warm and vibrant heart froze to a solid and impenetrable lump of ice, because he despised the real her so much.

She shuddered at the thought of meeting with him again back in Perth, perhaps bumping into him accidentally. She'd have to leave, get away, she couldn't face the pain. She picked herself off the sand, brushing herself down, and continued to make her way to the place that defined her sense of happiness if only for a stolen few moments - it had become her most loved yet most painful place in the world; the huge rounded rock on the beach at the basin - if only she could turn back time.

Sitting curled up on it, she felt a strange sense of warmth, the memory of Brad first seeing her there was so fresh in her mind, she dared herself to re-live it. A deep voice echoed somewhere behind her. "Cleopatra I presume!" She flinched for a second, either her imagination had re-kindled a life like auditory ability or she was actually going mad. She wanted to turn around, but although she could have sworn that she heard his voice with her own ears, she knew it was just a very clever ploy by her imagination and the sea winds gently whispering through the air - sent by the devil to drive the blade into her heart then twist it.

Brads' heart pumped out of his chest, she was there, the place they allowed themselves to be who they really are. He repeated himself, "Cleopatra I presume?" Again, she didn't turn. A cruel coldness crawled the length of his spine, he turned to leave - after all, she heard him, he knew she had, he saw her flinch - this was her way of punishing him, torturing him, driving his own knife into his gut and carving out the words, I don't love you. He couldn't leave, his feet wouldn't allow motor function unless it was to hold her. He reached out and tenderly stroked her neck, afraid to receive the cutting edge of her rejection, but driven on by his own burning ambition to hold her close and win her love. "Jessica, I'm sorry." He whispered, so softly, that it was almost lost in the rhythmic sounds of the oceans restlessness.

Jessica froze, not only was she mad enough to hear the great Brad Monroe apologising to her, she'd also felt the warmth of his caress on her neck. Was she really that insane? Had she become *that* desperate for his touch? She was now imagining the impossible? In a daring move she swivelled around to see Brad, unmasked, his lustre and sparkle departed. She jumped off the rock, hitting the ground hard, but immediately picked her skirts up and began to run, run away from the hurt, run away from the rejection, run from the vision of an eternal heartache.

"No, I can't - I'm …" Her words choked her as tears prevented her from telling him that she was the sorry one, sorry for the deception, for everything nasty she'd ever said, sorry she couldn't be the next Mrs Monroe, sorry she was an idiot and very sorry she was the loser. Her breath bit into her chest as a pain in her head drove deep like a javelin. Brad watched his love run away from his arms, devastated in the knowledge that she'd run away from him. He became angry, angry with himself, and angry with her, he ran after her, no more trapped nerve, he was physical perfection, his powerful sporting thighs easily beating down his prey.

He threw himself at her in a flying tackle and brought her down. Heaving with breathlessness caused more by anguish than physical activity he pinned her down. He pulled off her head dress and wig, ripping off her jewelled neck collar, and hurled them toward the ocean. Jessica cried out, humiliated, did he really need to do this to her? As usual he felt the need to punish her for being herself, Jessica Shackley, slightly too curvy and ordinary, and not some high flying stick thin perfect rich girl, the type he was far more accustomed too. She fought him, trying to punch him, but his strength easily overpowered her. He held her still, and just gazed into her eyes, his face was wild, his eyes more like burning lumps of coal, his mouth was held in a thin lipped mockery. The bastard was back, because *she* was back and she wanted to be gone.

She cried out, her voice carried away through the wind. "Leave me alone, I know you hate me, so just leave me, stop punishing me, I can't help being me!" He returned the sentiment with a passion. "Not until you tell me that you love me, for who *I* am, for what *I* am, you've no idea just how much I've fought loving you!" Jessica drew a breath for a second and threw him a quizzical stare of surprise, was he telling her that *he* loves *her*? Why did he ask her to tell him that she loved him for who *he* was, and what he was? Her mind held her tongue to ransom, holding back the words he had begged for to ease his pain.

She remained still, sporting a puzzled look, as she frantically searched his eyes. The pain in her head began to blur her sight as she scanned his face. Before she could respond with the words he needed to hear, with an impatient surge of disgust, he roughly released her. "Same old Jessica, of course you don't love me, it's a game to you isn't it? I didn't think my mother could be right and now, you've proved …your not worthy." He almost spat the words into the air, his bitterness of a love scorned now obvious. He looked down at her with contempt, the same contemptuous eyes he held when she first met him. The same scornful attitude when he made her leave his garage.

He began to walk, the cold heartless bastard was abandoning her. Seeing the only man she had ever loved walk out of her life jolted her vocal chords back into action. " But, you're wrong." He kept walking without looking back, shaking his head with disbelief, she loved a good argument and took every opportunity to make sure he knew how *wrong* he was. She stood up, desperate, watching him leave, then added with a scream above the waves crashing on the rocks. "You're wrong, because I *do* love you, I…" The wind filled her lungs with salt air as she fought for breath; her headache beginning to overcome her strength. He stopped, but didn't turn around, she took a final deep breath, "you see, I always have," and then added in a more hushed voice, afraid of his scorn, "and I always will."

He looked over his shoulder to gaze at her face, lit only by the huge glowing deep golden waxing moon - she was a goddess, *his* goddess. He sprinted back to her scooping her up in his arms with joy. "Why didn't you just say that before?" She gazed weakly up at his eyes shining like a god, *her* god. "I thought you hated me." Without speaking he lowered her down on the sand and laid next to her drawing her close to his chest. She wanted to make love to him, to touch him, to feel his body moving as one within hers. This was it, the one moment that she had lived for, if she never lived to see another day, she wouldn't care, because making love to him made her life complete.

"I want you, with all my heart. I love you, I always…" She broke off as she watched him lean back and smile, that incredibly perfect even solid white smile, the one that made any woman's heart beat faster - and he was smiling at *her,* the slightly imperfect, slightly too curvy, Miss Jessica Shackley.

He gazed at her beauty as he slowly and sensuously discarded his clothes. "You want me? Well my Queen, your wish is my command because I am all yours." She averted her eyes from his masculine nakedness, school girlishly embarrassed by his show of complete arousal yet hugely turned on by his nakedness. She wanted him, she wanted it, she wanted this moment to baptise her in the art of being a real woman for a real man. His eyes smiled with the warmth of a summers day, as he brushed his lips across her cheek. He found her mouth then smashed his lips against hers, he was taking no prisoners with the passion of his kiss - his tongue tenderly danced with hers. She felt as though they were spinning as the lushness of his lips caused a throbbing and mini eruption of molten lava in her loins. She had felt the need for sex for so long, but this ache was different the combination of the power of true love and sexual lust was the celestial grace granted to humans by God.

With a sudden frenzy of lust, he ripped her entire tunic into two, throwing it aside. He gasped as he drunk in the sight of her heaving naked body. She almost felt faint as his heady lust filled eyes made love to her without touching her. His breath burned into her skin, as he dragged his eyes across her nakedness. Appraising her he was whispering the sweetest lyrics of love from a man to a woman - even without orgasm, he was already in a carnal sense of heaven. He ran his hands tenderly caressing her soft virginal skin , oh so slowly, from her breasts, lingering at her inner thigh causing her to involuntarily writhe for a more intimate exploration of her eager body.

She could feel him inwardly controlling himself, as his breathing slowed down. "You are more beautiful than I could have ever dared to imagine," he murmured softly as he delicately brushed his lips against hers. He ran his tongue around the curve of her heaving breasts then pulled it away, teasing her delightfully. "Tell me you love me baby," he asked boyishly, making it clear that his tongue would not find the hardness of her nipples if she did not obey. She inhaled and shouted, "oh yes I do love you!" He immediately responded by plunging his hungry mouth over her breasts sucking hard until she begged him to make love to her, to give her every inch of his pulsating muscle.

She threw her head back, arching her spine as the thrill of his frenzied attack on her nipples felt as though they were connected by an invisible thread. Every stroke heightened the aching between her legs. "Touch me Jessica," he whispered in a satin velvet smooth voice, before running his tongue along her neck, down beyond the valley of her breasts toward her taut stomach. His hand guided hers until she met with a throbbing and twitching hardness, yet it was baby smooth and perfectly waxed. She moaned with desire as she instinctively rubbed her hands up and down his length, driven on by the increasing volume of his manhood. He had to stop her, his control was in new territory and could not be trusted. He laid on top of her, allowing his hungry hands to caress her. She twisted and moaned as his inquisitive and experienced finger tips found the hot wetness of her groin.

Her own aching was building into a crescendo, as he pushed them further and deeper inside her. He withdrew them suddenly to taste them while staring her right in the eyes. "Taste me Jessica." She thought she may errupt then and there just hearing him talk. She crawled down his throbbing body and for the first time in her life, took a mans throbbing rock hard manhood into her mouth. Her hormones were out of control at this point and she had no problem teasing and sucking and licking to the point he had to drag her off it for fear he would choke her with his love.

He was the master of fornication and in a deft movement he straddled her with his body before dropping his head between her legs. Tasting her lasted but seconds as he felt a growing surge of adrenalin and testosterone that he could barely control - nature had no intentions of allowing him any more self control tonight. He raised his head and crawled back to her lips holding her so tightly.

They were laying clamped together sweating and panting. She lifted her legs and wrapped them around his lower back, thrashing and contorting her body to push his incredibly huge throbbing cock inside her. She needed the ultimate penetration from a god amongst men. She looked up at him, the picture of sculpted masculinity. Her heart was bursting. In true abandonment of modesty, she whispered full of anticipation and love, "I want you inside me, take me, make me yours, only ever yours." His eyes closed momentarily with the intensity of the emotion he felt for her. He slipped his hands under her bottom squeezing and manipulating her, making her *beg* for him.

He spoke constantly to her in Italian, warm exotic words of love from a hot blooded man who loved her - her moment was here. He slowly lifted her legs one at a time, until they were fastened firmly around his neck. She gazed up at him, as she panted for breath gasping out loud with delight at the devastating smile he flashed her. He lingered with her in that position for what seemed a hundred years, desperately wanting to thrust himself deep inside her, but also savouring this, a most wonderful and precious moment in time. He had never felt like this - *ever.*

His own desires on fire, he could wait no longer, "Ti amo Jessica." He plunged his powerful body deep into hers in one powerful and most passionate thrust of his pelvis. Her cries of pain at the extreme depth of penetration ripping through the hymen that protected her innocence, then mingled with the pleasures of her own lust until only the flames of her passion drove her on. He stopped for a moment, with surprise, gazing at her beautiful face, his expression held one of intense rapture. He felt overwhelmed by the depth of his love for her -almost to tears.

She woke him from his momentary dream as she began to thrust her hips in and out with such fire and exertion that he moaned for her to slow down for fear he would not be able to exert any further self control. He wanted to make love to her slowly, for hours, yet he was rapidly aware that it would be impossible. Jessica had an effect on him like no other woman he had ever taken to his bed. He withdrew himself suddenly, causing Jessica to shriek with disgust and impatience, he gently rolled onto his back, and gestured for her to sit on top of him, her previous embarrassment at being seen naked and vulnerable departed, as she took command, throwing her breasts out before him in a porn star show of her virginal exit and entry to vixen like eroticism.

He rose up to take each hardened tip in his mouth, she rocked back and forward and side to side slowly, rubbing herself against him in a way that made her want to explode. He watched her give him her body rhythmically in a beautiful symphony of love making - hypnotised by her purity and beauty he called out. "I love you Jessica, I'm yours, if you want me." She returned the sentiment through adoring eyes. They moved together in perfect synchronicity - aware they were created for this moment in time.

Jessica, eyes closed, began to increase the speed of her gyrating with an animalistic and natural instinctual desire. Every stroke was gaining momentum, her need more desperate, she was making love to him in earnest as she approached the moment that defined her as a woman and the reason behind the chemistry of attraction. Like a jockey on the home stretch she rode her lover with an urgency that made him shiver and gasp - he was close to the finish line.

She screamed out "Oh my god, oh, you are my everything, I love you." Her rapture was more than he could bear he trembled as he watched her poetic movements climax and crescendo into an unrehearsed untamed and wonderful cloud burst followed by a waterfall of ecstasy which flowed through every nerve ending. Her moans, shivers, throbbing and shrieks of unfettered pleasure were more than Brad could stand.

As she opened her eyes which had been until now clamped shut with concentration, she caught the contortions of his face, he threw his head back, and uttered his profane love for her and how he needs to be inside her. He suddenly pulled her down on top of his belly and whispered with passion as his trembling became urgent "I'm giving you *all* my love." Their lips obsessively glued together; the rest of the world melted away as together they completed each other finalised by his high powered injection of hot male orgasmic love.

They lay in the sand, their hearts beating as one, entwined, spent, shivering and panting. Brad could feel hot wet tears on his chest, as the overwhelming experience caused her tears to rain down despite her extreme happiness. "Baby don't cry, did I hurt you?" She smiled a confident, satisfied womanly smile. "No - well, yes, but only at first, it was so, so wonderful, I don't know why I'm crying. I think it's because I truly do love you, beyond words." Brad squeezed her tight, "baby, I'm sorry, for everything, the way I was." After a brief silence she reluctantly replied, "I'm sorry too." Brad closed his eyes with satisfaction, he whispered gently, caressing her hair, "Baby, was this…? Was this, your *first* time?"

She felt embarrassed, " I was saving myself…for…for someone special… *you*. Was it… was *I* okay?" He was still gasping for breath as he spoke, his smile brighter than the moon now flickering across their entwined bodies, "*woman,* you were beyond amazing, you *are* spectacularly amazing." He panted for breath, "in every way."

She felt so warm inside, satisfied that love and sex in the movies is real, once you find it. "Well, I've waited a long time for *you* to come into my life - forgive the pun." She giggled as he rolled on top of her and pinned her down, "Would you believe me if I said it was *my* first time too?" She threw her hair back and laughed out loud, despite a sharp pang of jealousy knowing any other woman had ever had his body inside her. "Err, no - your reputation precedes you mister."

He cleared his throat in disapproval and threaded his fingers through the length of her hair. "Okay, you got me there, but it *was* the first time that I've ever made love to anyone that I truly loved so completely. You are my muse, my person, my soul mate - and I know that *now,* because *anything* I have ever done with anyone else in the bedroom, has just been a practice session for this most incredible spiritual experience - so believe me when I tell you I will *never* bed another."

She sighed with joy, as the overwhelming blanket of complete fulfillment warmed her entirety. She must be dead, because life had never, ever, felt so overwhelmingly perfect. She didn't ever want to wake up from *this* dream.

23

Like a scene from an epic Hollywood movie, Marc Antony and Cleopatra laid naked, basking in their new found intimacy. The silver moonlight glowed and danced on the ocean, throwing a soft backdrop further caressing their mood. They clung to each other, entwined as one, glued together by the heady perspiration of love and effort. Silently, they regained their breath as they shared each others sense of ecstasy after the purity of true love making. Stripped bare of the worries of the worlds injustices and cruelty, they lay locked in quiet admiration of a black canvas sparkling with flashing diamond spheres - only the soft rush of the tide echoed around them as their musical accompaniment.

Brad caressed her and kissed her softly "I want to be this close to you every day for the rest of my life." He added, edged with sadness. "But for now, I think we'd better get going, before they send a search party." Jessica sighed contentedly at Brads clear reluctance at returning to earth, mirroring her own sentiment exactly. She wrestled with a sudden urge to laugh hysterically, imagining being caught naked on the beach - which she realised was a distinct possibility. Laughing like children, they struggled to clothe themselves with the remains of their tunics. Jessica had to use half of hers to tie around her middle like a sarong, and the other torn piece to drape across her top, just barely covering her nudity - yet tonight she didn't care a fig about her slightly wobbly thighs or well rounded bottom; tonight, she felt like a Queen and walked like a Queen, because she was *his* Queen.

They walked hand in hand back to the resort enveloped by a completeness neither could put into words - Jessica broke the mood. "Why did you come after me?" He stopped dead and put his hands on his hips defiantly, "why did you leave?" His quick fired response was laced with irritation. "You know damn well why I left," she replied with more venom than she had meant. "Well," he started, while finding a group of rocks perfect to sit on. He pulled her down in close proximity to the warmth of his body. "I assumed, you left because you didn't want to have anything to do with me." She gasped, "oh my word, that's so not true," she shrieked. "I loved you… I do…love you. I guessed it was you when we were in the cave, I think I knew before I knew, if that makes sense. You were in my heart, right from the start, but I ignored it, for awhile.”

She hugged him laying her head against his chest, listening to the rhythmic beats of his heart. “I didn’t want the dream to end.” They both sighed in mutual reflection before Brad broke the silence. “So why *did* you leave?” He stroked her face with his finger tips. She sat up, gazed up at the stars. “You were enchanted by a raven haired Queen, not me. I couldn’t live up to being your disappointment.” He would never understand why women were so hard on themselves, “Woman, how on this flaming earth could you be a disappointment to anyone?”

She was the first to stab the bubble with a knife, “you made that very clear, because I’m a Pom?” Brad sighed deeply, his distress showing. “Me and my defence mechanism from heavy baggage. I’ve hurt you haven't I?” He nuzzled her ear with his lips, “can we get over this please ?” She was ruining the moment, but her hatred of racist jibes pushed her on. “I just don't understand what your problem is with the English, it’s such an antiquated racist attitude - and as far as I’m concerned, we’re all in the human race and should not be segregated by our place of birth, amount of melanin in our skin, our gender, our sexual orientation…” He had *really* hurt her, “wow you’re so fired up, I can see I’ll have to bare my pommie hating soul to you before you run for a presidency,” he winked, his sparkling eyes diffusing her rant in a second.

“Well you’ve bared everything else.” He took a deep breath, “actually, I haven’t.” He paused, his eyes pleading for compliance. “But first, the rules, hear me out and don't say a thing until I’ve finished. I haven't spoken about this to *anyone* for years, not even my own mother.” Jessica felt both intrigue and fear at what he was about to tell her, she couldn't imagine what could justify his bitter hatred of the English. Nodding, she closed her eyes, allowing him the dignity of silence. Brad kissed her nose and took a huge breath of air for courage.

“I was married once, a little over four years ago, to an English girl called Catherine Chandler, she was nowhere near as wonderful as you, but she was like you in many ways; long strawberry blonde hair, beautiful, intelligent, and witty. I fell for her, well, at the time I thought it was love. I was 27 years old, and had played hard as a bachelor, she was twenty five years old, and had been around the stables for awhile. I was warned about her by many of my friends, but I ignored all the warnings as people who are infatuated by physical beauty often do."

He began to clench and unclench his fists. "Even my father and mother warned me about her, they didn't like her at all. My mother fought me like hell when I told her I was gonna marry Catherine, but I won! Against my parents warnings I got my own way, we were married in the biggest society wedding you've ever seen. Catherine had wanted it that way, she said she wanted the whole world to see how lucky she was to marry me. The press were there and even local TV." He coughed nervously, as he recalled his wedding day. "I hated it," he whispered, through clenched teeth.

"Unlike you, Catherine was materialistic, a hard bitch, a showy lady, she liked to let people know that she had money, designer labels and obvious wealth meant everything to her!" Jessica squeezed him and they kissed for a few fleeting seconds, refuelling her heart - he then continued. "We were married for a year and I guess, happy. I worked long hours and was away allot on business building a car empire. She always supported me, never complaining about my absence. I thought I had married an Angel, and I had, but a fallen one, Lucifers sister!"

He paused for awhile, Jessica could sense his agitation, and clasped her hand in his, gently kissing his face. "It's okay, go on." She was struggling to hide her jealousy. "Well, as I say, we were married for a year, and then I received a big announcement, she was having my baby." Jessica couldn't help but let out a gasp of disappointment, but Brad was too racked by his memories of emotional pain to notice. Brad continued, "I was excited but also broken, my dad had just passed away and would never see his grandchild but over the moon for my mother. I'd always wanted to be a father, I know that you probably can't imagine me being the home loving type and all that, but I've always wanted to have a loving family around me, like the one I grew up in. I made sure she had everything. I hired a nurse to look after her, keep her company and cook for her, and everything was hunky dory. She wanted us to move into something more suited for a family so I bought the house in City Beach which was the perfect family home. When she went into labour, I got a call at the garage, I rushed to her side, I had her booked in to the most expensive private hospital in Perth, making sure her room had a view of Kings Park. Anyway, when I got to the hospital, the nurse tells me she's in early stages of labour. I can't tell you the elation I felt. Anyway, I try to go into the room but the nurse stops me…" He inhaled deeply his voice choked, "… saying that only the father can go in, of course I tell her proudly that I *was* the father, but the nurse gives me a dirty look and tells me that's impossible, because the father is right by her side"

He broke off to clear his throat, then continued sadly, "then she recognised me and almost fainted. She let me in and that's when I saw Catherine in bed kissing with my best friend Danny Taylor. I remember feeling as though I'd been hit by a train. I couldn't say anything, but she just smiles up at me and tells me, that she wants a divorce so that she can marry the father of her child. Can you understand how unbelievably wicked that was, even saying it, I can't believe she was evil enough to do it."

Tears streamed down Jessicas' face as she imagined how he must have suffered at the hands of the callous Catherine. Seeing she was crying, he kissed her tears away, tasting them with his tongue. "That's why I childishly felt a little hatred for British blonde bombshells. I spent the last three years of my life having sex with as many brunettes as possible and a few redheads, but really I was acting out, numbed, I was still in shock. I just never wanted to make a commitment to a woman again, I made a solemn vow to never marry, and definitely never fall in love…" His voice disappeared to a whisper, "… but then you came along and ruined everything!"

"I'm so sorry, what can I say." Jessica stumbled awkwardly over her words of comfort. He pulled her chin up so that she was looking into his soul, "it doesn't matter to me anymore, you see now that I've found out what true love prescribed by chemistry is, I know I never loved her anyway, I just wanted to believe I did. Can you forgive me for my behaviour and saying such nasty things to you?"

Jessica couldn't speak, she was overcome with her own tears, annoyed that she had made him relive his own personal nightmares. Eventually she picked up the courage to speak. "I really love you Brad Monroe, and I always will, no matter what happens between us now, or whenever or however we may be separated… please, always remember these words. I will never betray you, believe it and remember it, never!"

Brad held her close, "so now you know my terrible family secret. Any skeletons in your closet?" He squeezed her hand and flashed her a comforting smile. She gripped his hand tightly never wanting to let him go. "Well, I've never been married, never been in love - until now - my friends all say how I'm old school, saving myself for the right guy and I'm like, 28 years old now, you are what, 31?" He nodded, flashing her another heart melting smile. "I've had some boyfriends, one that was particularly weird, he was a paranoid schizophrenic, when I cooked for him, he always thought I was trying to poison him! Maybe I'm just a bad cook. What else can I tell you? My mum died of cancer a few years ago, and my dad couldn't deal with it and left me and Kevin. We had to overcome a lot of emotional hurt, but we're okay. I love Kevin, we are close and happy, my family is just me and Kev, so that's my life to date."

She swallowed a lump in her throat, glad the light wasn't strong enough for him to read her eyes, because lying to him didn't feel good. But a white lie, was necessary to protect him - and that's okay - wasn't it? Brad kissed her, and pulled out the ring, placing it slowly over her finger. He stared in earnest, forcing her to see his sincerity, the moon slivered from out of a cloud, laying bare his sparkling emerald eyes."So now we've been open and honest with each other, that is how we must *always* be - we must promise to *never* mislead, deceive or lie to each other - there's nothing you can't tell me, not for any reason. Sometimes the truth hurts, but it will always be the truth. Promise me, because I love you Miss Shackley, and now we've found each other we can't let anything drive us apart."

"I promise… honesty always… I love you more than anything too." Jessica rested her head on his shoulder, a pang of guilt surged through her, the shame of not telling him about Amber sending a sick feeling to her stomach and her cheeks a hot crimson. She snuggled up to him, her brain working overtime. In her head she kept repeating, white lies don't count, white lies don't count.

24

Brad had an early morning flight back to Perth for a emergency shareholders meeting. "I'll text you when I can babe, I don't wanna go, I really don't, if I'd have known I was gonna meet you and we were gonna… I would never have agreed to the meeting, but I *have* to go." He fondled her hair. "I promise, now I've found you, I'm never letting you go." She gazed up into his hypnotic green eyes finding nothing but sincerity and unflinching love; she wanted to cry with joy and pain. He reassured her again, "I'll text you as soon as I can."

A short hour later she watched him board the plane. She followed the Cessna until it was a tiny spec in the distance, her elation was marred only by the searing pain of lying to the man she had just made a heartfelt promise to be honest with - why couldn't Amber stay in jail? She made the lonely journey back to her room replaying every second of her stay - she decided to throw away her guilt, and focus on her heart. Feeling content, an overwhelming sense of peace washed over her. Finally, Cinderella no more because she did go to the ball and met her prince.

She spent the rest of the morning leisurely bathing with a contented smile, only to discover that Harriet had forgotten to leave her a change of clothes. She telephoned down to reception, then sat on the balcony wearing nothing but a towel, watching the guests leave happily chattering about their most fun weekend. After a long hour, Julia arrived at her hotel room door, sporting a huge smile, a bouquet of flowers and a change of clothes.

"These are for you my favourite daughter in law to be." She grinned, then added, "but they're not from me." She handed Jessica the flowers, an intoxicating scented bouquet of blood red roses, her mind flew back to the bunch of blood red roses in her flowers the night Brad came to her home - he'd come to see her with flowers but ditched them when he realised she was with Scott. She groaned at her own pig headed stupidity at not realising it then.

"He had them flown over from the mainland for you, looks like he's got it bad." Julia was obviously delighted with the results of her party. "You planned all of this to happen didn't you?" Julia winked at Jessica, intermittently shoving her nose in the flowers and sighing with pleasure at their heady aroma. "I just gave stubborn old fate an almighty shove. I told you…you were in love with him. But it was the computer test that paired you. I couldn't believe my eyes when they told me you were both a perfect match."

"Brad told me rule number one, you're always right even when you're wrong." She laughed happily. "Ha, did he now?" She chuckled throwing her hands to her hips. "Oh, here, I forgot, these are for you." Julia handed Jessica a bundle of clothes, a pair of stone washed denims and a white tee shirt. "I hope they're your size, I got a size 12 jeans and a 14 top. I was going to have a cup of tea, I'd love my daughter in law to be, to join me of course." It sounded so good, "I'd be honoured to have tea with my mother in law to be." Jessica quipped with a musical laugh. She knew better than to challenge the authority of Julia. She smiled inwardly at Julias' sentiment, daughter in law to be, her sense of insecurity started to question her worthiness.

"I'd love to marry him Julia, but I don't think that Brad could make that sort of commitment, you see, he told me about Catherine." Julia almost fell over, and plonked herself promptly onto a nearby sofa. "He told you about Catherine? Then my dear, your big day won't be far away at all, he's never even allowed me to speak her name, you see he was hurt very bad, very bad indeed. Catherine is a wicked girl, she must have been born to a jackal to do what she did to Bradley." Jessica could see that Julia was getting upset, and tried to change the subject.

"Shall I ring for room service? Then we could have that tea, would you like some muffins too?" Julia winked,"Tea, yes but no muffins for me dear," patting her tummy. Julia sat quietly whilst the tea was served, she punctuated her agitation by drumming her nails on the edge of the sofa. Julia continued her conversation sipping delicately on a china cup every now and then.

"Bradley is a clone of his father, which is why I know exactly how he feels and what he'll do. I knew from the way he looked at you, and the way he spoke, that he was fighting with himself over you. I also knew that you were exactly the type of girl that he needed, a feisty honest hard working girl, with no pompous airs and graces and some flesh on your bones in all the right places. That's what his father saw in me." Jessica grinned, making a mental note to go on a diet. "Tell me about Jesse, Julia, what was he like?"

Her expression dropped, her pallor whiter than any ghost. "His passing was a very hard time for us both. Jesse was diagnosed with squamous cell carcinoma of the lung, it was already in an advanced stage and only six weeks before he …" her voice trailed off in pain. "Jesse and I had a marriage made in heaven, I met him in Tellico Plains, Tennessee, he's American, just like you and Bradley, it was love at first sight. Back then, there was no such thing as email or smart phones, we were pen pals, wrote every week, snail mail. We got married in the US a year later and Jesse came to live in Australia. We started out with next to nothing, and we worked hard, by golly did we work! By the time I had Bradley, we'd been married for three years, and we had made our first million!"

Jessicas mouth dropped open with admiration as Julia continued, her eyes filled with light as she reminisced. "Jesse Monroe was a stock broker, he knew *everything* there was to know about the stock market. Once he had enough experience with a large stockbroking firm, he went out on his own, investing in up and coming companies, basically buying and selling at the right time. I remember he used to say all the time that timing was the single most important element when you're in business, if you make the right decision at the wrong time, it's no good, but you can make a wrong decision at the right time, and still end up a winner. My Jesse was a dedicated hard working and very clever man, and Bradley grew up in his footsteps.

Jesse eventually got his citizenship but as he loved cars, and had already made significant profits, he decided to slow down a little and began buying and selling cars. But nothing he did was every small and eventually he purchased a garage up in Wangara, he then took on a dealership, and it escalated from there! As you know, Monroes own almost all the large scale dealerships for Nissan, Honda and Toyota."

Jessica didn't know but hid her surprise. "Did you work at the garages?" Julia laughed, "Oh no, I kept away dear, I opened a fashion house, you see I used to be a dress designer. I studied needlecraft and design at college many moons ago, but now my main assets are in Melbourne and Sydney, there is far more interest in high fashion there you see. Perth is for beach bums. I don't get too involved these days and much of the trend these days is selling online." Julia glanced at her watch, "The time is getting on dear, I'd better be going, are you flying into Jandakot?"

Jessica smiled graciously, "I've decided to go back the scenic route, by ferry - I don't want this trip to end *too* soon." She glanced at her watch too, "Gosh, I'd better scoot, it's due in half an hour!" Julia held her close. "You've made me very happy Jessica, because you've made my son happy. l wish Jesse was here to meet you, he would have loved you too. I look forward to the day when you too have our family name, and I don't say that lightly. There's one thing you must be aware of …because of Catherine's deceitful legacy, you must be a hundred percent honest with him, it would always be better to tell him what he doesn't want to hear, than ever tell him a lie - deceive him and he finds out, you *will* lose him, forever"

Jessica hugged her tightly to hide the sense that her face was burning with the word liar engraved on her forehead. "We had that conversation, I would never betray him, or lie to him, I truly love him Julia." They hugged tightly, she could feel Julias' happiness radiating, but another surge of guilt chilled her stinging her eyes with her deceit. Jessica hoped and prayed that Julia was always right and that one day she *would* be Mrs Jessica Monroe - but first she had to deal with her deceit - Amber - but how?

25

The ferry boat ride reminded her how poor she was, and the kind of passenger she would have been on the Titanic - third class. As an evil wind howled, whipping the waves like a jockey to a racehorse she cursed herself for not taking the luxury jet back to Jandakot. The ferry rocked mercilessly from side to side - even the most hardened sea worthy travellers hung their heads green faced, over the side. Her paupers return to Perth mainland was in diametric opposition to her celebrity arrival - perhaps it had been a wicked trick, a cruel fantasy and she'd wake up in her bed, cold and alone - the whole thing being a dream. Saying goodbye to Rottnest Island felt like cutting out her own heart; the memories she had with Brad coursed through her veins like a teenagers celebrity obsession.

The only thing she could think about was being ripped from his chest and it hurt, it felt wrong, like encountering a snow storm on a sunny day. She couldn't wait to get his text, the last thing he said to her before he left was, "I'll text you as soon as I can" and "now that I've found you, I'll never let you go." She rehashed his words over and over in her head, as though her life depended on it - that's because it did. Her phone was at home so the journey was particularly agonising not being able to stare at it waiting for his text. She knew the next phase of their relationship would see her glued to his every text, every word, every kiss.

The anti climax of arriving back hit her like a wet rag, but as she watched her taxi career away, she stood, swaying ever so slightly from her new found sea legs. She appraised her home, a smart red oxide brick duplex with a pretty lace pattern - heritage green woodwork ran the width of the home. Her eyes followed the cream coping and inlay which matched the striking green Colorbond bull nosed verandah. She stopped at the front door where a huge planter housed a stunning hot pink bougainvillaea which had wrapped its way through the intricate cream trellis. She smiled looking at the bushes to the other side, remembering the roses unceremoniously dumped there when Brad had appeared at her door. She berated herself for not realising sooner that he was crazy about her. Of course he was - why else did he keep making waves in her life? Baiting her to visit him, knowing, she would go to him. She sighed, making a mental note to stop being such a stereotypical dumb blonde.

She loved her house, it was a reflection of the day she took control of her life. But that day had been tinged with sadness - it was the same week her mother had died and her father finally deserted them for good. Memories good and bad floated through her mind as she considered her house, small, but perfectly formed, just like her, she grinned. She immediately threw that notion away, casting her mind back to the likes of some of the amazing looking women she'd seen on Rottnest. A wide smile curved across her tired face when she thought how, no matter how imperfect she thought she was, she did win the most eligible bachelor in WA and recalled many expressions of disgust from the so called model perfect women. Love clearly had no boundaries - thank god.

She mindlessly floated through the front door on a wave of fanciful romantic aspirations with Brad, until she walked into the lounge. It was a far cry from the regally sublime surroundings with Perths elite, only hours ago and despite the picture perfect exterior, the interior was another reality and a biting anti climax. Days old washing up in the sink showed signs of another life form manifestation, the bathroom looked like a murder scene only missing the tape around it and there was no food or milk in the fridge.

She shivered and placed a cardigan on. Spring had kicked the Winter out with designs on morphing into Summer, but the weather was spiking between unusually hot and now unusually cold. With no wood to light the slow combustion fire, she also had no heat - life's tough at the bottom she grimaced. She pretended Brad had her in his arms and sashayed around the kitchen - but then again, she reminded herself, the only way is up! Finding some dried milk, she made a cup of coffee thankful for the radiant thoughts about Brad, at least she had his love to keep her warm. She was on cloud nine, despite the mess indoors that she would definitely kill Kevin for later, but today, *nothing* could ruin the unbelievable knowledge that he loved her the way she loved him.

The acute soreness she felt when she sat down was a testament to his love - a love that had become everything to her, but now, without him, she wouldn't be able to breathe again - love hurts. She frantically searched for her phone, finding it down the back of the sofa, she yanked it out in the hope of finding a warm message of undying devotion from her god - nothing, no missed calls, emails or texts - he was a busy man after all. Battery was almost dead, she just managed to text Kevin to get over and bring some wood for the wood burner - she got a glimpse of his churlish response before it died in her hands - damn, now she had to plug it in and charge it so she could pick up Brads text. She tried to ignore the stab of pain, at the girlish disappointment she felt knowing that Brad had not yet texted her with comforting words of lust filled love.

She slapped herself, she was being silly; he said he loved her and he said he would text her as soon as he could. She slapped herself again, he just couldn't right now, and that's the price she would have to pay to date a wealthy business man. It hurt, mainly because she had just slapped herself twice in the face. She sighed, focussing on the happiness he brought her; she'd gladly give anything to feel his strong arms around her right now. Huddled in her bed in a fleece onesie, she clutched her coffee for warmth - lost in romantic dreams she doodled hearts and roses aimlessly until a noise at the front door raised her hackles - someone was trying the door to get in.

It wasn't Kevin, because he'd texted her that he was south of the river, down in Fremantle with Scott and their surfie friends. Her heart beat out a tribal message of fear, she needed to call the police! Paralysed by fear she realised her mobile was in the lounge being charged. She tiptoed into the lounge but with a sudden click, her front door opened - she threw herself over the sofa crouching low behind it. Positive footsteps click clacked through the lounge. The intruders heels clicked slowly and firmly on the wood floors through to the kitchen. She heard a kitchen cupboard open and then the rattle of cups and the click of the kettle being turned on.

Jessica thought about it, a burglar wearing heels? Then she realised that intruders didn't usually break in for a cup of coffee either, or was this some new type of cereal burglar she felt the urge to laugh at her own joke as hysteria overcame her - she drummed up enough courage to peer over the top of the sofa, a harsh guttural female Australian accent rang out. "Yo sis when you're done hiding behind the sofa do ya wanna cuppa - and geez when did ya last have a clean up around here, its worse than prison?"

Amber cackled with laughter as Jessica stood up, "What the hell are *you* doing here?" Her voice wavered with anger at the thought that Amber would dare to break into her personal safe haven. "That glad to see me huh? Well don't chuck a wobbly, it might break your face, I told you on the phone, I done my time, parole board felt I was rehabilitated or some old shit like that, got out earlier than expected seems those acting classes really paid off. Did ya get my room ready?"

Amber kicked off worn bright red high stiletto heels launching herself unceremoniously onto a chair, putting her feet up on the coffee table with blatant disrespect. "Hey ain't ya got no milk, all I saw was some bloody shitty milk powder, are times that tough? There's me thinking *I* had it rough." Jessica sniffed the air, "you on the sauce already, I can smell your damned booze breath?" Reality was biting Jessica hard in the arse dispersing her weekend of dreams in an instant. "Only had a couple… had to celebrate my freedom didn't I? Don't see *you* cracking the champers?" She laughed a rough and ready laugh. "Anyways, so what if I am a lil bit tipsy? It's *my* life, and it's a free world, what's it to you anyway little miss righteous as ever?"

She scorned in a deliberate broad Aussie accent. "You still so perfect these days you don't have a little nip now and then?" Amber was already a big problem, "no I don't. What're you doing here anyway? How can you dare to come back here, after what you did, to me? And you break in! Please, I'd rather you leave, now, and stay out of our lives."

"Ooh, miss la di da, would you rather?" She mocked mimicking a high class accent, " break in ya say, ha, well you always did leave the spare under the pot near the Grevillea - still a dumb ass. Lucky it was me and not some murderer, or maybe after two years in the can I am one." Jessica sank down onto the sofa rubbing the back of her head where she hit it and cried, a throbbing headache beginning to take hold. "Please Amber, what do you want? Money? Yes, that's it, that's always it. How much? Take all I've got, but just fucking go."

Jessica threw her purse at her. Amber snorted with mockery. "I ain't here for ya charity, what d'ya take me for? I just need somewhere to hang out for a few weeks, that's all. Then I'm gone, me and my girlfriend are going up north, I've heard the tricks pay good money up there, those boys in the mine just gagging for it, and a few girls too."

Amber was worse than before she went into jail. "Where did you learn to become such a slut?" she hissed, disgusted with her own sister. "Where did you get off being Miss Virgin 2023, or have you finally tasted a bit of cock?" She scorned spitefully watching Jessica go purple as the old feelings of searing anguish ripped up her insides. She couldn't let Amber ruin her life again, she wouldn't! And she couldn't risk Brad finding out about her. "You can't stay with me for a fucking day let alone two weeks - you need to leave Perth *now.*"

"Why?" Exasperated tears rolled down Jessicas face, "cos you look exactly like me and you've used it against me once too often to ruin my life!" Jessica looked into the mirror and Amber stood next to her, almost identical twins. Amber had a slightly larger frame and was an inch taller but it was hardly noticeable. There was no way Jessica could risk anyone mistaking Amber for her - and now her love life depended on it. Jessica grabbed her bag, rummaging through it frantically, "Look, I'll give you a thousand dollars, it's all I have, if you go up north - now." Amber was astute like her sister, she grinned, showing off smokers teeth, "Ten, ten grand and I'll leave, in cash of course, no bank account for crims like me, my dear sissy." Jessica had the money it was her entire account for a down payment on a new car, but to rid herself of the archetypical evil twin, it was worth riding around in her mothers clapped out Datsun for life - she recalled Brads soft voice that said he would get her a car, she knew she would be okay, it was worth anything to rid her of her white lie.

"Okay, but I can't give you the money until Monday, its's everything I got, so this weekend you can stay, but you cannot borrow my clothes or be seen turning tricks on the streets, capiche?" Jessica stared down her arrogant sister. "I mean it Amber, I can't go through another Augusta again." Amber rolled up into hysterical laughter as she took up residence in the spare bedroom. "Oh my gawd, Augusta, how could I forget? That was a scream, admit it, I'm damn good at massage, at least all *my* clients got a happy ending."

She grinned wickedly at Jessicas face enjoying her pain. "Hey, dya think I should start a salon?" Tears coursed down

Jessicas' face as she thought about Brad, should she reveal her dirty little family secret before she could get rid of Amber? After all he'd revealed his, but she knew she should have told him at the time, so now it already looks like she was the one thing he couldn't forgive - a deceitful liar. In one cruel twist of fate her whole world had come crashing down around her - she knew something would go wrong, it was like the universe didn't want her to be happy. She felt ashamed, she was honest and hated deception more than anything - just like Brad.

"I'll never betray you," she whispered to herself, picturing his expression of utter faith in her. If she had told him or Julia, what would they think of her? She imagined their faces if they knew that she had a jail served, drug taking con woman and part time hooker as a *twin* sister? She was sure that they would tar her with the same brush - let's face it, twins kinda share the same DNA - no she couldn't tell him.

After Brads' disastrous marriage to an English blonde cheating bitch with no morals, Brad wouldn't dare chance it with the twin of a monster! God no! She'd keep Amber in the closet and pay her, then in a few days she'd be gone, out of her life forever, it would be worth sacrificing her new car to get rid of her and be with the love of her life.

With her phone now fully charged she scanned it for a text from Brad, nothing. She quickly texted him, "I love you and miss you." Then frantically texted Kevin just as he sauntered in through the front door. "I got the wood" He grinned, plonking down a pile of cut logs. Jessica whispered, afraid she may hear them."It's Amber, she's here - she's gone to bed in the spare room - I think she's asleep in a drunken stupor, she looks worse than ever, jail hasn't taught her a thing."

Kev flashed a stoners grin as he started lighting the fire. "Don't worry sis, we'll sort her out once and for all - don't sweat it, she knows your achilles heal or whatever they call it so don't let her get to ya! Hey, how did the weekend of love go?" He winked knowingly. "I don't know what you mean," she insisted innocently. "Yeah?" Kevin pulled out his phone and logged into his twitter page. "Didn't ya know *he's* trending number one on twitter with pics of him and you …" He paused for added suspense and read out loud. "Brad Monroe, aka Marc Antony, Perths notorious and most eligible bachelor - finds true love on Rottnest Island with a beautiful mystery woman his stunning Cleopatra, will they win the $100k prize? Some say it is a fix."

Jessica turned several shades of red, her embarrassment instantly proving her guilt. Amber pulled her ear away from the door making a mental note with a wicked grin, £100k prize for being in love with a guy called Brad Monroe, and Perths most eligible bachelor? No wonder she wants me gone. Looks like my family may be worth sticking around for after all. She laughed herself to sleep - the only way, was up, and she'll make sure this Brad Monroe, gets his way up…with her.

26

Tuesday morning, Jessica checked her phone, no texts, a sinking empty stomach invaded her thoughts - why had he not texted? She tried to ignore the sick sense of darkness pervading her heart. She whispered frantically to Kevin over breakfast Weetos, "should we wake her or just leave a note?" Neither fancied going into battle with her before work so opted for the latter, leaving a large set of house rules under a magnet on the fridge.

Amber peeped through the blinds, watching Jessica and Kevin tip toeing down the drive whispering to each other. A fag hanging out of the side of her mouth she almost coughed herself to death with amusement. Wearing one of Kevins' best sweatshirts she made herself a coffee while texting a random man she picked up at the Wannaroo bus station; he was waiting for the all clear so he knew where to go for a morning session.

She laughed like a drain as she read the note, then promptly tore it up. She flipped the bird out of the window to whomever was passing. "Sorry sissy, I don't do rules," she cranked up the stereo and indulged in a luxury shower using Jessicas salon quality products. She smirked, free at last, this is the life. Padding naked to Jessicas' wardrobe, she slid the mirror glass door back to reveal a very average and modest taste in clothes. She shrieked her thoughts out loud ,"fuck, don't worry sis, can't see me borrowing much of this shit!"

She pulled out a skimpy Aussie style beach dress, although she was taller, Jessica was a little plumper than Amber and it was baggy in places. Next, the underwear, she pulled everything out of the drawers scattering them like a burglar searching for cash - she settled for turquoise gold panties that tied up at the side with a matching bra. The bra was baggy, Amber had never had implants and it showed, but stuffing some toilet paper under her boobs she lifted them so a decent cleavage showed, she grinned at herself in the mirror then set about Jessicas' make up box. A bit of concealer, and then the final touch, perfume - a new box of Angel sat in a gift set with a beautiful thick body creme the kind of luxury Amber had never worked hard enough to buy. She lavished it all over her body and sprayed the room and herself with the perfume - the place smelt like a whore house, perfect. Her phone bleeped a text, the first customer of the day was outside.

Jessica had no time to lament about Amber, she had to fit in Mondays work as well as Tuesdays, but her heart lurched every time her phone rang and it wasn't *him*. Each and every call or text that wasn't from Brad felt like a knife to the heart. Her social media marketing campaign offering a discount treatment for Derma planing and Micro-needling had been successful and she would have usually been pleased with the unusually high response, but, unwittingly showed her disappointment in the tone of her voice to every client that called.

She *had* to hear his voice, she was sick to her stomach - was this love sick? His voice, his touch, his presence had become her addiction, injected with force into her bloodstream, and now she had it, she needed it, more than anything ever in her life - in fact she would die without it. She texted friends, who all advised he was a playboy, and for him love just meant at the time, it was a holiday romance. It hurt, like hell, she disagreed, but inside the fear began to mount - was he really lying? No, she knew in her heart, he was a good man. But she felt discarded, dumped after a hot passionate fling.

She knew she wasn't like most girls her age, liking classical music when her best friends were partying to pop hits. Although her closest friends were married or in long term relationships. Checking her phone for the third time in the last minute, she felt schoolgirlish tears welling - why hadn't he texted like he said he would? He was well connected, perhaps Julia had her checked out? Could they know about Amber already? Or had he just been play acting the whole time, saying the right things to carve another notch on his bedpost?

After a gruelling day of insecure thoughts Jessica arrived home with a heavy heart, her mind weaving multiple possibilities. She walked headlong into a new carnage - Amber was half way through a bottle of vodka while on the net putting her photos on a sugar daddy web site - there were clothes and mess everywhere. Jessica stood like the scene from 'Carrie' covered with pigs blood, just staring disbelievingly at the wreckage which was once her home. She was too tired for arguments, her mind was consumed and her heart racked with the pain of no contact from Brad.

Ambers upturned expression challenged her for a row, but to Ambers surprise if not disappointment, Jessica failed to engage. She sat in the kitchen pretending to do the business paperwork but was really staring sadly at her phone for hours before giving in to her tiredness and retiring to bed. Should she text him again? But he hadn't even replied to her last one! Should she call? Even email? She didn't have the guts to hear a rejection or a matter of fact attitude from him… no, *he* should contact *her* , after all, he said he would - he promised, he even *vowed.*

She had a sudden thought, what about social media? He mentioned he would friend request her, she had issues with passwords on her phone and couldn't get into Meta Facebook, that was it! He's contacted her on facebook and messaged her a long love letter full of affirmations of his undying love for her. Excited and re-animated she pulled out her MacBook air and logged on - she felt a massive sense of relief remembering his words, "I'll friend request you as soon as I can babe, it's easy to communicate on there." She stared at her facebook, no friend requests. She checked in case he had messaged her and it had gone to her "other" file, there was nothing, except the odd message from someone claiming they were the king of Nigeria and wanted to leave her millions.

That night, the void was huge, the emptiness in her heart overwhelming. She clutched the phone, tears coursing down her face as she sadly relived her weekend with Marc Antony - it felt more like a dream now. He was *always* in her head, and as every minute elapsed without a text she felt the noose around her neck tighten. Was that the noose for guilty liars?

A text sounded in the middle of the night, like an eager puppy she scrambled in the dark to read it, her heart dropped to the pit of her stomach, it was Kevin, he was out late again with the boys from work but promised he'd move in properly tomorrow to keep an eye on Amber. She seized her opportunity and texted him to find out if Brad had been at work, perhaps he was sick. Her phone dinged straight away. *"Yes, he was at work"* She responded needing to pump him for information. *" How was he? You know was he happy?"* The reply came back immediately. *" He was quiet - I guess. He didn't really say much to anyone, neither happy nor unhappy, just busy I guess."* Okay so that was it, he was busy, her mind refused to not walk the plank and spell out the obvious - too busy to even text the so called love of his life?

Eventually she fell asleep clutching her Iphone to her heart, the pillow was soaking with her disappointment, her mind was furious but her heart was at war with it, as it kept telling her they had a higher love and something *must* be wrong. But her mind won - agreeing upon the inevitable judgement, she'd been nothing more than a fantasy play thing for the weekend. She mused angrily, of course, he was a renowned playboy, he was also considerably wealthy, why the hell would he want to be with what Julia described as 'an ordinary girl'? That description of her, hurt.

She sighed in anguish and pain, how embarrassing to be described as ordinary. They were rich types, used to making derogatory comments about mere mortals like her. If she were a beautiful rose her petals would be falling one by one because she was drooping and dying, second by second - he didn't want *her*, he didn't *love* her, he was the cruel Brad Monroe she had first met. She hated him so much, because she loved him more than life itself.

27

Amber shook the Vodka bottle into her open mouth - dammit, empty. She needed some action; Jessica was in bed, it was the middle of the night so no one to argue with, suburbia was boring as hell. She was about to relent and go to bed when she heard a light tapping at the door. She quickly tidied her hair, and answered it. Scott bounced in full of beans, he was back from his fishing break and was determined to apologise to Jessica about dating Tanya - even at this late hour. He'd missed Jessica so much, he needed to plead his undying love for her in the hope of winning her over again.

"Glad you're up sweet cheeks, I'd have texted you babe, but my phone's dead, dropped it over board, fucking thing, gotta get another one, that's the third one this year and its only end of March. About the Tanya thing she's nothing to me and …" Amber clamped her hand over his mouth. "Shut the fuck up, it's late baby boy, you might wake the cat." Scott looked at her, puzzled. "You done something to your hair? There's something different about you." Then whispered, "hey, wait a minute, you ain't got a cat, did ya get one?"

Amber laughed, and picked up her cigarette lighter from the floor, making sure Scott was watching. He almost fell over at Jessicas' short skirt which displayed long lean legs. He stared up at her, still confused; heavier than usual make up and reeking of expensive perfume. "Wow, babe, you're looking *very* sexy tonight." He pushed her back gently and looked at her frowning momentarily. "So who's the new guy? You didn't know I was coming over tonight?" She was quick off the wicket, she didn't know who he was but presumed this must be the famous Brad Monroe she heard Kevin and Jessica talking about.

"Geez take a chill pill baby, Kev told me you were likely to show up." Scott looked surprised, "he did?" Then broke into a cheeky smile, "he knows me *far* too well." He kissed her teasingly on the cheek, expecting her to push him off - she didn't. "Mmm love of my life," she purred curling her fingers under the young mans' chin. "I'm so lonely tonight, how would you like to forget about the world, it's just you and me?"

Scott stared into Ambers eyes. Then he caught a whiff of her breath and laughed. "Oh my god, you're wasted - that explains this look, crazy talk, *everything*." Amber laid on the sofa and parted her legs just enough so that he could almost see between her legs. "I'm just teasing you baby, so I'm gonna introduce Perths most eligible bachelor to my cat, but first, here's a question for you, what colour knickers am I wearing." She teased, gyrating her hips ever so slightly.

Scott began to stammer, he couldn't believe his luck, he clocked the empty Vodka bottle and grinned, joking, "if I'd known that Vodka had *this* effect on you I'd have invested in a vat of it." Amber sniffed her nose in disapproval, "answer the question then." Scott awkwardly attempted to peer between her legs. "Er, I guess a kind of light brown I think." She laughed, opening her legs a little wider, "Wrong! I ain't got any on." It took Scott awhile to process the point; He stood dumbstruck.

"So you want me to play with you a bit?" Scott straightened up and loosened his shirt, a sex game, excellent. He took a good look at her legs, they were longer and leaner than he remembered, his breathing becoming a little more rapid. "What about I play with you baby?" He grabbed at his hardened crotch. Amber purred with approval moving her body sensuously. Without any more prompts he roared with youthful desire, leaping upon her, he'd never seen her so uninhibited before; he made a mental note to get some serious liquor in. "Shouldn't we go to the bedroom?" Amber took control, "no, lets do it in the lounge and then the kitchen, I'm gonna adore your macho sex stick baby, tell me what you want me to do to you."

Scott couldn't believe his luck, she was behaving like an animal, a total porn star and even with *his* reasonable carnal knowledge, she had him at her mercy. He straddled her, unbuttoning his jeans with one hand trying to hold her down with the other, but she was surprisingly strong, she flipped him over like a rag doll and pulled his jeans clean off. He let out a moan as her lips and tongue found his mouth in a frenzied passion as though she'd not had a man for years. Amber began to slowly, very slowly slither the length of his belly until she found his throbbing erection urgently twitching and begging to be fondled. She had him, he was powerless, under her spell, they locked eyes as she let the tip of her tongue flicker like a snake across the head of his swollen manhood.

She could tell he was holding his breath, silently begging her to swallow everything he had. With a sudden lurch she forced his steel like muscle down her throat, Scott screamed as she took no prisoners. She raked her long overstated red finger nails across his thighs. He begged, "let me fuck you Jessica," he was trying to pull her up, but she held him down, he was shocked by her brute strength. "I want to taste *you* baby." She made no secrets about the sound of her efforts, the sucking and licking in earnest creating an audible tinder to his inner and most explosive fire. Crawling back up his body she finished him off by talking dirty, using her hand while whispering her deepest darkest sexual fantasies - he wanted to penetrate her but her frenzied dirty mouth caused him to suddenly explode - Mount Vesuvius had nothing on him.

In the throws of his ecstasy he pushed her head back down, to clean up the love she had so deftly released. When she finally let him leave, he was exhausted, confused, and very *very* happy determined to fulfill some of those whispered fantasies tomorrow! As Scott almost skipped to his car she shouted out to him, "hey Brad, let's hang out again tomorrow." Scott stopped abruptly turning slowly, his face like thunder. "You're so drunk you think you've been sucking off Brad Monroe - is *he* your fucking fantasy?" His tone was menacing. "You don't even know who I am do you?" Amber giggled, "ooh so touchy, don't be silly, I was kidding, see you tomorrow."

She shut the door and laughed to herself. Scott walked to his car unconvinced - so that's why she didn't let him touch her, she was saving herself and fantasising about Monroe while giving *him* head - a hatred for Monroe and Jessica began to ignite.

Amber looked in on Jessica while she was sleeping, rasping under her breath. "Hey sissy, think I just got you into some trouble again." She laughed to herself, "Oh well, shit happens."

28

J essicas' phone rung and vibrated along with a rain forest wake up song, exotic birds singing their dawn chorus, but not in *her* empty soul. She checked her messages, nothing from Brad. A wave off desolation started her day off with a sense of emotional agony and despair - she couldn't shake the feeling that something was dreadfully wrong. He really should have called her by now and she was out of excuses for him. She wanted to drive over to one of his garages and find out where he was or beg Kevin to hint to him to call her, but she knew he would disapprove of that. It would look as though she were checking up on him, she daren't upset him - especially as she needed his support with Amber.

She had to resign herself to discover the merits of patience, which up until now, had not been one of her strong points. It didn't help shouldering the guilt over neglecting to tell him about Amber, especially as she was now in the house and destroying it. She was drawing the cash out for her the next day, she couldn't wait to part with the money to see the back of her. Perhaps it was better that Brad wasn't around for now - getting Amber out of her life was imperative. At least the delay in being with him again was a weird, albeit very unhappy god send.

The salon was very slow that day, leaving Jessica time to obsessively stare at her phone in a never ending cycle of checking social media then crying, feeling worthless, unloved and generally lament her situation with Brad. She thought perhaps she should see a Psychiatrist and that she'd hallucinated the whole event! It was all over so quickly, she couldn't believe that she had made love to him that night, he had taken what she valiantly guarded for so long, it was like living out a fantasy, where everything was perfect.

Could she have scared him off in some way? Perhaps he *hadn't* meant the things he said? Perhaps he didn't love her at all and was just getting into the theme of the event - surely not? She tried to ignore the nagging seeds of doubt that kept entering her head, and again tried to give herself hope by pursuing the idea, that he was just too busy at the moment. A dark depression lurked at the back of her mind because she seriously doubted that *anyone* could be too busy to even text a new flame and especially the one they said they loved! Her head was going around in circles - yearning for him was killing her. Her phone beeped for the hundredth time that day, this time, another odd text from Scott saying he was prepared to forgive her as she was such a sexy mare.

She didn't even read his text properly, he was nothing but a stupid idiot. Her whole being was screaming inside for Brad. She was possessed with the crawling notion that Brad had been simply performing an act the whole time, fooling even his own mother, or was she also play acting? No, Julia was genuine. Should she contact Julia? Would she support her? Or would Brad become irate knowing she had gone behind his back? The hopelessness of her reality deflated her so much she couldn't talk to *anyone.*

Scott didn't stop texting but she ignored them, didn't even read them. Jessicas' spirits were lower than ever as she packed away her things for the day. She was living in hope by trying to convince herself that Brad would turn up on her doorstep with a huge bunch of those scented red roses and a perfectly good explanation. Whatever his excuse, she would fling herself into his strong arms and accept it. As she switched off the lights to leave, she let out a startled cry - a man dressed in black, wearing a ski mask with only eyes and mouth visible approached her menacingly. She backed away toward the wall, as he stepped towards her, she begged. "Please, take all the money in the safe, you can have it."

She threw the key towards him, but he ignored it, concentrating only on his victim. He leered at her, in a way that terrified her, she realised what his intentions were and began to scream but he clamped a gloved hand across her mouth. He pounced on her, pulling her arm almost out of its sockets, wrenching it high behind her back. She winced in pain, as he led her to her own massage table. "Get on it bitch." His commanding voice terrified her but she refused, shaking her head and crying. He jerked her arm, making her cry out with pain. Reluctantly she climbed up onto the table, feeling helpless and alone, she cried for Brad to save her, to come and rescue her in her moment of ultimate terror, but her cries were in vain - never had her life felt more futile.

The masked man, ripped off her salon gown, and then with a strange gentleness, unclasped her bra and pulled down her knickers, folding them up, and placing them on a chair. He ran his eyes greedily over her body, and then stopped for a moment, seemingly confused about something to do with her chest. "Please, I beg you," she gasped, "please don't do this, my boyfriend will be here at any moment, if you leave now, I won't say anything." The masked man, suddenly threw her a towel to shield him from her nudity. "It's okay you can cut the little girl scared act," came a cold yet recognisable voice. "I can't do what you want anyway, I guess I'm the failure you already had me down for."

Jessica sat up and shouted, "Scott? Is that *you?*" Her face turned purple with anger, as he pulled off his mask, and looked her straight in the eyes, his face was hard and seemingly unrepentant. Jessica began to cry. "Scott, why? How could you do this to me?" "Jessica," he began, scratching his head in a puzzled way. "That's a bit rich, after all you said and did to *me* last night. Anyway I didn't really want to do it, but last night you said it was your ultimate fantasy you bloody begged me to do it. So I did it for *you* - guess it was the drink talking. You were like, like a different person last night, seeing as you really aren't into me, let's face it you've been rejecting me for long enough."

His words were edged with a cold hostility she'd never seen before. "I told you to do it? My fantasy? Last night?" Jessica mouthed the words as the jigsaw pieces flew together in her head. "What happened last night and where? Tell me." Scott showed his irritation, "don't tell me you've forgotten after the crazy shit you did to me! You admitted how you liked it rough, bondage and all that stuff and wouldn't let me really fuck you unless I did it like this. Gotta say you made my cock ache last night, I can still feel your damned tongue on it, where the fuck did you learn to suck off a bloke like that? I must admit I knew it was the booze but it was kinda fun seeing you let your hair down for once and oh my god, I couldn't walk properly after. But it pissed me off that you needed to down a bottle of Vodka to even touch me. His tone took on a chilling air - he was distinctly unfriendly. He screwed up his face in thought closing his eyes momentarily. "But what I don't understand, I noticed you had tattoos on your stomach, were they like those temporary ones? Because they've gone."

Jessica knew she was gonna have to explain that Amber had set both of them up. She calmed down enough to explain this to Scott. "This is gonna sound crazy, I've got a twin sister, yes, the classic evil twin who throughout my whole life has got me into trouble because she's pretty much the spitting image of me. Yes, she's got tattoos and it was *her* who did those things to you, while I was in bed. She's a thief a con artist, a drunk a whore you name it, if it's bad she's into it. She was sent to prison two years ago, I didn't ever think she'd come back here after what she did and in my name, but yeah, she's back stampeding into my life to cause trouble. I'm sorry me and Kevin didn't tell you this before but when she got sent down, we thought we'd finally purged her from our life and to be honest we just wanted to forget her."

Scott held her protectively. "Wow, what a piece of work, I should've known you wouldn't have wanted to do that to me in such a violent way. No wonder she didn't know who I was, the stupid bitch me Brad." Jessica turned white and froze, "she mentioned Brad to you? How the hell would she know about him?" Scott shrugged his shoulders, "dunno, but one thing I do know, she's one dirty and slutty troublesome bitch."

Jessica was shaking with possibilities, could the deadliest thing her sister could have done - happened? She thought about the media article, had she seen it, spoken to Brad and driven him away - already? "Scott, will you come home with me, and help me kick her to the curb? Maybe the humiliation of being confronted by you will get her to leave." He didn't want to, these Shackley women were fucked up. "Okay, but let's do it now ,I got other shit to do."

When they arrived Kevin was already there, he stared at them both in a strange way pacing back and forth like a caged lion, he pounced on them immediately, "how could you do that to Brad?" He hissed at Jessica. His face was several shades of crimson fury. "You sat there after your weekend and told me how much you loved him." Scott stared at Jessica, but she neither noticed, nor cared." I do love him, have you not noticed the broken heart I've been carrying around with me since Rottnest? I've been waiting for him to contact me, but I'm still waiting Kev. Anyway, what the hell do you think *I've* done to *him* ?"

She had never seen Kevin so angry, he erupted like a volcano raining his lava of disapproval. "So you thought you'd heal your broken heart by going down on Scott 'on the sofa? I thought your morals were a little higher than that Jessica. Not only do you fuck my best mate you fuck my boss and now you're gonna fuck my one job opportunity that means everything to me. Because if you and Brad are what you say you are after your weekend of love on Rottnest and Brad finds out what a cheating bitch you are - he'll fire *me* for sure! Why couldn't you just be happy with Scott? Why pretend to be in love with Brad then cheat on him?"

The colour had drained from Scotts face, the happy go lucky expression wiped clean. "You went to Rottnest with Brad? Our boss, the guy you hate? Is this all some kind of alternative reality I've fallen into while I've been fishing? One minute you're telling me I've been blown by your spitting image and now I find out you've been fucking my boss?"

Jessica threw her hands to her hips spitting chips at Kevin, "I didn't go down on Scott! How stupid are you? It was obviously Amber. Yes, I'm in love with Brad and I'm faithful, and no, Scott is just a friend and yes, I'm heart broken because Brad hasn't contacted me like he said he would, so do me a favour you couple of absolute fuck-tards and wait till you get the facts before you both fucking tear me up."

Tears were rolling down her face. Scott launched himself between Jessica and Kevin, angry, "whoa, hold up you two, I'm not hanging around for a seat to a sibling pity party so fuck all this shit!" He stormed out of the door slamming it so hard a piece of plaster fell away. Jessica ran after him but it was too late she watched as his red sporty car over revved with tyres screaming as he sped away. She shouted after him. "Scott, please, come back!" He screamed at her out of his window, "do me a favour lady, unfriend me."

Back inside Kevin was standing fists clenched he was so angry. Jessica sighed, tears continuing to fall down her cheeks but Kevin was un-relentless in his disgust for her. Finally finding her voice, Jessica challenged him before he could judge her any further. "Tell me one thing, how did you find out about this supposed blow job on the sofa? Were you there? Because *I* wasn't." She snarled, her eyes flashing with anger. "Amber told me," he retorted coolly, his face dropping as realisation began to hit him like a kipper in the face.

"There it is, you actually believed *her*" She screamed, losing her cool rapidly. Kevin looked surprised for a minute, "are you saying it isn't true then?" She sighed deeply, but wanted to scream and shout, "of course it isn't true, you fucking clown! Now you've hurt Scott shouting out how I love Brad for fuck sake. He's loved me for so long, its hurt him - his stint with the lovely Tanya didn't bother me at all. I was gonna talk to him and tell him gently about me and Brad but in you went like a fucking steam roller and now he's gone, feeling angry and hurt and driving like a bat out of hell - I'm worried he'll have an accident! And by the way our dear sister pretending to be me told Scott my fantasy was for him to rape me. So tonight he attacked me with a ski mask in my salon - it's why I came home with him as I had to explain about Amber. So no, Kevin, I'm innocent and I'm carrying around a broken heart … all this shit is more than I can bear." She sobbed uncontrollably.

Kevin realised he'd once again been duped by his very clever and manipulative sister. Kevin held his face in his hands, his foot was tapping with anxiety, he always did that when his father was hitting his mother. "There's gonna be a bigger problem then." He bit his lip until a trickle of blood escaped he was staring at the floor. "Amber wanted Brads address, so that she could explain you're twins and apologise on your behalf." He paused for a while, his face white as a ghost.

Jessica screamed, "please, oh god please, Kevin say you didn't fucking give it to her? Even *you* are not *that* stupid - or are you?" Kevins' expression confirmed his stupidity. Jessica let out an anguished howl that even the gods could hear. "What was she apologising for?" Kevin, scarlet faced stared at the floor. "Blowing Scott."

Jessica ran to the bathroom to vomit. She returned quietly, "she's ruined the one good thing I found in my life. I love him so much - I can't lose him, you don't understand how I feel - I'd rather die than lose him. Kev you have to help me, we *have* to stop her, that is, if it isn't already too late. Because if I've lost him, then the world has lost me."

29

An angry knock at the door interrupted the heavy silence between Kevin and Jessica who were so lost all they could do was stare at into space. Only their thoughts of how to remedy the situation kept them occupied. Kevin leapt up to open the door - Scott dominated the door way like a black cloud, his face displaying his hurt, remorse and embarrassment for being with Amber and what he did to Jessica.

Jessica hugged him, and tried to let him know how much she cared, but her words of friendship bounced off his 'rejected in love' force field. Kevin also apologised for his stupidity about Amber and they all gazed at one another thoughtfully, as they each tried to come up with a suitable plan to fix the situation. The front door suddenly opened, so hard it that made them all jump. Amber marched in, unaffected and obviously very pleased with herself, she leered at Scott. "Yo sexy boy, whats going down or should I say who's going down?" She laughed hard.

Jessica let out a strange noise as she flew at Amber's throat. "I'm going to fucking kill you, our Father hated you, I used to wonder why, but now I know, because I hate you too." She screamed in a voice strangled with the memory of years of embarrassment at the hands of her demented sister. Scott and Kevin subdued Jessica pulling her away still spitting murderous threats.

Scott walked around her looking at Amber then at Jessica, "you ain't kidding, peas in a pod!" Kevin appointed himself mediator and approached Amber who was poised in the centre of the lounge scorning them all. "Have I missed the point of all this or what?" She sniggered, opening a packet of chewing gum throwing a stick into her mouth and chewing it vigourously. She shimmied up to Scott. "You back for more babe?" She sniggered again, lighting up a cigarette and puffing smoke straight in his face. Scott snarled also lurching at her throat, he shook her hard yet she maintained her laughter which seemed like more of a witches cackle.

Kevin pulled him off and whipped the cigarette out of Amber's mouth throwing it quickly out the door. "Scottie, I'm sorry man, but our dirty family laundry is about to get washed with bleach." Kevin pushed Amber onto the sofa, and turned to Jessica and Scott, "everyone just sit down." He then turned to Amber, speaking to her like a social worker to a lunatic, "look what you've done to everyone, why do you take such pleasure in hurting us Amber? We're supposed to be family - don't you want a family?"

Amber smiled as though butter wouldn't melt in her mouth ignoring Kevin she turned to Jessica. "Family? Oh yeah, I forgot we're family, though I kinda recall being left alone crying, getting picked on and hit for no reason, you were Dads favourite, you have no idea what shit I went through." She winked at Scott and blew him a puckered up kiss. Kevin had to restrain both Scott and Jessica. She grinned and spoke matter of factly while looking at her chipped red nail varnish. "Hey, sissy, your new piece of ass got a mighty nice pad ain't he? What is he? Some kind of millionaire or summat? Fuck, no wonder you wanted *me* out of the way, you're obviously doing alright for …"

She didn't get a chance to finish her sentence as Jessica hurled her drink at her, narrowly missing her head. "If you've ruined things for me with him, I'll kill you Amber." Jessica sank onto the floor, and began sobbing her heart out. Amber sneered and spoke with zero remorse, "can you speak up I can't hear you with that great big pity dick in your mouth. You'se think you're so high and mighty and better than me don't cha? Pretty lil Jessica, the good twin, yeah yeah, sure."

Scott sat on the sofa with his head in his hands to hide his boyish broken heart - knowing Jessica was in love with Brad was hurtful. Amber didn't let up. "Anyways, I didn't see that Brad dude, the house was empty, I just admired it from a distance, that's all, there ain't no law against that is there?"

They let out a unified sigh of relief at the prospect that at least she hadn't seen Brad and even better, he hadn't seen *her* ! Amber retained her pitch in centre stage, "anyway, I thought I'd tell you my news and you'll all be happy, I'm out of here tomorrow, I met a guy who wants me to do some photographic work, modelling, he likes my legs, he's out at Midland, so I'm staying at his place. I'm gonna collect that ten grand from you sissy and split. Happy now?" Jessica stopped crying, it was worth, every cent to see her leave.

"Don't you mean Pornographic work." hissed Scott, disgusted and ashamed. "Now now, lover boy, you weren't exactly saying no yesterday were ya? And oh my didn't you gag for more, you even made *me* gag." She laughed hard and ignored the dangerous looks that he threw her, then haughtily swayed across the room and back out the front door. They all caught a whiff of whiskey as she passed. There was a united sigh of relief when she was gone. Kevin whispered, "Ten grand? That's your savings for the car, you can't give it all to her." Jessica sighed, "if it means peace for us it's a worthwhile sacrifice." Jessica hugged Scott, "I'm sorry about my sister and the Brad thing, I'll explain properly another time. I promise I didn't mean to hurt you, I didn't even expect to fall for him the way I did, it was a fluke, on Rottnest, but you had kinda dumped me for Tanya anyway, remember?"

Scott interjected, "yeah but I thought you knew it was just a fuck with her - it's always been about you and me - I thought we were gonna be together, you know, in the end. Anyway, go to bed, I wanna talk to Kev." She gratefully obeyed his command, hugging Kevin and then disappearing into the sanctity of her room.

She could hear the muffled voices of Scott and Kevin talking for hours, but all she could think of was Brad - the same old questions whirled round and round like a washing machine on an endless cycle. Why hadn't he texted or rung her? She was sure that he would, he'd said he would, so why hadn't he? And Amber had gone to his house, it was in darkness she said. Was he partying with another woman?

She went over and over his parting words, but nothing could ease the tormenting realisation that he had no intentions of calling - he was clearly a bigger bastard than she could have imagined. She cried herself to sleep, wondering if the women in her family were cursed when it came to finding a *good* man. She had to accept it, the idea that Brad Monroe was gonna be her husband to be, was now dead to her.

30

It was a sullen and dull morning, unusually overcast for Perth, accurately reflecting Jessicas' mood - no more blue skies for me she thought. She felt like sleeping in, there was nothing worth getting up for. She felt as though she had no reason to live or breathe again. She spent an hour typing long abusive texts to Brad, but deleted them before sending them. She needed to unload the burden of her betrayed heart and true to her style, this needed to be done face to face. She *had* to confront him, she'd show him she too was a game player and she didn't mean on the PS4 pro she had sitting in her lounge.

No, she'd show him that she didn't want him or love him either and she'd throw as much spite and hatred at him as was expected of a woman scorned. Visions of his magnificent loving green eyes flashed before her. She wiped away tears, if he came up with a reasonably believable excuse for treating her with yet more contempt she would forgive him. Her gut was telling her he wouldn't. But really, she wanted to throw herself at his mercy, and beg him to take her in his arms again - this time never ever letting her go!

She felt as though she were on the verge of a nervous breakdown, if this was what love was, it's why she needed to avoid it. Her mind was on him, every minute of the day, she stared at her Iphone daring it to ring, it didn't. She went to the bank at lunchtime amazing staff by wanting her ten thousand dollars in cash stuffed in an envelope, a security risk they warned her of, but she took it silently and left. Once home she saw Amber who had packed a bag full of Jessicas make up, perfume and a few clothes. Jessica said nothing, it was pointless she was already operating on empty.

She handed her the ten thousand dollars and without a word Amber took it and had the cheek to count it all out as though it were owed, and then without a thank you she left slamming the door in rebellion behind her. Relaxing a little Jessica sat down and stared at her phone again - why hadn't he called? At least he didn't even know about Amber, but that meant he had zero excuse. She was going insane, there was only one thing left to do - she had to go to his home, whether Kevin, Scott or Brad liked it or not. She simply couldn't live another day without at least knowing why he would torture her so cruelly.

She threw open her wardrobe then let out a scream, Amber had helped herself to several of her favourite clothes. Jessica felt the urge to cry and just end it all, but until she heard him tell her he didn't want her, she carried the flickering hope of being held in his arms again which was enough to temper any suicidal notions. But she could see why there was a lovers leap - its more pain than pleasure - didn't Brad say there was pleasure in pain? Was *this* what he meant? Did he enjoy inflicting this kind of pain?

His sincerity had moved her, out there under the stars on Rottnest, he couldn't have been lying to her, could he? He'd confided in her about his first wife, she *did* mean something to him, didn't she? Whatever his reason for not calling her, she was sure it would be genuine, and she'd forgive him! She struggled to fit into an old pair of jeans, too tattered for Amber, although there were so many rips in them, that they were now the height of fashion again! She teamed it with an off the shoulder broderie anglaise blouse which coupled with her hair carefully arranged over her bare shoulders made her look and feel slightly worthy *almost,* beautiful.

Driving down the west coast highway the memories of that iconic weekend were so alive, so tangible within her soul, she refused to allow the dark thoughts of doubt to creep in and torment her. She was invincible, she'd always been a fighter - like her mother to the bitter end. She parked a little way up the street again, not wishing to give her arrival away to him, she wanted to catch him unawares - she had forgotten her car announces her arrival for miles.

The house was as Amber had described, in total darkness. She could see that it was most probable that he was not at home, she didn't know whether to be pleased or not, at least if he was out, it would be due to business, and that's why he hadn't rung her, after all, he was a very powerful man, running allot of businesses, of course he would have to be out at all hours of the night - wouldn't he?

She stood on the tiled doorstep staring up at the hot pink Bougainvillea adorning the white render - just like hers, and considered what she would do next. He was out, there was no point in knocking on the door. She began to walk away, then felt an overwhelming sense of curiosity, she wandered around the side of the triple garages, startled momentarily by the security solar lamps that would light up her path. She found an arched wrought iron gate open leading to the back of the house.

She was in the middle of a mature scented tropical garden. She strained her ears, as the faint sound of gentle music wafted through the stillness of the night. Following the sound, she found herself in the deepest corner of the garden, she looked up, and realised that she was directly under the spa area. She remembered how his sculpted athletic body emerged slowly from that spa exactly like the greek god of the sea Poseidon, the memory flooded her eyes with tears that she forced away.

Curiosity pervaded her good sense; the music was coming from up there, on the balcony! It was a mellow, pan pipe type of sensuous music. As though a can of petrol was suddenly ignited in her mind she reeled with the tumultuous possibilities of what he would be doing up on his balcony maybe in that spa listening to sultry music in the dark! There could only be one explanation, he was making love to another woman! Tears exploded within her, but the burning internal anger vaporised them before they dared to manifest. How could he do that to her? How could he lie? She wanted to catch him, she wanted to embarrass him, humiliate him, she wanted to see him suffer the pain that he'd forced her to experience.

Her eyes burnt deep into her sockets, begging her to allow them to release the tears that bubbled there but fighting with herself, she denied herself the weakness of crying. She could not, and indeed would not stoop to crying for such an inhumane creature; her verbal contempt and loathing hatred was all that she would give him and that was something she had a doctorate in! She spotted a large drainpipe rising to the first floor, it wouldn't be easy, but she was sure she could manoeuvre herself well enough to get onto the first balcony - yeah and catch him in the act of cheating.

It hadn't crossed her mind that it was breaking and entering. For once she was grateful to Amber for stealing all her dresses and good clothes, at least it had forced her to wear old things, suitable for climbing up drainpipes. She stifled a giggle at her own love crazed behaviour and texted a tag on Meta Facebook, then thought better of it and removed it flicking onto

Brads page with sadness staring into his beautiful amazingly light green eyes - he still hadn't friended her - oh how empty she felt.

Driven on by the stabbing indescribable pain of rejection and hurt, she heaved her body against the solid drainpipe and got a good foothold on the ridge that ran around its perimeter at regular intervals. She was also thankful Kevin had taken her mountain climbing a few years ago. An old man shouted up at her as he passed with his wiry fox terrier. " Need some help there darl? Lost your keys?" Jessica giggled like a silly schoolgirl, "oh, hi, yes, I'm so daft, but I'm okay, a good opportunity to practice my climbing skills - but hey, thanks." The man smiled and nodded, even if he didn't understand why a pretty blonde wanted to practice climbing skills, but he did get how one would be dumb enough to lock herself out - girls these days, absolutely pathetic.

Jessica tempered her rising hysteria, having to swallow a bout of crazed laughter ending in tears. She mused how she'd make a great cat burglar, because stupid men were so gullible to a pretty blonde - she went cold, yes Brad was a man that could have his head turned by beauty, she recalled the Marilyn Monroe woman on Rottnest, maybe it was *her* he was with. It was clear, *she* liked him and he clearly found her drop dead gorgeous - the cold hearted bastard.

She struggled for ten minutes persistently trying not to slip down the smooth surface, eventually she placed her hands over the top of the wrought iron railings. She peered over the top, but couldn't see anything, the whole place was cloaked in darkness. She scaled the railings silently, and did a superman roll to the floor, keeping still, hoping not to be seen. Her pain had mutated to madness, she struggled not to laugh hard until someone in a white coat took her away. She remembered her mothers favourite British advert. "*All because the lady loves milk tray,*" she whispered, amused by her own wit.

Laying still in the dark, she pondered her entire life, and then silently and painfully re-lived her weekend with Brad on Rottnest, he was the best thing that ever walked into her life - how could he dare walk out without looking back. Wiping away hot tears she listened, she could still hear the music, it was coming from inside, he must be entertaining the slut in there, her anger instantly re-ignited.

There was no one there, but listening harder she could just hear the unmistakable bubbling of the jacuzzi clearly on a low setting and not the usual vigorous full bubble mode she mused. No, he's in there with a new victim. Stepping cautiously she tip toed to the patio doors and like a crazed jackal was about to jump out and do a 'ta da' but she froze - there *she* was, a slim woman, balancing elegantly, feet dangling in the spa.

She strained her eyes to scope this woman out, her heart sunk deeper than the Titanic, she'd hoped she'd been wrong - she hadn't. She appraised the shape, the woman's back was to her and she was wearing an unusually wide brimmed hat, quite old fashioned she thought. The woman was certainly trim but not quite the celebrity type slut she'd imagined. No long hair embracing a naked back, the woman wore a modest one piece bathing suit. She watched curiously, a thousand thoughts pulsing through her brain, if she left now she could remove herself from this situation, but the desperate need to *know*, drove her on.

The woman was sitting on the edge of the spa still dangling her feet in it's swirling depths, she was doubled over as if in pain, and held her hands over her face. She hadn't noticed Jessica and seemed oblivious to anything - the atmosphere seemed almost… She hardly dared think or breathe, the scene was overtly melancholy. Perhaps Brad was in the bathroom or cooking food or something? She cursed under a jealous breath, more likely getting a condom although did he use protection? She realised in *their* love making frenzy he had not used one!

She remained still, shivering in the night air. She felt an overwhelming sense of utter foolishness at not respecting his privacy - yet she couldn't rip herself away. More than twenty minutes passed, Brad had not shown in all that time - the silent woman was there, alone. She had to do something, she couldn't stay hiding in the bushes like a freak. The creep song started to play in her head, she smothered a laugh. With a deep breath of courage she stepped toward the woman, just one delicate step at a time - each time optimistically hoping that Brad would show up, see her, and greet her with enthusiastic emerald eyes his love affirmed - then kick this other strange woman in a hat to the curb.

The woman wasn't going anywhere, she continued to kick at the water with a heavy air of sadness that totally enveloped her.

Jessica couldn't contain either her anonymity or her silence any longer, she stepped over, and said the first stupid thing that came into her head. Her voice cracked slightly as she broke the silence, "enjoying your evening?"

The woman didn't hear, her face lowered and focussed on perfectly manicured and tapered delicate fingers adorned with crystal clear white diamonds - the trappings of the rich. Jessica stepped a little closer, her fear making her heart pulse wildly. She was now standing so close she could smell a distinctive and favourite aroma; "Mon Guerlain: notes of a woman," she whispered, but a little louder than she had meant. The woman turned to face her and let out a startled scream.

31

J ulia?" Jessicas' heart beat out of her chest as she witnessed despair laying naked in Julias' eyes. How stupid she felt, of course she had forgotten that Julia lived with Brad! "Jessica, my dear." She half spoke to herself, managing a weak smile, and seemingly not surprised at Jessicas' sudden impromptu appearance. Julia turned away again, to resume her previous position. Jessicas stomach lurched with a deep dark sense of dread, no Brad anywhere to be seen, and Julia, almost catatonic with a lost sadness.

The ground began to sway beneath her - was he? Could he be - dead? She fought tears, but they won. "Julia, what's wrong? Is it Brad? I haven't heard from him since Rottnest - I know he was at work, I …" She held her breath awaiting the inevitable news that would destroy her world. Julia pulled away from her, standing up and walking away, only stopping to lean heavily on a near-by chair as she covered herself with a wrap. Her voice wavered, it was apparent to Jessica she was fighting to dominate her emotions. "Oh my dear Jessica, I don't know how to tell you this, I know I should have called you as soon as it happened…I didn't know what to say to you and I… just couldn't face you." Her voice cracked to a strangled whisper, "yes…it's Brad."

Jessica choked for breath as an imaginary plastic bag smothered her face until her eyes bulged black from asphyxiation. She fought for breath as her mind raced with the multiple possibilities of the impending bad news she was about to hear. "Tell me." She pleaded. Julia continued staring at the floor, pausing to clench and unclench her fists. "It's Brad, I'm afraid, he's, he's gone." An excruciating stabbing twisted in the back of Jessicas' head preceding a desensitising blackness which enveloped her as she dropped immediately into a dead faint.

When consciousness revisited her, she found herself on the floor but propped up by large velour cushions. A soft voice, someone quietly talking on their mobile, pacing back and forwards brought her back to the land of the living - she struggled to sit up. "Brad?" A sharp head pain reminded her to lay down - the voice finished the call and was by her side.

"The doctor will be here shortly dear - you hit your head really hard on the pavers, exactly where you had that contusion before, you're almost certainly concussed again and you absolutely have to rest now, you feel hot so I'd say you have a temperature." Jessica's body trembled as she stared up bleary eyed. Julia put a cool compress on her forehead and dabbed a cotton pad at a wound that was now bleeding at the back of her head. "I'm afraid I couldn't carry you to the bedroom, are you comfortable enough for now?"

She plumped up the array of cushions behind her. Jessica managed a weak and embarrassed smile, "yes, yes, thank you." Julia mopped her own brow which had gathered beads of perspiration. "Now then," she smiled. "I think you've got the wrong end of the stick." Jessica repeated her words in a daze. "Did I catch a stick?" Julia stroked her forehead. "Brad, has gone to England, he had to go urgently, he literally took the next plane, didn't even tell *me* properly, I just got a hurried call from the airport and a note."

Jessica bolted upright immediately remembering everything, "you mean he's not, he's not…" Julia smiled, "dead? Heavens no my dear, he's alive and kicking." Jessica heaved a huge sigh of relief, Brad was alive, but then immediately felt sick she couldn't shake the depressive notion; Why didn't he text her then? And if he'd merely had to go on some urgent business trip to England why was Julia so depressed? It didn't make sense, surely Julia didn't need to be with her grown up son *that* much.

She spoke quietly through confused out of focus eyes. "Julia, why didn't he call me or text since Rottnest? I've been sick, heartbroken and worried out of my mind, if he loved me, he would've …" Julia placated her softly, "of course you'd think that, but he dropped his phone on the runway Monday - the workers said it was smashed beyond repair. When he left you, he was walking on air, all fingers and thumbs, you really put his mind and heart in a whirl. He called me from a pay phone at the airport."

Jessica let out a larger than life, in love, happy screech, no phone, then an urgent business trip, of course, that explains *everything*, she snapped back to the land of the living, beaming, overjoyed. "I'll be waiting right here when he gets back." Her eyes reflected the intensity of her love for him - her whole being felt reborn at the thought of him holding her in his arms again.

Julia let out a sharp breath through her teeth, her deadpan expression said it all. "That's the thing, and the reason I'm here, now, alone and very unhappy because I've been wondering how on earth I can tell you this." Jessica struggled to sit upright, the pain in her head throbbing in tandem with the creeping cold hand of dread strangling her windpipe tight. Julia continued looking straight into Jessicas' misty eyes. "It isn't a business trip." She paused to let this new information sink in, as she witnessed the corpse like pallor return to Jessicas face before she delivered the final death blow, "you see, he won't be coming back."

Julias words hit her like a baseball bat to a recent double contusion. Jessica stared into Julias' eyes, her face combusting into the kind of love lost despair all mortals fear. She repeated Julias' words in disbelieving staccato, "he won't be coming back? But, that's not possible, he told me he loved me, more than anything, he said… he said…" She struggled to control the waterfall of heart break. When it finally released, her tumultuous despair affected Julia too, she broke down into tears, all upper class restrain't unleashed.

Being strong for Julia helped to release hidden pockets of her own strength enabling her to briefly forget her own sorrow. Julia sobbed, "I wanted to tell you as soon as I put the phone down," she whispered, "I couldn't! I couldn't face you Jessica. I *made* you love him, I pushed you together and now like the classic Casanova that he is and has always been, he's broken your heart! I'm so sorry, I'm ashamed and so guilt ridden, I just can't face *anyone!*" Jessicas' heart was in her throat, "Casanova? Is he there for another *woman?* He can't be…he… he said he loved me. I believed him." Julia gasped in between breaths, then added, "I'll tell you what he said, but I need a strong cup of tea first dear and I'll get you one too." As Julia left to make the tea, Jessicas' head screamed out of control with anger, as her life spun into a new world of pain.

Why did Julia refer to him as a Casanova? A stab of fury enraged her. That was it, he'd left her for one of those stick insect models. The notion felt unthinkable, yet at the end of the day she knew, perhaps their weekend of love had just been a hell of a one night stand. Visions of his love making, tender, loving, passionate - everything he said was heart felt, wasn't it? Could it really have been a playboy at his most masterful? Even Ted Bundy couldn't have put on an act as good as that - could he?

She cried into her hands, she was such a gullible fool, her father had always told her she was a dumb blonde, today she realised he'd been right. Julia quietly returned with a tray of tea and lammingtons and sat next to Jessica after checking her head. "Here, take two of these, it's codeine and paracetamol they'll help with the pain." Jessica grabbed her hand and held it tight. "You called him a Casanova - why?" Julia remained silent, feeling sick, fighting with the words she needed to say. Jessica broke the silence rambling, as random thoughts tumbled out of her mouth. "He loves me, I know he does…it was *real*. He won't stay there, he hates England. He told me his ex wife is there."

Then it hit her. Julia seized the moment to elaborate. "He's gone back to her …Catherine. I don't know what's happened to Danny, her husband, I don't want to know, and I don't know *what* he sees in her..I never have. Maybe when he told you about her it unleashed hidden feelings he still felt for her. Perhaps you reminded him of her… a little too much. I don't know. I'm furious with him and for the first time in my life, ashamed to call him my son. Believe me, I'm as devastated as you are."

An overwhelming and suffocating panic made her heart beat out of control. Jessica stood up, swaying with concussion, "I'm so sorry, I gotta get out, I've got to go, I'm spinning like a living ceiling fan." Julia grabbed her wrist and held it tight. "No, lay down, you're having a panic attack, please, you *must* rest, the doctor is on his way, you have serious concussion and now you're in shock, don't go, stay here, in the house for a few days, until you want to go. I could really do with the company - if you can bear to be with me." Tears gushed from Julias' eyes. Jessica looked away out of respect for her pride until she composed herself. Julia stroked her hair as though it were spun gold, "here, drink your tea, hot sweet tea is a good start." Jessicas' eyes were red and swollen, her face glistened, wet with pouring tears as though she had been swimming in a pool of despair.

Julias' grey blue eyes had lost something, it was as though a light had been turned off. The zest and energy that had amazed

Jessica so much had departed, she was a shadow of her former self and for the first time, she looked her age.

"What did he say? On the phone?" Julia sighed. "He was brief, he never liked good byes." She swallowed hard. "He said, he *had* to go back to Catherine." Jessica swallowed hard, the pain in her heart, wanting her to just lay down and die. "He didn't even mention *me*?" The pain was laid bare. "I'm sorry dear…no, he didn't. I tried to talk sense into him but all he could say was that he had his reasons, his decision was final and he knew I wouldn't understand, but he didn't know if he would *ever* come back and he had already put a long term strategy in place to keep the businesses running with him living abroad."

A bitter bile rose in Jessicas' throat; a weighted torturous pain filled silence ensued, neither knowing what to say. Julia watched Jessica turn a shade of bilious green, "I knew this would be hard for you, I didn't realise just *how* hard." Jessica was choking on the information as she attempted to absorb it. "Why would this Catherine woman want him now? I mean, did he contact her? What happened?" Julia pulled a face. "He didn't tell me, but you and Brad set the party alight, even trended on Twitter. Your instant intense attraction was reported in many tabloids and let me tell you, you're very photogenic and you looked wonderful together. Australias' most desired Bachelor finally tamed by a beautiful young Cleopatra. I'm guessing Catherine read it, she also still has family here in Perth and of course knowing the woman that she is, she will have been incensed with jealousy - you see it's her nature to own everything. I'm guessing she called him, but I can't be sure dear. But one thing I *do* know, he found love with you, and for a moment in time and space, you had the man of your dreams and he had the love of his life - but *now,* that time has gone, maybe in another life…"

Blackness smothered the pain in her heart, as Julias' words drilled an empty hole into Jessicas' head, her world became dizzy, a forgiving peace released her earthly mortal suffering as she sank back into a comforting state of unconsciousness. Jessica awoke again in a sweat, it was still dark, temporarily confused, she ran her hands across sateen luxury 1000 thread Egyptian cotton sheets - where had she felt these before? Brads' bed - a huge brass four poster with wonderfully puffy duck down pillows. The pain returned like a jagged blade followed by an acid bath to all her internal organs. Her brain repeated Julias' words over and over again. How could he not at least try to use someones' phone to text her? At the very least, he could have admitted that when he rehashed his stories about the evil Catherine, he realised he still loved her!

Hot tears tracked the length of her face finding a resting place on the pillow. She curled into a fetal ball. Julia was her only ally in love, she'd acted on her deepest instincts, she knew Brad was somehow meant for her and she went to a great deal of trouble to unite them - and it worked, so how? How could it all be gone in an instant? She felt a deep sense of emptiness as the realisation hit home, that she had no choice but to let him go, even Julia seemed to accept the inevitable - and had urged her to do the same! Perhaps Julia was right - in another life… But she was still in *this* one! The futility of her life without him cut a deep valley in her gut. She knew, she had to forget love, forget happiness, and forget Brad, in the way he had so *easily* and *cruelly* forgotten her.

32

Jessica woke up stretching weakly, her world filled with a sense of absolute nothingness. She was somewhat thankful Brad couldn't see her face which she knew without looking was grey and drawn. She sent a text to Kevin - he ignored it - after five minutes she called him. He was asleep enjoying a dreamy menage-a-trois, and most put out to be woken up half an hour before he needed to.

"I need a favour," she put on a brave face. Kevin yawned and burped. "You just killed the best dream I've ever had! You're pushing this brotherly love thing," he growled at her with real menace, totally unaware of her turmoil. "What's the favour?" He added reluctantly, hoping he could go back to sleep and rekindle that fantasy.

"I need you to put a note on the door of the salon, I'm closing it down… I can't face it anymore." Kevin sat up in bed suddenly wide awake,"what the fuck? Why? You've only just opened it, what about the lease? And all the people who you said are booked in this week? Anyway, where are you?" She ignored all the questions and drew up her strength, "that's the next favour I want you to do for me," She hesitated, imagining his tired face. "I want you to get the keys to the salon, you know where I hide them, get the appointments book and take it to work with you, then bring it to me. I'm in City Beach, at Brads, I can't drive right now cos of my head, can you do that for me? Just don't ask questions."

Kevin smiled, "can't drive, cos of your pigging head? Oh I get it, been on it ave ya? Yeah, bathing naked in Prosecco with lover boy yeah? I should've known, you're more interested in shagging your man than work, mind you, he's minted so you don't need to work anymore I guess." A stabbing sadness and overwhelming loneliness strangled her soul. "It's not like that" The emptiness in her voice was hard to miss, but Kevin managed to.

"Just get my appointments book and come to his place in an hour - *please*." Kevin hissed unrepentant and unsympathetic to whatever she was going through. "Not in a freaking hour, I can't." He moaned, "how about I ring your punters myself from work, yeah that's what I'll do, so what shall I tell em?" Jessica sighed sadly, "okay, well tell them, due to unforeseen circumstances, I've got concussion, had a fall… erm, tell em, I've had to close the salon for a short period of time."

Kevin smirked,"well you'd better make sure lover boy is okay with me using the phone, cos he flips at us doing private stuff in work time." He grinned, imagining what a crazy sex session they must have had to prevent her from working. "Is Brad okay now? I didn't wanna worry you but he was so moody on Monday?"

She grabbed onto his words instantly. "What do you mean moody?" Kevin really wanted to go back to his dream but answered quickly. "Well he was like one minute all smiles like he'd won the lotto and the next minute he was stalking about with an expression that said fuck off, he was beyond evil to everyone. Linda put a call through to him and said it got nasty." Jessica became even more animated, "what call? Who from?"

Kevin stared at his Iphone, "I don't know sis, I'm not psychic, Linda said it was a posh English woman. Oddly he hasn't been seen since, and ignored everyones calls, texts and emails. Then this morning we get a message that a new Manager is coming in. So lemme guess, you shagged his brains out so much, that Prince Charming is running off with you my Cinderella sister."

Jessica exploded, "why the hell didn't you tell me about this woman's call on Monday? You cretin, please stop smoking that shit it's making you like a real drongo! Wasn't it obvious to you that something was wrong? Why else would he suddenly disappear? You could've saved me from days of despair and misery! And you didn't tell me he'd disappeared! The last thing you said he was busy and didn't speak at all." Kevin was getting ready to click off from his angry sister. "I don't know what the dude does, it could've been business, he gets loads of fucking calls, and he's a moody bastard at the best of times, I'm not your keeper am I?"

A pregnant silence prevailed for a moment, Jessica hissed at him, "clearly not and just as well! But you *are* my brother; I wish that you'd have more common sense!" A few more minutes of silence, gave Jessica a chance for remorse. "I'm sorry Kev, I'm not well, I'm here with Julia and she's given me some bad news," a lump in her throat strangled her to silence. "Well the news can't be *that* bad if you're quitting work and living with lover boy and the mother in law. So spill em, what's going down?" Jessica took a deep and painful breath, "you must promise me you won't tell anyone else, and I mean it." Kevin cut his eyes to the ceiling, really wishing he could carry on with his erotic dream, "yeah, yeah, just spill em miss Marple." She gave it to him straight,"Brads gone to England."

She took a deep breath to find the courage to state the worst thing that could have happened to her. "He's gone to be with his ex wife - he's broken me Kev." A loud smash caused Jessica to pull her phone from her ear, Kevin had dropped his phone. Eventually he spoke, "what the fuck? He's got a fucking wife?" Jessica didn't want to talk about this anymore, "ex." Kevin repeated what she didn't want to hear. "Not very ex if he drops everything to be with her." A solitary tear tracked her already pallid face. "Thanks for rubbing it in, please don't say any more, you're tightening the noose, believe me, I can't breathe, I'm more than gutted - okay?"

Kevin tried to make her feel better, "don't let that selfish prick make you feel like shit, you've been like a zombie since you got back from Rottnest, he's no good for you, you deserve better. Scottie confided in me last night, he said he still loves you, you could do worse you know." Jessica could feel the bile from her stomach rising at the mention of Scotts name. "Kev, I can't think about him right now, I'm injured, I hit my head, and don't ask how, it's concussion, but I'm dizzy. I'm gonna stay here with Brads' mother, a few days or even weeks maybe. I can't face working, I'm struggling not to jump off a cliff right now. Please do me that favour and ring those clients. Look after Scottie for me, I feel terrible about what Amber did and all that - but at least the bitch has gone." Kevin failed to leave her with a positive thought, "yeah with all your fucking car cash."

"I know, but you know Kev, shit happens, and as we know, it usually happens to me!" Jessica stared at her phone, tormenting herself. The lack of contact from Brad held nothing but intense suffering. The phone vibrated in her hand, a new Meta Facebook text from Hilary, an old school friend. "Hey, have they let your sister out now?" Jessica called her, she hated texting. "Yes, why?" Jessica listened with dread,"check out the front page of the Midland Echo online." Jessicas' blood ran cold. "Why, what's she done now?"

"I'll read the headlines, are you sitting down? Druggie, jailbird attacked. The story says she was found half naked, badly beaten and left for dead. She's in the Royal Perth Hospital. Luckily the photo wasn't clear, but I knew it was her from that tattoo she had of the mocking bird. I hope she's gonna be okay, she stole my purse the last time I saw her, but I'm over it, I think she just got a big dose of karma."

It was hard to hear others curse her twin even if it was true. "I wish she hadn't got so messed up by drugs and alcohol years ago when mum died, I try to forgive her but it's hard. I'll go see her, thanks for letting me know Hilary." Jessica scribbled a note to Julia, according to Julias' doctor she wasn't capable of driving, but she *had* to see Amber. Her head was throbbing, and her vision was blurry but she managed to get dressed, and stumbled down the stairs of the grand staircase in a mesmerised stupor. She found the front door so heavy, but eventually managed to heave it open.

Staggering to her car she knew she was out of her mind, blinded by concussion and with a broken heart; she was a danger to herself and others and shouldn't be driving but she *had* to get to the Royal Perth hospital. She would always bear the curse of her evil twin, how could she *ever* lead a normal life when someone who looked identical to her, insisted on causing so much public trouble?

She managed to drive there, even though she knew she was far from fit enough. A tired nurse ushered Jessica into a private room, away from press who were making a commotion all jostling for an interview or pictures with her. Jessica tip toed towards the bed, Amber was asleep, her black and blue arm outstretched to accommodate a cannula half way up it. She looked angelic for once, then she opened one eye, the other swollen shut. She tried to smile but couldn't, her lips were split and swollen. Jessica noticed bruises around her neck. She tried to soothe her.

"The nurse says you're gonna be okay, you just need bed rest to get over shock and bruising, you've broken a few ribs but nothing that won't heal. Here, this arnica cream will help with the bruising." Jessica gently massaged the cream into Ambers face, a tear sprung from Ambers eye and then another until Amber began to convulse with emotional and physical pain. Jessica held her "It's okay, I'm here, you're safe now."

Amber motioned for her to move towards her lips so that Jessica could hear her whisper, "I'm sorry for everything, I wish I could be with mum, I wish I was dead." Another nurse bustled in dragging a large drugs trolley, she plonked a small paper cup of pills on the side - she stopped suddenly. "Identical twins - thought I was seeing double for a minute - talk about long hours." She smiled and spoke softly, "make sure Amber takes the large one now, its methadone, heroine replacement, here's another she needs to take after she's eaten but she won't eat at the moment, so she's on a liquid nutrition alternative, needs to keep her strength up."

The nurse beckoned for Jessica to go out of the room where she continued in a hushed voice. "Terrible what happened, she was attacked says she was robbed of all her savings almost ten thousand dollars, the men then left her for dead in the forest. Doc says she'd been violently raped but put up a struggle, forensics got some good skin samples from under her nails; she's seen the psychologist and we'll keep her in for a good while yet. One thing you might be able to help us with, she was unable to give admissions her address, do you have it?" Jessica sighed, "Yes, she's living with me, I'll give admin the address details."

Jessica stroked Ambers forehead, "you need this pill Amber it'll help you deal with needing a fix okay? But when did you get on heroine?" Amber opened her eyes and swallowed the capsule almost choking on it. She mouthed the words, "go, don't worry about me, your money, they …" Jessica interrupted her, stroking her head. "It's okay, it's only money. I'll come every day, and when you're better you'll be moving in with me. Brads left me anyway. Seems we are in synch as usual as we both wish we were dead." She gulped as tears immediately flushed her eyes deep blue. "I'm gonna help you get clean this time, once and for all, we need each other Amber, we're family not rivals and despite everything, you know, I've always loved you, it's the drugs I hate. I know mums cancer affected you, deeply, but you gotta get over it now - she wouldn't want to see you like this, destroying yourself, and our family."

Amber closed her eyes and nodded, muddy tears escaping her usually belligerent eyes. As Jessica drove home she burst into gut wrenching tears, hearing herself say the words, Brad had left her, provoked an earth shattering empty despair, it was her reality, not a dream, he'd left her to be with his ex. Despite the intensity of his love for her and their love making he couldn't even offer the courtesy of a good bye and explanation. The evil ex won the day - she really *did* want to die.

As she drove precariously her mind ruminated constantly, she didn't care about the road. There were no men left like *him* in the world, he was one of a kind, carved by the gifted hand of the creator - she was *so* alone, alone in the world without him. She needed him, she wanted him, she loved him with a passion that she'd never felt before. He was prince charming, and had rescued her at the ball, and now, her carriage was a pumpkin and her life was destined to be in tatters.

She veered her car too fast, around the narrow cliff road by the sea. Her head was hurting, spinning and throbbing, her heart bleeding out. She couldn't see, her tears blinding her already blurry view. It wasn't worth living with out him. Nothing mattered in her life any more - she couldn't live without him. A low ride red sports car speeding up from behind played with her bumper, seemingly enjoying another rev head chase. It stuck to her like glue, and for an instant she played the F1 game without care forgetting this was not a computer game.

Her mobile beeped, a text message, maybe it was him? With a careless rush of hope she fumbled in her bag pulling out her phone, she strained to read the message, but her heart dipped, it was Kevin, "Scottie says he'll take you to the movies tomorrow night, he loves you sis, lets face it, Brad's always been kinda out of your league."

The words punished her like barbed wire wrapped around her heart and pulled tight, until it bled and beat no more. Through sad eyes, she glanced at her rear view mirror; her eyes connected in fleeting recognition with the sports car driver who was playing to win - it was edging towards her tail and was showing no mercy. She floored the old cars accelerator, but a violent jolt from a rear end shunt showed her who was boss - it was the final death knell. She didn't stand a chance - the red car screamed past, its hoodie wearing driver flashing by in a momentary blur.

A sharp stab burned where she'd hit her head, she closed her eyes for a second, her hands of their own volition grabbing at the source. The steering wheel screamed erratically on the bend enjoying the momentary freedom from its driver. She caught it, but despite a valiant battle of control, the universe had already heard her death wish and accommodated her fate. It was then, that she realised, she *did* want to live. She fought a valiant battle to stay on the road, but it was too late, despite her best efforts, she lost.

Her brains last sensory moments left her swooning at Brads' smile, melting to his deep soft voice and crying with ecstasy from a stolen shivering sensuality as his warm strong arms pulled her tight against his chest. The heady scent of imaginary vanilla musk mingled with a dense and smothering acrid burning odour that caused her to cough. "I love you Brad Monroe - find me in heaven," she murmured as the heart stopping vision of his smiling face pervaded her entire being.

Reality bit hard - a searing heat accompanied a deafening and high pitched engine scream in surround sound. Like crystal chandeliers smashing on a granite floor, shards of glass rained down in time to a twisted metal grinding chorus. Her world exploded around her in high definition technicolour juxtaposed with the absolving peace of absolute nothingness. Her body was set free, she was flying, then the darkness rose to envelope and comfort - nothing mattered anymore. The deep dark blue waters rose up to greet her, enveloping her body in a final act of the ultimate deliverance.

Jessica felt an overwhelming sense of tranquility as she was released from the pain in her heart, body and soul. Brad's smiling face flickered, fading into the ether until her whole world dissolved to the blackness and finality of nothingness.

ABOUT THE AUTHOR

CJ Webb, is a natural born soap opera writer, as she loves discovering skeletons in closets, and in her books, she exposes many. *"I like the story to be fast paced, and every word, action and situation has a meaning further into the story, so I always tell my readers to pay attention, it will make sense later on."* Suspense, intrigue and outright scandalous goings on are her forte in every

novel. Having spent time in Hollywood writing movie and TV scripts she is a visual writer, and transfers the visual medium to the written word with a rare ability according to critics. She has won an award for her debut novel '**The Immaculate Deception'**an abridged version due to be re-released**.** She also won the TV Soap Magazine National Australian Writing Competition for The Bold & The Beautiful TV show. She has a Masters in Screenwriting and a first class Psychology degree; she is academically accomplished and keeps her readers hooked.